DALE MAYER

Zonked in the Zucchinis

Lovely Lethal Gardens
REWIND 01

ZONKED IN THE ZUCCHINIS: LOVELY LETHAL GARDENS
REWIND, BOOK 1
Beverly Dale Mayer
Valley Publishing Ltd.

This is a work of fiction. Names, characters, places, brands, media, and incidents are either the product of the author's imagination or are used fictitiously. Any resemblance to actual events, locales, or persons, living or dead, is entirely coincidental.

ISBN-13: 978-1-778866-59-3
Print Edition

Books in This Series:

Zonked in the Zucchinis, Book 1
Yipped in the Yams, Book 2

About This Book

Doreen is slowly recovering from the mad yet joyous ending to last year, as she faces the new year and what it might bring. Since she's now engaged to Mack—and everyone around her is pressuring her to pick a wedding date and hopefully soon—she yearns for another case to keep her busy.

So, when an older gentleman calls and needs help fulfilling his wife's last wish, Doreen is right there to help. The case is beyond cold, which means she gets free rein. However, when it starts to butt up against a new case Mack has, he's quick to move her back into her lane—only he's not quite quick enough.

Doreen and her trusty animal trio traverse the Joe Rich area to downtown Kelowna and back, as her cold case curls back around in on itself—and Mack's current case. Solving these two cases will be worthy of a mention in the history books!

Chapter 1

End of December ...

"IT WASN'T MY fault," Doreen stated, as she glared at Mack. "You said we would wait until the new year, and I agreed to wait until the new year. It's not my fault that somebody just called and asked me to come over and look at his garden bed."

"What garden bed?" he asked in frustration. "Why do you want to go look at a garden bed?"

"Because he thinks a murder was committed in it."

He closed his eyes and whispered, "Dear Lord."

"I know. I know, but I didn't call him, Mack. I didn't have anything to do with it."

"You don't have to anymore," he noted, with a sigh. "They just seem to come out of the woodwork now."

"I know," she exclaimed, beaming so brightly. "Isn't it great?"

"And what do you mean, somebody was murdered in the garden bed?" he asked. "Shouldn't he be calling the police?"

"Apparently it was a while ago," she noted, nudging him, "so that should make it a cold case."

"Not if it's still on the books, it's not," he countered.

"I was hoping you could be more … considerate about that. I did call you, thinking you might want to come along."

"Yes, I definitely want to come," he replied, glaring at her. "I don't know why people always think they can go straight to you instead of the police." She didn't say anything to that, and he sighed. "You definitely get better publicity than we do."

She burst out laughing. "I do, and I'm sorry about that because I'm really not trying to make you guys look as if you don't do anything."

"That's exactly what it looks like," he declared. "Anyway, who on earth does he think was killed in his garden bed?"

"He says—back then, a long time ago, when the murder supposedly happened—he found an awful lot of blood in his garden bed, and he took a lot of pictures, and he phoned the police right then. However, he hasn't been able to use his zucchini patch ever since then because he's been afraid it would destroy evidence."

"But he did contact the police?"

"Yes, a long time ago, though."

"So, we don't know if a human body was there. We don't know who was killed there. We don't know who he contacted at the department. Meaning, we don't really know anything. *Great.* Another case bound to damage our reputation."

"But those were the old days," she noted, with a bright smile. "Not the new ones. Are you ready?"

"Ready for what?" he asked.

She smiled. "To start the new year, and to start a new

year with … are you ready?" He nodded, yet with a sad smile. *"Zonked in the Zucchinis,"* she declared and burst out laughing.

After a moment, it tugged a grin from him too.

She added, "Come on. Let's go. I can't wait to start a new year with you … and another round of cold cases." And, with their arms linked, they headed out to check out this case.

Chapter 2

As Doreen walked outside, Mack at her side, she offered, "I'll drive." When he stopped and raised one eyebrow, she frowned. "What?"

He asked, "Where did you say this guy lives?"

"Joe Rich area," she replied, frowning. "Can't say I've been there much. At least not enough to know the roads."

"In that case," he stated, "I should drive."

Instinctively she asked, "But what if I want to drive?"

He shrugged. "You could, but then we might need a tow truck." Her hands went to her hips, and Thaddeus poked his head out from behind the curtain of her hair, staring at Mack as if in astonishment.

He grinned. "They have a different ecosystem up there."

She frowned again, not sure what he meant by that.

"You don't have any snow down here," Mack explained, "and it's been a relatively warm winter. However, depending on how far back into the Joe Rich area this guy lives, he could have a lot of snow at this point."

"Snow?" she asked in horror, turning to look at her little car, sitting on the driveway. "Oh."

"Yes, *oh*. My vehicle is a 4x4, and I would rather have it

and not use it, than need it and not have it."

"Okay," she conceded, "you've convinced me."

He laughed and motioned her toward the far side of his truck. As he stepped forward, Thaddeus made an awkward hop from her shoulder onto Mack's arm and waddled his way up, squawking, "Thaddeus is here. Thaddeus is here."

Mack grinned at him and asked, "Do you ever stay home?"

Thaddeus gave him that snickering laugh of his. "*He-he-he-he.*"

"I'll take that as a no," Mack muttered, then turned to Doreen. "Did you ever consider letting them stay home?"

"I do let them stay home sometimes," she replied, as she walked around the truck, opened up the passenger side, and helped Mugs do his awkward jump into the higher-up truck. Then he found himself a place to sit on the back seat. Goliath, not to be outdone, took an easy graceful leap right up, as if trying to show up Mugs. Goliath proceeded to sit atop the seatback, with his paws crossed in front of him, looking to all the world as if a king for the moment.

Doreen laughed. "It's really not quite so simple to get up into Mack's truck, you know," she muttered to the cat. Goliath just gave her that enigmatic stare that he always did. Even she struggled to step up and get into Mack's truck, but she wouldn't say anything. She climbed up awkwardly, managed to close the door, and, once she was seated, realized that Thaddeus had no intention of coming back to her side. "You probably don't want to drive with Thaddeus perched on you like that," she warned Mack.

"No, I really don't," he agreed. "Have you got a way to change his mind?"

"Sure." She made a weird little whistle that she had

learned from Jerry to use just for calling Thaddeus. His head swiveled in her direction, and she patted her shoulder. "If you want to come with us, big guy, you'll have to come over on my side."

Immediately he started a chorus of "Big Guy, Big Guy, Big Guy," flapping his wings in joy.

She winced. "No, not your friend Big Guy at Jerry's house." Yet Thaddeus wasn't listening. He kept up the Big Guy refrain until they headed out of town toward East Kelowna and then he fell silent. A peaceful silence reigned for the first time during the drive. "Do you think he understands?" she asked pensively.

"Considering that he's just now quieted down, I would think so," Mack replied, glancing at her. "The bigger question is, do you think he knows how to get to you-know-who's place?"

"I would suspect so," she agreed, with a nod. "And we do go there on irregular occasions."

"Sure," he pointed out, "but you haven't been there in a while—or have you?"

"No, we're due to go for another visit soon."

He smiled. "At least you're making friends in town."

"I am, indeed," she stated, with a big grin in his direction. "I'm not sure about *friends* per se, but, at this point in time, it's just nice to know that I'm not being laughed at."

"You'll never be laughed at in this town." He raised his eyebrows at her. "You've done too much good for everybody."

"I don't think people remember that though, do they?" she asked. "It's human nature to remember the good and to forget the bad, and very quickly they forget the good too."

He looked over at her in understanding. "You have done

a marvelous job in town," he noted. "Don't ever let anything get you down about that."

She looked at him and smiled. "Even though I do a better job at PR than your department?"

He snorted. "You certainly get the better PR. I'll give you that. I even suggested to the captain that maybe he should hire somebody to write some good news about us to help override all the good news about you."

She winced. "I'm sure that didn't go over well."

"I think he considered it, … for all of five minutes." Mack laughed. "I didn't mean it. The department is doing just fine on its own."

"Particularly since you're closing so many cases," she pointed out, happy for him.

"Absolutely," he muttered. "It would just be nice to think that we could do it on our own."

She frowned. "I was thinking about this a while back. You really couldn't have done it on your own." He stiffened ever-so-slightly and turned to glare at her. "I mean, you didn't even know about many of these cases, and, even if you did, it's not as if they were at the top of your priority list. You have only so much manpower and only so many hours in a day," she explained. "For me, it's a whole different story. I was bored anyway."

"And now?" he asked, with a small smile twitching his lips. "How do you feel now?"

"*Boredom* was the right word for it back then," she noted, with a wry smile. "Yet I'm happy to have this case now." Her voice drifted to a soft whisper as she repeated, "I'm happy." Even she recognized a sense of wonder in her tone.

"I'm glad to hear that," he replied, his tone softening to match hers. "You've had enough bad times. It's all about the good times now."

She nodded. "I hope you're right."

"Nope, no *hope* about it," he declared. "You make your life what you want it to be." When she frowned at him, he asked, "What?"

"I guess I never expected to hear that New Age mumbo jumbo from you."

Mack rolled his eyes. "I don't know that it's New Age mumbo jumbo, or that it's coming from me," he clarified, "but you have to understand that I worked hard to get where I am too. It wasn't a walk in the park all the time, and I definitely did things wrong along the way. However, at the end of the day, I set a goal to reach the position I currently have," he shared, "and I achieved it."

"You did, indeed," she agreed, beaming at him, as she squeezed his hand on the steering wheel. "You're a great detective." He chuckled. "Sometimes I think everything would be so different if we were living together."

"Absolutely. Anytime you're ready for that, you just let me know."

She stared at him and noted, "You never mentioned it before."

"You weren't ready before," he replied. "I don't think you're quite ready now either, but you brought it up. So I'm just telling you that, anytime you want to go that route, I'm there right with you."

She smiled. "You've been very patient with me."

He glanced at her and nodded. "I would like to think so."

She sighed, realizing his eyes were twinkling at her. "I know that I've been quite a trial," she admitted.

"You've been nothing but wonderful," he stated. "Don't

go down that road."

"If it weren't for Nan, I wouldn't have come to Kelowna at all."

"I know," he agreed, "and honestly she does like to remind me of that."

Doreen burst out laughing. "I imagine that she does. She's always been quick to take credit for things that she's done. And, in this case, we do owe her all the credit."

"And you owe yourself some credit too," he pointed out. "Since you arrived, you've been a huge force for good in this town. Besides, we had a great Christmas, and now we have lots to look forward to in a brand-new year."

She couldn't argue with that. What a different future she now faced versus one year ago. "And, one of these days, all that lovely lawyerly stuff will be over and done with, and I can move on."

"It will," he said, with a smile. "Though I have no idea what's left to be dealt with." He looked over at her. "Do you?"

She shook her head. "No, not really. Something to do with Mathew's estate, but I'm not sure what. Of course we still have the court cases involving him and my ex-lawyer Robin," she added. "I don't know whether the police have dredged up all of what they need out of it yet or not."

"I can always ask, if you want."

"Sure," she replied. When he passed a major turnoff road, she eyed the ugly corner but had missed the road sign to the turnoff. "Where are we?"

"We just passed Big White," he replied.

"It's so"—she looked around—"different up here."

"Have you ever been to this corner of Kelowna?" he asked curiously.

"Once, I think, for one of my cold cases. Bernard may have helped me on one up here. I just don't remember it all," she noted. "Funny, I wasn't expecting it to be like this." She frowned, as her gaze searched the country fields amid the mountains.

"You weren't expecting this countryside landscape?" he asked.

"It's really beautiful."

"It is, but it's a very different ecosystem here."

"You mentioned that before," she murmured. As they drove on, she saw snow piled high off on the side of the road. "I guess the skiers are happy."

"Exactly," Mack agreed. "We have a thriving winter wonderland recreation center going on here," he stated, with smile, "and a lot of people come here for the skiing."

"That would be wonderful."

"Do you ski?" he asked.

"No, gosh no," she said, frowning at him. "My ex-husband would never have approved of that."

Mack asked, "What? The *cute snow bunny on the slope* look didn't appeal to him?"

She smirked at him. "I would probably be the bunny falling off the slope," she pointed out. "That look would never appeal to him."

"Too bad," Mack said. "I think it would be adorable."

She laughed. "You have a skewed idea of a sense of humor though," she noted. "I'm not sure that counts in this case." When Mack took another corner up ahead, she looked around. "It's really wintery here."

"It is," he confirmed. "They get a lot more snow up here than Kelowna does. Most of ours is gone in town, and, with your being on the river, you have access to a lot more sun in a day," he explained. "So, although Kelowna will get more snow at various locations in town, out here they get quite a bit more." He gave her a bright smile, as they passed the entrance to the ski mountain. "Anytime you want to learn how to snowboard, I'm in," he offered.

She looked on with interest, as several of the cars behind them and the one in front turned and headed up the mountain. "I'm not the athletic type. Yet drinking hot chocolate and sitting around the fire and looking outside at the snow sounds like fun," she replied wistfully.

He nodded. "If you're serious, we can always go away for a weekend."

She looked at him and smiled. "Now that would be fun, although I have no one to look after the animals."

"My brother might agree to get roped into that—or we could rent a cabin and take them with us too. Maybe we could start you off with cross-country skiing instead of downhill."

"I always wanted to ski," she muttered, "yet I just never really imagined that I would be very good at it."

Mack swore under his breath.

"I know. I know. I know," she muttered, sighing at the remnants of hearing Mathew's voice still in her head.

"Yeah," Mack admitted, "those statements just make me all the more determined to take you up on the mountain to see if you would enjoy it." Then he looked over at the animals and added, "But the animals are not invited for that."

"Really?" she asked, looking at him in surprise.

"Yeah, really," he stated, his lips twitching. "I don't know how you'll carry Mugs and Goliath and Thaddeus while on skis."

"I have carried them in the past," she stated, "but it's not exactly an easy combination."

"No, you're not kidding," he agreed, "and I can see them dumping you into a snowbank at the first chance."

"Mugs might, if only to sit on top of me and to warm his feet."

At that image, he burst out laughing. "I can so see that too," he said, still chuckling. "What was the address again?" She looked it up on her phone and repeated it for him. He frowned. "I did check our database earlier, but I don't have anything with that address in the files."

Doreen asked, "Was this one of those areas where things were rezoned and new postal codes were given and others changed?"

"I don't think so. Up here everything would happen in a pretty standard way, although I won't say it couldn't have happened, because you know how things go."

"Right, the wild, wild west," she said helpfully.

He grinned and nodded. "Exactly. So we don't really know what's going on along some of the backroads up here," he explained. "We've pretty much input our paper files into the online database, and other areas in the department are up to speed in many ways, but you never really feel as if everything has been included."

"Right, I can imagine," she murmured. As they headed around one more corner, she smiled. "It's a long way out of town."

"And yet it really isn't that far," he noted. "It's just a short drive, but you're not used to driving very far."

"If you say so," she muttered, but inside she was quite happy that he'd driven, even if Mugs wasn't terribly impressed. She looked down at him stretched out on the back seat, and he woofed at her. "It's okay, buddy," she said gently. "We're almost there." And, sure enough, Mack slowed and came to a turnoff onto a narrow dirt road. "Is this it?"

"It is," he declared, "and, as you can see, it's not paved." He carried on up the road, and the dirt turned to mud and slush. By the time they reached the house, piles of snow were all along the roadsides.

"Wow," she muttered.

Mack nodded. "The owner probably had the lane plowed before the last snowfall, which melted and left a muddy mess behind. You can see that the snow was all heaped up as we drove in. ... So definitely more wintry conditions are up here than in town."

Chapter 3

A S THEY HOPPED out of Mack's truck, the front door to the house opened, and an old man wearing bright red suspenders over a pair of khaki pants stood in the doorway. He had on just a T-shirt, which really surprised Doreen, since it was clearly wintertime here. As he studied the two of them, he frowned.

Doreen ushered Goliath out of Mack's truck, but he immediately balked. "What's the matter, Goliath?" His ruff stood out in warning, and he immediately returned to the truck. "You want to stay here?" she asked him.

Mack came to her side, wondering what the delay was. When Doreen explained Goliath's reaction, Mack nodded. "Better leave him here. He's smelling something he doesn't like."

"But Mugs is yanking on the leash and can't wait to get inside. Plus, Thaddeus is calm."

Mack shook his head. "I would defer to the animals then. To each their own."

With Goliath safely inside, and the windows cracked to circulate some air, Doreen let Mugs pull her to the front door and the owner of this property.

As soon as the old man saw the animals, his face rippled into a huge smile. "Doreen?" he asked excitedly.

She smiled right back and nodded. "Yes, that's me. Nice to meet you, Milford."

"Welcome, welcome," he boomed, his voice echoing through the air. Mugs raced toward him, and the old man bent down to give him a big greeting. Thaddeus, not to be outdone, called out, "Thaddeus is here. Thaddeus is here." The old man laughed and laughed. "Oh my, you have made me a happy old man today." He ushered them inside, and, as soon as he looked at Mack, he asked, "Are you her assistant?"

At that, Doreen snickered, and Mack turned on her, his eyes beading into a frown. She paused between her giggles to speak. "This is my fiancé," she replied. Mack's frown fell away, and he beamed. He reached out a hand and introduced himself as Corporal Mack Moreau, Kelowna detective.

"The police?" Milford asked, his eyebrows soaring upward. He turned to face Doreen. "You're engaged to him?"

She nodded. "He asked me to marry him over the holidays."

"That's good timing," The farmer faced Mack and added, "Besides, you probably need to keep her close, don't you?"

"I do, but maybe not for the reasons you're thinking of," Mack replied, with a chuckle.

"Oh, I imagine she's a handful," Milford declared. "That brings back good memories of days gone by." He pushed them farther and farther into his house, which was simply one big room with a wood-burning stove in the center. He walked over, crouched down, and checked that enough wood was in the stove. Then, with a nod, he turned back to them. "Can I get you some coffee?"

"Sure, I would love a cup," Doreen replied.

Mack added, "Me too. Thanks."

Doreen looked around, noting the single couch and the solo old chair, both which had seen better years, but the old man appeared to be in decent health and in a good humor. "Have you lived here long?" she asked him.

"All my life," Milford stated proudly. "It's hard when you lose your partner of fifty years," he shared, "but that's what happened to my Rose last year. Breast cancer took her away from me. I've got no use for that cancer stuff," he muttered. "It's got no business taking such a beautiful person from me."

"I'm so sorry," Doreen said.

He nodded. "That's the problem though. Everybody's sorry, but just nothing nobody can do about it. It's like, tag, you're it. It's downhill from there, like a line of dominos falling, with the lack of medical treatments, particularly at her age and her stage of cancer," he muttered. "Life hasn't been the same since."

"Do you want to move back into town?" she asked. "You would be closer to everyone."

He snorted at that. "If I were to go anywhere, I would move farther away from people. Good night, absolutely nothing to be gained getting close to people."

She smiled. "You've got a lot of snow out here."

"Yep, I sure do," Milford stated proudly. "I kind of like it myself."

"The snow?" she asked.

He nodded. "I like winter. I like the hibernation. I like the fact that the road is impassable for most people." His lips twitched as he looked over at Mack. "I was a little afraid that Doreen wouldn't make it up here."

Mack smiled and nodded. "I wouldn't let her drive here, since she didn't know the area."

"Good thinking," Milford said. "You never know. You may need to keep a leash on that one. Lots of guys like me are out there who would try to steal her from you." Then he went off in a cackle of pure joy.

Doreen grinned at him. "And, if you weren't still mourning the loss of your beloved wife, I might even be interested."

That set Milford off again. "Oh my, this is definitely a good day now." He motioned them over to the couch. "Take a seat. Take a seat."

Almost as if understanding what the couch had once been used for, Mugs quickly hopped up and settled in immediately, without her even getting the chance to tell him off for his bad behavior. She gasped and rushed over to get him down, but the old man was having none of it.

"He found Old Boomer's place," Milford shared. "That's where he sat all the time."

"What happened to Old Boomer?" she asked, without thinking it through.

His face quieted, and he sighed. "Lost him a few months back. … I don't want to say it was almost as hard as losing my Rose, but, at that point in time, it was a second deadly blow." He shook his head. "Ain't fair. None of it's fair."

"I'm so sorry." Doreen winced, as she appeared to be constantly saying the wrong things.

"Oh, don't you worry about that," Milford said. "It was his time to go, and he was just as heartbroken over the loss of my beloved Rose as I was."

Mack, as if sensing more pitfalls ahead, interrupted, "Doreen mentioned something about the zucchini plot."

"Yeah." The old man turned a little more belligerent as he faced Mack, as if seeing the cop in front of him now, not Doreen's fiancé. "I have been planting in that zucchini patch since time began, until all that blood appeared one day. And my beautiful Rose told me that the murder needed to be resolved, once and for all. I told her there weren't nothing I could do about it, but then I read about Doreen here. So, I thought, well, maybe I would give it one more try to solve the mystery. For Rose, you know?"

"I'm glad you did," Doreen replied. "Now, if you wouldn't mind telling us what happened?"

"Not a whole lot to tell," Milford began, with a shrug. "I went out one day to check on the zucchini patch. Boy, was it overflowing with zucchinis." A fat grin covered his face at the memory.

"It was one of those bumper crops, where anytime somebody came by to visit, we sent them home with zucchinis, basically forcing them to take some in order to get rid of it," he shared, with a chuckle. "I've got to admit that there were probably a few times when people didn't even want to see us because I would send them home with half a dozen each." At that, his expression again filled with happy memories. Then a cloud passed over his features, and his smile faded.

"And then one day I went out there, and blood was everywhere. I mean, fresh blood, soaking into the ground. It was all over the place. And the ground was chewed up some, as if some big fight had happened."

Doreen frowned at him, and he nodded.

"I went back inside, told my wife, and she just shrugged, saying some coyote or whatever must have gotten a rabbit or something," he murmured.

"I hadn't put up much in the way of fences for the rabbits, and honestly, I would have kept that zucchini crop outside the rabbit fence to let them eat it anyway, just to slow its growth," he explained. "Some people have trouble with zucchinis, but they grow like crazy here. Anyway, I looked around for a carcass, but I didn't see anything. As far as I was concerned, it was way too much blood for a rabbit." The old man shrugged.

"Back then we had a Kodak camera, and I tried to take some pictures, but the light was funny, and the blood just didn't show up." He sighed. "It's one of the reasons I didn't worry about really forcing the issue because it seemed I had no way to prove it was blood. Plus, the ground soaked it up very quickly. I had no way of knowing whether it was something else, though I couldn't figure out what else it could be.

"So that was part of the problem too. If it wasn't blood, then what was it? And, if it was blood, whose was it? I thought maybe a deer got taken down, and it was certainly that level of blood, but why would there be a dead deer when I hadn't killed one? And, if the blood was from a deer, where was it? We do have bears and mountain lions up here, cougars for sure," he added, "and wolves definitely."

"So, it could have been a nonhuman predator, is what you're saying?" Mack asked.

"Yeah, it sure could have been, and I was prepared to let it go. Honestly, I didn't want to start any big hullabaloo about it. I didn't want nothing to do with any headache and hardship, particularly with the police," he said, his gaze narrowing on Mack.

Mack just nodded and didn't say anything, something he seemed to be really good about when it came to reading people.

Doreen patted Mugs, pleased to see he was being very well behaved. She looked back at the old man. "So why now?"

"Because of my Rose," Milford replied. "One of the things that she wanted me to do was get that settled once and for all, so her soul could rest easy. Mind you, I figured that, once you're dead, you're probably dead, and your soul don't care no more. Still, she told me that it would bother her into eternity, and I don't want anything to stop my beautiful Rose from having a good sleep," he explained. "So, I've fussed. I've fumed, and I've thought about it. Then I figured there would be no help for it. I would just have to find a way. Then I heard about you," he declared, with a beaming smile in Doreen's direction. "I'm not even sure how I stumbled on you," he admitted, looking at her, as if she were suddenly here out of the blue, without his even understanding that much.

Dorren watched him, noting some of the same symptoms she saw at Rosemoor starting to show with this man as well. She looked over at Mack to see if he'd picked up on it, and it was obvious that he had. "So," Doreen asked, "did you keep any of the soil from that patch?"

"What do you mean?" he asked, looking at her. "I didn't plant in that patch no more. If it was people blood, which I don't know why it would be, I felt it would be bad juju if I were to plant something in that soil."

She studied him for a long moment. "I would have thought maybe giving some of that back to Mother Nature would be the circle of life."

He looked at her, then nodded. "I do think about that every once in a while, but my beloved Rose wanted this mystery solved."

"Right," Doreen agreed, as she turned to look out the window. "Where is this zucchini patch?"

"Ah, after coffee, I'll take you out there." He got up to tend to a big black kettle, boiling on the stove. He took off the lid, tossed something in, and then proceeded to pour two cups, which he then handed to each of them. She took hers and accepted it gently. It was hot, far too hot to drink.

Mack was busy getting them back on topic. "Did you have any visitors around that time?"

"*Nah*, no visitors. We don't get much in the way of visitors out here."

"How long ago was this?"

"Oh, twenty-five years or thereabouts," Milford replied, with a frown.

Doreen's eyebrows shot up.

"As I already told you, I was totally okay to ignore it for the rest of my life, but my beloved Rose wouldn't have it."

"Right." Doreen noted that everything Milford was doing now was being orchestrated by a woman from the grave. However, if something was nefarious about all that blood … "When you say there was a lot of blood," she began.

He nodded. "A lot of blood."

"Okay, can you tell me what *a lot* looks like?" she asked.

"Oh, it's at least this whole patch, some six feet wide." He shook his head. "Never really thought there would be that much blood."

"Six feet? So, like a six-foot circle?" Mack asked.

The old farmer pondered that. "It weren't no circle. It was a big mess, not exactly neat and tidy like a circle would be, but, yeah, I would say about a six-foot circle. You know, six feet across the diameter."

Doreen nodded, pulled out a little notebook that she kept with her, then started making notes. When she looked up, Milford was giving her a big wide smile.

"See? Now if you were here twenty-five years ago, I would have brought you down to look at this. I called the cops, and they told me that it was probably a cougar or a deer or something along that line."

"Did they come out here?" Mack asked.

"Nope. Sure didn't. 'Course, at the time I wasn't exactly too interested in having them out here. So I probably didn't make it all that clear what I thought should happen."

"Right," Mack muttered, with a nod, "but maybe now you could tell me what you think happened."

The old man looked at him. "It's obvious, isn't it?"

"Not to me it isn't," Mack replied. Then he looked over at Doreen, who grinned at him.

"It's obvious from our corner," she declared, with a knowing smile to Milford.

"What's obvious?" Mack asked in confusion.

Doreen explained, "That somebody was murdered here."

"Exactly," the old man agreed, grinning broadly. "Now I know I got the right person." He cackled hard, slapping his knee. "Drink up your coffee, Doreen. Drink up, and I'll take you out to the crime scene."

At that, Mack rolled his eyes and whispered something under his breath.

She nudged him, but she also knew where Mack was coming from. She worked to finish her coffee, which she had to admit was a struggle to get down. It was strong and thick and black, yet somewhat appealing. She would take a sip and almost choked as it was so strong. Yet still she had to have another sip because it had a very unique flavor.

"Campfire coffee," Milford shared, with a nod. "It takes a bit of getting used to, but, once you're there, you'll crave it."

"At least now I know where to come to get another cup," she said, with a smile.

"Oh, yes. Anytime you want a good cup of coffee, you just come right on up here," he declared, "and I'll get you one."

"Thank you."

Thaddeus poked his head out from behind the fall of her hair and whispered, "Thaddeus is here."

"I know, buddy," she said, then felt a little shiver pass through him. "Are you okay, buddy?" Thaddeus rubbed against her cheek. She stroked his feathers and murmured, "Doreen is here. Doreen is here."

"Does he ever come out of your hair?" the old man asked, staring at the bird.

She looked at him and shrugged. "At home, yes, but not always when we're out. Sometimes he likes to walk. It depends on how comfortable he is."

Milford nodded. "He probably smells Ragtag."

"Who is Ragtag?" she asked.

Milford grinned. "He's my cat, and he's huge, so a bird like yours? He would be a goner for sure."

She again felt a slight shiver in Thaddeus, as he quickly tucked back behind her ear, as if understanding full well what the conversation was about. "That is good to know," she replied, looking at Milford. "I don't want anything to happen to Thaddeus here."

"No, I wouldn't either," he declared cheerfully. "So, it's a good thing you're not letting him down on the floor."

She frowned at that, then looked over at Mack, who

studied the old man carefully. "Now that the coffee is gone," she noted, standing up as she held her hand close to Thaddeus, "how about you show us the old zucchini patch?"

"Righto." Milford hopped up, grabbed his jacket, and waited for them to get bundled back up again. "Let's go. It's out here in the back."

Out of the corner of her eye, Doreen caught sight of a huge monster-size cat, watching them as they headed toward the door. She stopped, looked at the cat, then asked Thaddeus, "Is that what's bothering you?" Thaddeus nodded.

"Oh, that's him," the old man said, laughing. "He's a great hunter, been hunting all his life."

"Thaddeus is not on the menu," she stated.

"Of course not," Milford agreed. He turned, cast a gimlet eye at the cat, and barked, "Did you hear that?" And, with that, he walked out ahead of them. A little unnerved, realizing that she had a cat of her own, and that cats were cats and required a different set of acceptance in many ways than other animals, Doreen quickly exited the house, keeping a close eye to ensure the other cat was shut up inside as they left.

She looked back at Thaddeus as they stepped outside and muttered, "See? That's why not all animals are friendly for you to interact with." Thaddeus just looked at her, and she nodded. "I know, but those are the facts of life." Outside, they walked around the house to the back, where a walled-off garden was. She stepped up, looked at it, then frowned.

"Oh, it's not here," he declared, with a bright smile. "It's over here." And, with that, he led her around to the far end of the garden, to another patch that sat empty and forlorn, more or less weeded over, except for winter plants and old brown weeds, plus a couple sprigs of green still frozen in time, with snow atop them. "This is the patch," he announced, pointing it out.

"Interesting," she murmured.

"Right, but, ever since then, I haven't been able to do anything with this garden," he muttered.

She stared at the patch. "This is about ten by five?"

"Good eye." Milford nodded. "Good eye."

"Okay, and did this only hold zucchinis?" she asked.

"Yeah, it sure did," he proclaimed. "That's why we had to get rid of so much of it."

"You could have grown less," she suggested, turning to look at him.

"Could have, but my beloved wife, she loved zucchini, so we grew lots of it. We just gave away the surplus."

She frowned, not quite sure she understood why anyone would grow so much, yet she also understood that zucchini plants tended to take on a life of their own. As she surveyed the patch, she asked, "And the blood filled the whole thing?"

Milford nodded. "Yeah, it sure did."

"Interesting," she murmured. "Did you ever dig it up?"

He looked at her. "What do you mean, dig it up?"

"Turn over the bed or do anything with it?"

"Nope, nope, nope, nope," he said. "It's exactly as it was."

"Right," she replied, staring at it. She wasn't sure what she was supposed to say at this point, but her mind was already seeking answers. "Now," she began, and Milford eyed her expectedly. "You say you haven't turned it over, and you haven't used this plot."

"Nope."

"So, are you saying that, if I took a sample of the dirt

right here, we would end up with blood in it?"

"Sure would," he said, "although, there's been however much rain and snow and ice thinning it down, watering it out, or whatever."

"Right." She turned to Mack, who just frowned at her. "Do you have a baggie?"

His eyebrows shot up, but he whispered, "Do you really think the city will pay for a soil analysis at this point in time?"

She frowned because she hadn't thought about that. She also knew the captain wouldn't be supportive just because of budgets and all. They might have solved a lot of cases, but they had done so without a ton of expenses. So incurring more would be a constant headache for everybody. As she considered this, she noted, "We can't proceed if we don't have a sample, so let's at least do that."

"I'll get you a container." The old man raced back inside.

She looked at Mack as Milford took off, his jacket flapping around as if this was the most excitement he'd had in a very long time. "What are you thinking?" she asked Mack.

"I think he's nuts," he stated. When she rolled her eyes, he smiled.

"Maybe this really is something that bothered his wife," she suggested, "and he's just trying to clear up loose ends, before it's his time to go."

"I get that, and I'm not against your theory, but I don't think we'll get this analyzed."

"You don't think the captain will go for it?"

"I know the captain won't go for it," he stated. "We've had a hard time getting approved for things like this on current cases that we have a shot at solving. We don't know if this was even a crime. Oh, and I didn't get a chance to tell you this, but we've just had another round of cuts."

"More?" she asked, her eyes growing round.

"Yeah. We haven't got the new budget numbers yet—and we might not for a while, I guess. Yet what I can tell you for certain is that we don't have the money for this kind of thing."

She frowned, as she went over that. "What kind of money would it even cost?"

"I don't know. I would have to look into it."

"Are there private labs?"

His gaze turned wary, as he frowned at her. "I suppose there are, but I don't really know."

"If I give the captain the money to get it analyzed, would he allow that?"

"*Hmm*, maybe," Mack replied, "but I don't really know the answer to that. Because if it *is* blood—"

"Right, if it *is* blood of human variety," she clarified, "then it would be a case we need to look at."

"*We?*" Mack repeated, with a note of humor.

She looked at him and then nodded. "Yes, *we*, because this would be a cold case, so it would be a *me* case," she explained, beaming.

"Right, a *you* case, not a *me* case. Unless of course we find the body," Mack added.

"Which is why I was wondering if Milford had turned over the soil."

"Meaning, you think a body is buried here?" he asked, as he looked down at the ground.

"I don't know that there is. However, I also don't know that there isn't," she pointed out. "In cases like this, it's always hard to know."

"Cases like this," he repeated, his lips twitching.

She threw up her hands. "It might sound as if I'm trying to put on airs," she admitted, "but I'm really not. But what if a body is here?"

"I don't know. I can't imagine."

"And what if there was evidence of a murder here but no body? Or what if you have blood that goes to a cold case of a body that was found and not identified?"

"That's all possible. All of those possibilities are viable, or it could be a figment of the old guy's imagination," Mack pointed out, staring off in the distance. "But let's take a sample back with us, so we have it. No guarantees though," he stated pointedly.

"No, of course not," she agreed, with a bright smile. When he rolled his eyes at that, she grinned even more.

"You are interesting to have around," he muttered. "I'll give you that."

"More than that," she declared, with a cheerful grin on her face, "but I know it's hard for you to see it."

"Oh no. No way. You don't get to say things like that. I'm always happy to have you around, and you bring up a lot of very fun information," he noted, waving his hand at the house where the old man had gone.

She laughed. "If nothing else, it will make Milford feel as if he's doing what he promised Rose that he would do."

"I'll give you that," Mack muttered, "but we're not into therapy or grief counseling, so remember that."

"Right," she confirmed. "We appear to be into the stage of getting answers as to what happened, as to the cause of that grief right now."

"His wife died of natural causes, remember?"

"Breast cancer," she noted. "I guess that would be classified as natural causes, although sometimes I don't see how there could possibly be anything natural about breast cancer."

"I won't argue that," he replied.

She laughed. "Good. Some things you just can't argue."

"And, with you," he muttered, "there are a lot of those things."

Chapter 4

RETURNING TO TOWN in Mack's truck, Doreen frowned at the mason jar she clutched, full of dirt from several layers deep. "So Milford never dug up that plot since that first night where he found the blood because his wife claimed it was sacrilegious to disturb the site now. So, something should be in the sample, right? But how degraded would it have gotten over the last twenty-five or so years?"

Mack shrugged. "Surely it would have degraded a certain amount, just from being out in the elements for decades. Still, if the sample isn't too degraded, then forensics might be able to tell us if there is human blood in it. That is the main question here. Remember how we find bodies many, many years later and have managed to find all kinds of forensic information," he replied, taking his gaze off the road for a second to glance at her.

She nodded. "It's just so sad to think that maybe something happened that long ago, and yet nobody cared enough to do anything about it."

"But we don't know that anybody was notified," he clarified. "If Milford did call the police, we can't confirm it. Plus, the passage of time and history may have changed his viewpoint on some part of this event. That happens a lot with witness statements."

"I guess it really does, doesn't it?" she muttered. "You would think that people would be more open to the truth over time."

"I think that's probably why he's doing something now," Mack suggested.

"Maybe." They came up to the turnoff road for Big White. She watched as several vehicles took their turn and headed up toward the local ski mountain.

"Interested?" he asked, with a smile.

"Maybe," she replied.

He chuckled. "It might be fun."

"I highly doubt that. Most of the deaths up there are ski- or snowboard-related, and they happen fairly quickly."

"Meaning?" he asked.

"Meaning that there aren't any cold cases."

"I don't think Nan thought Kelowna had many cold cases either," he noted, followed by a moment of silence from Doreen. "Does that bother you?" he asked.

She turned to him. "Does what bother me?"

"That so many cold cases seem to be here in town."

"No, it doesn't bother me at all. I just think it's good that we're getting to the bottom of them."

"Do you think you'll get to the bottom of all of them?" he asked, a wry note in his tone.

She shuffled in her seat, causing Thaddeus to shift with a squawk. She laughed as she petted him. "It's okay, buddy. Thaddeus sure didn't seem to like that cat out there at Milford's farm, did he?"

"Cats on a rural place," Mack noted, "are hunters. Chances are, they're mostly self-reliant and feed themselves off squirrels and anything else they can drag in, including birds."

"I would hate to think of Thaddeus going that way," she whispered, with a shudder.

"Of course not, but unfortunately, a lot of cats are great hunters." He cast a glance at Goliath, sprawled out on the back seat. "Goliath must have smelled Ragtag and knew better than to go inside."

"Thank goodness. I don't want Goliath getting hurt in a fight."

"Yet Mugs was pretty quiet back there."

"He was, and I was quite surprised." She frowned. "He didn't try to get friendly with Ragtag either."

"I'm pretty sure that Ragtag would have had something to say about it. Good thing you locked Goliath in the truck."

"Yeah," she agreed. "Once I realized Goliath refused to come with us, I just locked him inside."

"Good, the last thing we want is two cats fighting. That would be a tough thing to separate."

"Maybe so. … When I stumbled across Mathew's body, Goliath got into it with a town cat and didn't really win that fight, from what I saw. I sure don't want him fighting any more cats, especially a feral hunter of a cat."

"He's fixed, right?" Mack asked.

"Goliath?" she asked. "Yes, he's fixed, and so is Mugs." Then she frowned. "I don't know how to protect Thaddeus from wild cats."

Mack laughed. "Just keep him close, or at home and just love him," he suggested, "but you could always ask your grandmother about that too."

"That's true. I hadn't considered that. I'll do it when we get back again."

"I'll take the soil sample to the lab and speak with the captain. However, I'm quite certain the timeframe is too long to get definitive answers about whether this is blood. Even if they suggest it might be, there won't be any DNA to identify who might have bled there. Keep that in mind."

"Thanks for doing that." She gave him a beaming smile. He dropped her off back at her house, and she unlocked the front door and stepped inside, with the animals in tow. Mugs and Goliath headed for the rear kitchen door, wanting outside again. So she propped open the door for them, as they wandered around the relative safety of her backyard. They were much more content now that they were home again. However, they were all in an oddly quiet mood, as if they hadn't found anything joyful or easy about the trip to Milford's farm.

"It was very different, wasn't it, guys?" With no answers forthcoming, she noted, "Interesting that you guys didn't like that trip." She carefully watched them for a moment. "Then again, it was an odd one for me too. It's a different world over there."

Thaddeus didn't seem interested in getting off her shoulder either.

"It's okay, Thaddeus," she said, stroking his beautiful feathers. He nuzzled his head against her neck and just stayed tucked up against her. It was such an odd reaction for all of them that she decided maybe a trip to Nan's might be a good idea.

"Anybody want to go Nan's?" Mugs looked at her, as if waiting for her to say it one more time, and she repeated it. "How about a trip to Nan's?"

Mugs jumped up from the patio and woofed at her. Goliath headed down toward the pathway, ahead of the game.

"Hey, hang on a minute," she called out to Goliath, but, no, he was on his way.

"Dang," she muttered, as she quickly grabbed the leashes, closed the kitchen door, and chased down Goliath. She called Nan on the way.

Sounding distracted, Nan asked, "Where are you?"

"We're on the river," Doreen replied. "We were hoping to come say hi."

"Oh." An odd tone was in her voice. "Sure."

"Unless it's a bad time."

"No, no," she replied. "When you're my age, you take the time. No such thing as a bad time, just time or no time." Then she gave a cackle of laughter. "I'll go put on the teakettle."

Goliath seemed to pick up his feet and moved rapidly, almost at a lope down the river. Not to be outdone, Mugs stayed very close to him. In fact, Doreen had to walk at an uncomfortably fast pace, just to keep up with them.

When they finally turned the corner to Rosemoor, they both seemed to calm down slightly.

She frowned at them and asked, "What on earth is going on with you two?" Oddly Thaddeus was still superquiet. The minute they got near Rosemoor, a mellow relaxing wave seemed to wash over all three of her animals. She crossed the lawn hurriedly, still remembering being told off for doing such a thing by one of the cranky gardeners, and stepped onto Nan's patio.

As soon as she did so, her grandmother asked, "Good Lord, are you still not coming in the front door?"

Doreen shrugged sheepishly. "Old habits die hard."

"Yeah, but you'll mess up my carpets if you come in this way. Everything is wet and muddy out there."

"I don't know about muddy," Doreen noted, "but you're right. It's definitely not very dry out here." With Nan tsking all over the place, Doreen quickly removed her wet boots and then stepped into the main room of Nan's apartment, closing the door behind her.

"There you are," Nan said, sitting in her big rocker. She had Goliath on her lap, and Mugs was stretched out on the footstool. The only one she was missing was Thaddeus, who was still perched on Doreen's shoulder, but not for long. Thaddeus gave a squawk, flew off her shoulder, and landed awkwardly on top of Goliath, who turned to swipe at him. Nan nimbly picked up the bird and deftly moved him to her own shoulder. "There we go," she told Thaddeus. "It's all okay." She looked over at Doreen. "Why are they all so out of sorts?"

"I'm not sure. I was hoping a trip down here would set them all to rights."

Nan attempted to reach them all at once, nodding carefully. "I don't normally see them acting quite so needy."

"No, neither do I. It's definitely a little concerning."

"You can pour the tea and then tell me all about it."

"Who says I have anything to tell?"

Nan looked at her and raised her eyebrows. "The animals certainly have something to say."

"I know," Doreen agreed, with a sigh. "It was just such a weird trip this morning."

"Ooh," Nan replied in delight. "Have you got a new case?"

"No. Maybe. I guess. I don't know," she muttered. "I'm not sure what this one is." She walked into the tiny kitchen area, picked up the tea tray already sitting there, carried it out to the living room, and set it down on the coffee table.

"You might as well go ahead and pour. It should be ready now," Nan stated.

Doreen obediently poured the tea and then sat back, looking at the animals in wonder, because not a one of them was moving. "Did you have a good morning?" she asked her grandmother.

Nan shrugged. "I was a little out of it this morning. You know, just one of those pensive days. Not a good day, not a bad day."

"Maybe it's not me that the animals are feeling but you."

Nan frowned at her, then looked down at the animals and gave them a fond smile. "That could be true."

"They certainly wanted to dash down here and see you."

"I won't ever be upset about that," Nan shared. "The older you get, the more you realize how important it is to have friends and family you want around you," she added, with a delighted smile.

Doreen just nodded, didn't say anything, hoping that whatever was bothering her grandmother would pass quickly.

"So, tell me," Nan said. "What's this new case?"

Doreen laughed. "You're as bad as I am."

"Ooh, I am, indeed," she agreed, with a big nod. "You have no idea how much we're all enjoying your cases."

"And yet they're all very sad."

"Sure." Nan gave a dismissive wave of her hand. "It's not as if we can change what happened. The best we can do is provide some closure for these people left behind."

There was definitely some truth to that, so Doreen proceeded to tell her grandmother about the weird phone call she'd received from Milford, and then about Mack wanting to make the trip with her.

"I see that Mack wants to be involved in your cases."

Nan burst out laughing at that.

"It's not that he wants to be involved in my cases. I think he's trying to keep me out of his."

Nan gave her a sly grin. "You could be right. Still, it's good for both of you. You have no idea how happy I am that the two of you are engaged."

"Agreed, but no pressure," she warned. "That was the agreement. He wouldn't pressure me into setting a date or locking down the details until I'm ready."

"Of course not," Nan stated. "You have to be your own person."

"If you say so," Doreen quipped, with a headshake. "Sometimes I think you guys are all just conniving your way into our wedding."

"Hey, Thaddeus won the pool."

"And how did *Thaddeus* win the pool?"

"Don't know," Nan replied, with an innocent smile. "So the contents of that pool go to you."

"Which means, it'll go toward the wedding."

"Yes, exactly, and we really love that solution," Nan crowed in delight. "I think you should get married here at Rosemoor."

"Oh." Doreen's eyebrows rose. "I hadn't considered that."

"Do," Nan urged. "Then we could all attend."

"Are you telling me that you wouldn't attend if it was somewhere else?"

"Of course we would, but then we would have to steal the Rosemoor bus again to get everybody down there."

Doreen laughed. "I'm sure everybody wants to avoid a repeat of that."

"Richie still has his driver's license, you know?"

Doreen winced. "Not sure for how long though."

"I know. Richie is getting on."

It was all Doreen could do to hold her smile back at that because, if Richie was getting on, so was Nan. Although, true enough, Richie was possibly five years older than Nan, if not more. Doreen couldn't remember their ages, but they were certainly having a lot of fun in their golden years.

"It may not matter, since we don't know how many people will be alive by the time you get around to getting married," Nan declared in a woebegone tone. "It would really be sad if we lost a bunch beforehand."

"Oh, no you don't," Doreen snapped in alarm. "No trying to guilt trip me into making this wedding happen sooner."

"No, I would never do that," Nan replied, looking at her askance. "How could you possibly say such a thing?"

Doreen rolled her eyes. "Have a sip of tea, Nan. Your wiles are lost on me."

Nan burst out laughing. "Still, it's a valid point. We're not getting any younger."

"Oh, and I guess that goes for me too then, right?"

"We'll consider all options," Nan noted. "Just so you know, some people here would be heartbroken if they weren't invited."

Doreen nodded. "I imagine inviting as many people as we can, and that, in itself, will be an issue in terms of venue. But also," she hesitated and then added, "as much as I'm happy to have a nice wedding, I don't want to end up with a big spectacle that everybody weighs in on."

"No, of course not," Nan said, "but I really would love for you to get married while I'm still here."

She stared at her Nan for a long moment. "And I very

much want you at my wedding," she pointed out. "So, why don't we just accept *that* as the plan, so you can relax and let me work on the details?"

Nan nodded.

"Or, is it that you think I won't work on the details?" Doreen asked, eyeing her grandmother shrewdly.

"I just don't think you'll work on the details fast enough," Nan clarified, with a bright smile. "And I know you're busy, so you should let me help."

"Letting you help is like letting a fox into a hen house," Doreen replied. "You'll make things happen, but I won't necessarily enjoy the clean-up."

Her grandmother stared at her for a long moment, then burst into peals of laughter. "Oh my, that was absolutely perfect." She was still chortling, as she added, "And you're right. You might not like the clean-up, but you know I would get the job done—if you don't have time to handle it."

"We're not having the wedding for a long time, so relax and forget about it for now."

Her grandmother grumbled, as she settled back in her chair. "Not sure what you're waiting for. It's not as if you're getting any younger either." Doreen glared at her, and Nan gave her a beatific smile. "Now, let's get back to the case you were on today."

"Yeah, sure." Doreen sighed. After all, anything was better than getting grilled by her grandmother about wedding dates.

"Besides, we'll figure it out, and, if need be, we might have to talk to Mack about it," Nan suggested, sitting up straighter.

"Oh goodness, Nan." Doreen shook her head. "Feel free

to talk to Mack, but, if he pushes me about a date, I will back off," she pointed out. She almost never spoke to Nan in that tone of voice, but she didn't plan on being railroaded into a wedding she wasn't ready for.

Nan slumped and once again glared at her for squashing her plans.

Doreen added as an afterthought, "I need to go visit Millicent too."

"Oh, yes, that's a good idea. I'm sure she's thrilled."

"I think so," Doreen said with a smile, as she thought about Mack's mother. "We always got along pretty well up until now."

Nan nodded. "Honestly, I think she would be happy with anybody at this point." When Doreen gasped, Nan blinked at her and then grinned. "Didn't quite mean that the way it came out, but—"

"*Right,*" Doreen grumbled, standing up. "Okay, on that note—"

"No, no, no, don't go," Nan called out, waving her hand. "Richie hasn't gotten here yet."

"Why is Richie coming?"

"What do you mean, why is Richie coming?" she repeated. "He hasn't heard about the case either."

Doreen frowned at her, and Mugs just threw himself sideways on the footstool, stretching out with a deep happy snore.

"See? Mugs doesn't want to leave yet either," Nan said.

With a sigh, Doreen sat again. "He didn't appear to be very impressed at Milford's home today," Doreen noted, "and neither was Goliath. He wouldn't get out of the truck." At that, Nan frowned at her. Doreen nodded. "I really don't know what was upsetting them, but another cat was in the house and was *not* friendly, which definitely terrified poor Thaddeus too."

"Oh my," Nan muttered. "That's a good reminder that not everybody out there wants to have the animals up close."

"I know," Doreen confirmed, "and some people don't like the animals at all."

"That's just dodgy," Nan declared.

Doreen laughed. "I won't argue with that, but we have to keep in mind that not everybody is an animal lover."

"Which is just weird," Nan stated, with a headshake.

Just then the door opened, and Richie walked in, pushing a walker in front of him.

"Hey, Richie," Doreen greeted him, eyeing the old man. "How are you doing?"

"I'm doing great. How are you, Doreen? All ready to get married?"

She winced. "Nope, I'm really not. Not at all ready to get married." She watched as Nan desperately tried to signal for Richie to be quiet, but either he wasn't seeing her signal or wasn't interested in listening, a trait Doreen had come to recognize in a good part of the residents here. They all seemed content to work on their own agendas, with no particular concern about anybody else's.

Richie continued on. "You should be ready. Mack's a fine young man."

"That he is, no doubt about that," Doreen agreed and tried to steer the conversation back to dead people. "Nan told me that you wanted to hear about my new case."

"Ooh." His face lit up. "You've got a new case, do you?"

"I'm not completely sure about that," she clarified. "It's all a little bit odd."

"Your cases are always odd," Richie said. "That's what

makes them so much fun." With that, he collapsed onto the couch, gave Nan a big smile, and asked her, "So, is it one we can help on?"

"I don't know yet," Nan stated. "Let's hope so."

Then Doreen went through the explanation and the visit they'd made this morning.

"Oh my," Richie noted in astonishment. "That much blood?"

"That's what Milford told us, and we did take samples for forensics. So, first we'll have to figure out if there is blood present and whether it's human or some animal. After so long it's likely to be nonexistent."

"Right. That would be the first thing to check, of course," he stated, with the air of somebody who knows all about it.

Which, at this point in time, Doreen wasn't sure if they did anything but watch cop shows, just so they could keep on top of all these cases. Crime shows seemed to be pretty popular right now.

"You would think that the cops would have gone to the scene," Nan stated.

"Supposedly Milford called them, but Mack has no record of that," Doreen pointed out. "But if nobody was reported missing around that time, or the cops didn't have any reports of violence, and nobody was seen in the area, the cops probably couldn't do much with this case. And way back then, there probably wasn't any DNA testing."

"Or, if there were DNA testing back then, it would have been very expensive and not something they would use to investigate random blood in a garden plot out in the middle of the Joe Rich area," Nan added.

"Ooh, Joe Rich, in the southeast part of Kelowna,"

Richie pointed out. "It's not really the wild, wild west, but it's definitely out in the boondocks. It's a really nice place to visit, but you've got to prefer to live without most of society around you in order to thrive out there. Of course, more recently, a lot of those properties have been incorporated into town now," he noted, "but, way back when, it was still pretty wild."

"I would imagine that, in some ways, it still is," Doreen stated.

"I would guess you're probably right." Richie frowned. "I used to know somebody up that way, but I don't remember who it was." He turned to Nan and asked, "Did we know anybody up there?"

Nan shook her head. "We've met a couple of the volunteer firefighters and whatnot," she noted. "There are definitely a lot of people in the Big White area these days, but I don't know that we've ever really met many people who live farther out. According to Doreen, this guy Milford's farm is way out there."

"Yeah, way back in the boondocks, so to speak," Doreen repeated, with a smile.

"But I wonder if *back in the boondocks* means the same thing to you as it would to me," Richie noted, studying her. "An awful lot of remote land is back there."

"This was about forty-five minutes off the main road."

He thought about that and nodded. "Yeah, that probably qualifies. No power, so wood heat. Nothing along the line of utilities. It's definitely a living-off-the-grid situation. I think they are pretty much on their own."

She frowned at that. "I didn't ask him about that. He did have a phone, but I don't know whether he had service there or went down to the highway to use it."

"Oh, that's good thinking too," Richie said. "And his wife died of breast cancer, you say? Man, that's just not fair, is it?"

"No, it sure isn't." She glanced down at her animals. Mugs stretched out a paw, and she sighed. "The way the animals reacted was over-the-top too."

At that, Nan explained a little bit more, and Richie frowned at Doreen. "You know how these animals are really canny, and if they don't like somebody—"

"It wasn't that they didn't like Milford necessarily, but I don't think they liked the situation. Goliath didn't like anything about it, but then he likes his creature comforts. Poor Thaddeus went very quiet and just hid in my hair the whole time. Milford has a huge cat named Ragtag that is apparently a big hunter, so Thaddeus probably would have been his main meal." At that, Thaddeus gave a squawk and lifted his head, turning to look at her.

She rushed to say, "No, I would never let him get you." She walked over and pet him gently, as he sat on Nan's shoulder. Still, he didn't appear to be very appeased at the concept of her successfully defending him. She sighed and returned to her seat. "As I said, it was a very odd visit. Milford was nice enough, and I certainly don't have a problem with the way he acted. And honestly, I do under-stand why he wants to sort this out now."

Nan and Richie both nodded, as if they could under-stand as well.

Doreen frowned. "I guess what I don't really understand is why they waited to follow up on where all that blood came from and why they never used that plot again."

"It would be sacrilegious," Richie noted. "They felt the need to preserve it."

"That's exactly what Milford told us was that his wife had said too. I just don't understand that process or that point of view, I guess."

Richie stared at her. "What if somebody did die there? By rights they should have put up a little monument or something to remember them by."

"And yet who died?" Doreen asked, with a wry look at him. "Think about it. We don't even know if anybody did die out there."

"Ah"—Richie pointed a finger in her direction—"but you don't know that somebody *didn't*."

Chapter 5

D OREEN WOKE THE next morning, rolled over with a yawn, and cuddled up close to Mugs, who was stretched out beside her. He grunted ever-so-slightly and shifted but not so much to show he intended to get up.

"I feel you, bud," she muttered, snuggling in. As she opened her eyes a few minutes later and stared outside, she saw snow falling gently. She laughed. "Look at that. *Snow.*" She knew that most people wouldn't share her happy reaction, but she hadn't ever spent enough time in the snow to worry about all its disadvantages. Neither did she consider plowing her driveway much of a chore. However, maybe a few years of it would become something she didn't want to do. But, right now, the snow was still a novelty that she enjoyed.

She dragged Mugs out of bed and went downstairs, where she put on coffee, opened up the back door, and stepped outside. Mugs stepped out too, his nose quivering, as he lifted his head to sniff the fresh air and, of course, that lovely snow smell. Then he turned, looked at her, and walked back inside. She burst out laughing but followed Mugs back into the kitchen. "Okay, I guess you're not impressed with the snow."

She grinned as Thaddeus squawked in the living room, where he'd been sleeping on his perch. She walked over to him, picked him up, placed him on her shoulder, and asked, "What about you?" As she carried him outside, he burrowed deeper into her neck, and she agreed, as the wind was picking up. Stepping back inside, she closed the door and poured herself a cup of coffee, then sat down at her laptop to do some research. Her mind was now obsessed with her new case.

Were there any missing persons from that far back? Would the police still have open files on missing persons from over twenty years ago? Mack hadn't gotten back to her on that issue or on the DNA either, which probably would take a lot longer. When he phoned about an hour later, his first question surprised her.

"Have you eaten yet?" he asked.

"Wow, not exactly the first thing I thought you would say."

"I just figured that you'd probably gotten up and gone straight to work and forgotten to eat."

She winced, as she stared down at her coffee cup. "I haven't really eaten yet," she muttered. "I'm still enjoying my coffee."

"Are you on the computer?" he asked, with a note of amusement.

"Maybe"—she frowned at her phone—"but that doesn't mean anything."

"No, it just means that you haven't had breakfast," he stated pointedly.

She sighed, not needing to confirm that. "Did you find out if a case was opened on Milford's bloody garden bed?"

"Haven't found anything as a case," he replied, "and I don't have anything logged in anywhere to say that Milford called or that officers went there."

"So, do we even know if anybody did?"

"That is a good question," he noted cheerfully. "I did talk to the captain, and he was at least in a good mood this morning. So, while he didn't exactly say it was a good idea to check out our soil sample, he did say it would likely be it would be too old for any blood to be identified within the sample."

"That's good," she replied, "and, if it's nothing, then it's nothing. I appreciate him being open minded about it."

"That's what we're hoping," he said, with a laugh. "Anyway I've got to go." And, with that, he disconnected.

She stared down at her phone suspiciously, then called him back. When he answered, he was already distracted. "What?" he asked. "What did you forget??

"You just seemed way too cheerful."

He stopped and asked, "What? I need an excuse to be cheerful?"

"No, but I worried that you have a case."

After a moment of silence, he chuckled. "Even if I did have a *current* case, it would be *my* case."

"Right," she conceded, "but not if it connects to my case."

"*You* don't have a case yet," he countered, "so nothing can connect. Plus, I don't think anything I have on my plate will connect to any cold case."

"You could at least tell me what's on your plate."

"Nope," he stated, his amusement leaking through the phone. "I'm about to head into a meeting. Bye." And, with that, he was gone again.

Frustrated at the lack of information from Mack, she dove back into the internet, checking out the local news to see if anything new had happened overnight. She scrolled through the pages, until she found a reference to a shooting up in Glenmore.

"A shooting," she muttered. She looked at the little bit of information that had been offered to the public but not a whole lot was there. The report noted that the police felt the shooting had been targeted and that the public was not in any danger.

"You guys always say that stuff," she muttered, as she stared at the newspaper story on her laptop screen. Still, any shooting should make citizens wary. Yet Doreen understood those public statements were a tactic used to avoid causing people to panic. She got up to put on some toast, going over Mack's comments. As she was adding butter, her phone rang, and it was Nan.

"Did you hear about the shooting?" Nan asked.

"I saw something about it, but it didn't seem to be fatal."

"Nobody died," Nan stated, "so that's good. At least not yet, they're in the hospital."

"And how do you know so much?"

"Ha. One of the women here has friends who are neighbors. They phoned her this morning with the news."

"And who got shot?"

"A young woman named Lynda Mahoney."

"Oh dear," Doreen muttered. "Is it a domestic violence case?"

"We're not sure. We thought maybe you could find out."

"I can't find out because Mack's not talking to me about

anything current right now." She couldn't stop the grumble in her tone.

Nan laughed. "But he will soon," she suggested, "and, when he does, just remember that we're here, waiting for an update." And, with that, she ended the call.

Doreen groaned. The last thing she needed was to have any more people waiting for her or expecting her to get news from Mack. As the day went on, no new updates were forthcoming on that recent shooting case, and she found nothing about anybody going missing up in the Joe Rich area for years. She went back as far as she could, then wondered about the possibility of a visitor or a traveler, maybe stopping overnight in Kelowna.

She shook her head as she considered the location of Milford's property in relation to anybody traveling. If the visitor stuck to the main highways, they would totally bypass that area. Surely nobody would have gone to the Joe Rich area accidentally. Now, going to Big White made more sense, especially for a ski nut. So she headed back to the online news columns to see if anybody had gone missing from up there, even some fifty years back. She found a few, but they had been found over time, often within a few days if not the same day—usually at something called a tree well. So Mack was correct on that point.

She didn't even know why she felt the need to check it, but something niggled at her about that whole Joe Rich area. Milford was way out from the city proper, so it wasn't long before her mind locked on to another idea. What if Milford wasn't telling the truth? What if this old farmer knew more than he was talking about?

"But if he's lying, withholding information, why would he call me? Why would he want the police to do something about it now?" she queried out loud. Mugs woofed at her, and she looked down at him and smiled. "You're right. It makes no sense, unless his guilt was preying on him all these years. If he withheld info way back when, why would he give us more information now?" She frowned at that and realized she hadn't asked enough questions. She was contemplating going back up there, except for it was snowing here. With the roads up there, the weather could be even worse.

Maybe she could phone him. She quickly picked up a notepad, wrote down a few questions that she wanted answered, and called him. The call went straight to voice mail. She wasn't sure if he would even check his voice mail but figured it was worth a try. So, she left a message, asking him to call her back, saying she had a few more questions, leaving her number for him.

With snow on the roads here she didn't want to go all the way to Joe Rich area, but the local library archives beckoned her out of her home. She told her animals that she would be back soon and put on her coat and grabbed her keys and purse.

She snuck into the microfiche area without a librarian seeing her. She was glad, as she had nothing to share. She decided to start fifty years ago and move forward, searching for any missing persons. Just two hours later, her back was aching to get out of the hardwood chair. And Doreen was frustrated, wishing for a designated Missing Persons section in all newspapers. With a sigh, she muttered, "No such luck."

She vowed to return again. She had a least covered ten years, starting with fifty years ago and working her way up to forty years ago. She would start there the next time.

Chapter 6

DOREEN DIDN'T HEAR back from Milford until the next day. His voice was that of an old man, yet it still boomed on the phone, as if he thought he had to yell.

"What questions?" he asked.

She laughed. "For one thing, were you guys home at the time this would have happened?"

"We'd been gone but were home again, somewhere around the same time period," he noted. "I don't rightly remember, but I think we'd gone into town."

"And you hadn't had any company?"

"Nope, no company."

"And your wife wouldn't have had anybody over to visit?"

"No, nobody was here."

"What did you do for work back then?"

"I worked in the logging industry," he replied. "Gone for a while and back for a while, then gone again for a while and back. We needed whatever work we could get to augment the farm income."

"Did your wife work?"

"Sometimes. Before she had retired, she had been a

nurse. In her later years, she was in town cleaning houses, but often it wasn't worth the trip."

"Right, I can imagine," she agreed. She asked him a few more things about missing people around the area and whether they had any regular visitors over the years.

"Sure, but most of them have gone by the wayside now, just like my wife," he said. "It's hard to keep track of people, especially when they don't really want to be kept track of."

Such an odd tone filled his words that she asked, "What about family? Do you have any family? Did Rose?"

"Not now." Then a note of suspicion came into his tone, when he asked, "You don't think we killed somebody off, do you?"

She laughed. "No, I can't imagine you bringing this to my attention if you did the deed."

"That's good," he said, "because I know a lot of stupid killers are out there, but I'm not one of them." And, with that, he added, "Now, I've got to get back to work."

"What work?" she asked.

"I've got to chop some more firewood," he muttered, and he ended the call.

She thought about that for a long time, then realized that, of course, chopping wood would be a daily chore on the farm, even in the summer to get a fire started in a wood-burning stove, should he not have electricity. He may do a lot of chopping wood upfront to get a stockpile going. She didn't know how much firewood he would go through, even trying to keep that little place warm, especially in winter conditions. It was cold and ugly outside still, even here in town, although the snow had stopped. That was a good thing, as far as she was concerned.

The snow was pretty for the one day, but, after that, she

complained.

So when Mack called and that was her first comment, even Mack had laughed at her. "We don't get to pick and choose when Mother Nature decides to dump on us. She dumps, and we just react as fast as we can to clean up the streets."

"That's not your problem though, right?"

"No, but you can bet that the number of accidents increases tremendously when the roads are bad. So, yes, it does affect us. It's just not our jobs to keep the streets clear."

"And nothing new on the DNA?"

"That could take months," he pointed out.

"I know, but it's not a hard thing to do. It's just a spray bottle thing to show if it's human or not."

"I'll check in with the lab in a few days," he offered, "but, meanwhile, things are a little busy at my end."

"Right. I did phone Milford and asked some further questions, but, so far, nothing is really popping."

"Not surprising. I did go back through all the cold cases I could find of missing persons in that area and related to that time frame. While the Joe Rich area doesn't pull in visitors, Big White does call to a lot of tourists," he pointed out. "So, in theory, any missing person could be a person coming here from anywhere."

"Right," she muttered. "That's not helpful."

"Nope, it sure isn't," he agreed, "and that's one of the reasons why these things can take a long time to solve." They spoke for another few minutes. "If you want to get adventuresome, putting on a hot soup or stew would be good."

"You're suggesting that I cook?" she asked, dread in her voice.

"Only if you want to."

Hearing how his tone had gentled completely, she groaned. "When you expect me to cook something by myself, it upsets me, and I immediately think I won't do a good job. Plus, it just makes me feel as if I need to get up and do it."

He burst out laughing. "No pressure. If you don't want to, I can always make something when I pop over."

"Are you coming over tonight?"

"I thought I would, unless you've got plans."

"My only plans are with you," she said, and, with that, she disconnected on him.

Grinning to herself, she headed over to the computer to see just how hard it would be to create a soup. Everybody always talked about stuff being so simple, but their version of simple never seemed to match her own. She was doing okay on some things, but, once winter had hit, food took on a whole different meaning. People mentioned stews and soups, casseroles, and a wide variety of things that Doreen had never eaten in her life. It had been both fascinating and daunting to realize that the salads and cold light fare she was more accustomed to eating had been replaced by hot foods. And that presented yet another challenge amid the cooking challenges she had already. But still, it couldn't be that hard. Right?

She searched for an easy recipe and clicked on one and read the list of ingredients and then the instructions, frowning as she realized that she surely could put on a hot soup. She went through more recipes, looking for something incredibly easy, then finally decided she could manage a vegetable soup and maybe even one with noodles. So, with that emboldened choice on her mind, she got up and started prepping for it.

She hadn't been working on it for very long, yet had the onions stewing, when Nan called.

"So, about that shooting," her grandmother began, "it wasn't targeted, at least as far as they can tell, and nobody knows who the shooter was."

"Really?" Doreen asked, frowning at the conflicting information. "How is that possible? I thought they said it was targeted, plus had somebody in custody?"

"They let the poor woman's husband go. And Lynda's not doing very well in the hospital either."

Doreen didn't even bother to ask how Nan knew this. "I'm sorry to hear that. That's not very nice to contemplate."

"Of course not," Nan replied, her voice deepening in reverence. Then she popped up again and added, "But it's already happened, so we should do something about it."

"And what would you want me to do?" Doreen asked in a wry tone.

"Question her. I'll head down to the hospital to see if I can visit her."

"Do you know her?"

"No, but women's groups go in to comfort patients they don't know. I'll blend right in."

"Perhaps, but you won't just go in and see her. That will be limited to the family."

"Sure, but how do we know who is family if we don't go down there and check it out?"

"Nan, please don't. Don't, don't, don't," Doreen muttered.

"Either I'm going or you are," Nan declared. "We can't just sit here and wait for people to get around to filling us in. We have to be on the ball here. This is a whole new case."

"But it's Mack's case, not mine," she reminded her

grandmother, trying hard to slow her down. Mack would have a fit if he found out Nan was meddling in one of his current cases. "And I'm not sure we even have a case."

"Just because he hasn't told you about it," Nan stated in a crafty voice, "doesn't mean we can't do something to get more information on our own. And, besides, if he hasn't told you, he doesn't know that you're even on it and probably thinks you don't know anything about it."

"I suppose," Doreen admitted, trying to be patient with Nan.

"But honestly, he shouldn't be that silly because he knows very well that all of us are right on these things," Nan declared, with a glow of importance.

"Oh, Nan, good Lord," Doreen replied. "If Mack has some shooting victim dying in the hospital, we should be looking at other things."

"Oh, like what?"

Doreen frowned, as she thought about it. "First off, the current shooting of that poor woman Lynda is not a cold case, so we need to keep that in mind."

"Yeah, we already checked that box," Nan replied. "Next."

Nan was barking orders, looking for her next set of instructions to be given. Frustrated with the old woman, yet somehow intrigued, Doreen considered that issue. "Do we have anything on the victim? Who she is? What her history is? How long she's been in town? Things like that."

"Oh, I can get right on that," Nan stated. "As I told you earlier, one of our residents here knows the neighbor." And, with that, Nan disconnected.

Doreen sighed, sent Mack a quick text. **Uh-oh. Nan is determined to work on your shooting case.**

He called her and asked, "What do you mean, Nan is on the shooting case?"

"It was in the news, and she figures we should be helping out with it."

"It's not a cold case," he declared, his tone ominous.

"I know, and I explained that to her, but she wants to be ready for whenever I catch it up."

"Catch it up?"

"Yeah, you know, whenever I put my cold case together with your current case," she explained, followed by a sigh. "I don't know where they get these ideas from, but they've already got the idea in their heads, so—"

"Good Lord," he muttered, with a groan.

"At least you can use whatever information they dredge up."

"In what way will I use it?"

"One of the Rosemoor residents knows the neighbor next door to where the victim was shot. So Nan and that other resident have been talking, and I sent them some simple questions to ask, to figure out how long the shooting victim's been in town, what she does, where she comes from, that kind of a thing. This info won't come through regular police channels but from the local gossips. In this case, a neighbor, so it will be more reliable."

He interrupted her. "Hang on. The captain's calling me. No wait. You tell Nan to back off and to stay off. I can't have you guys in this."

"I know," she grumbled. Nan would definitely get Doreen in trouble one of these times. As soon as the call with Mack ended, Nan called her right back.

"She was just visiting," Nan shared. "That poor girl was just visiting."

"Do you know where she came from?"

"Nope, but," Nan's voice dropped to a whisper, "she was here looking for information."

"What do you mean? Information about what?"

"I guess her father disappeared in this region a long time ago."

At that, Doreen straightened. "How long ago?" she asked. "And from where?"

"They don't know, and it could be from here to Kamloops or maybe even South Okanagan."

"That's hundreds of miles."

"Sure, but he was a rancher, buying and selling cattle and quarter horses. His big cattle ranch was in the Joe Rich area, I thought, but he may have had another parcel of land in the more northern regions. Yet I seem to remember that he had a personal residence in Kelowna or nearby, to escape the harsher winters up north. So he could have gone missing somewhere local too."

"Maybe not, but why was his daughter shot?"

"I knew it," Nan crowed in delight. "I knew you would be on this one. Wait until I tell Richie that we have a case." With that, she was gone.

Doreen stared down at the phone and groaned. "No, no, no, no. That's not how this works, Nan." But, of course, for Nan, who was a law unto herself and becoming a little bit unmanageable at times, that was exactly how it worked. Doreen wondered if she should call Mack back, then realized he would already be in his meeting with the captain. So, the last thing she needed was to be in even more trouble for the multiple phone calls.

Only since she'd learned how the rest of the world lived did Doreen realize how much jobs meant to people. When you didn't have money, it was everything, and, as she'd found out, having money seemed to be everything when you didn't have it. Still, even when you did have it, it was almost meaningless. At least that's how she felt about it now, but maybe that was foolish of her.

Multiple court cases were coming up where she might have to testify in, both criminal cases and estate matters. She really hoped she didn't have to appear. One criminal case in particular that worried her involved Steve, who'd buried many bodies on his property, close to her own place. With that thought, she decided to go for a walk up the river, maybe take another look at Steve's place. It should be nice-enough weather for that.

She called out to Mugs, "Hey, do you want to go for a walk?" He came running, his leash in his mouth. She laughed, hooked him up, and then put Thaddeus on her shoulder. Now she looked over at Goliath. "What about you?" His tail twitched as he stared at her. He didn't say a word. But then what did she expect him to say? *Yes, no, maybe?*

She grabbed his leash, put it on him, and he didn't resist, so she figured he wanted to go too. But when *didn't* he want to be in the middle of everything? After all, Goliath had a nose for trouble.

Chapter 7

LATER MACK WALKED in the door and called out to Doreen.

"I'm in the kitchen," she called back.

He walked through the house to join her there, his nose raising appreciatively. "Now that smells good." He wrapped his arms around her from behind and tugged her into a hug.

She rested there for a moment, before twisting and looking up at him. "It does smell good, doesn't it? Of course that doesn't mean it'll taste any good."

He chuckled. "You're doing just fine."

She frowned. "I'm not so sure about that."

"I'll give it a taste, and then it might just need some seasoning adjustments."

She watched worriedly, as he picked up the spoon and grabbed a little taste from the simmering pot in front of her. She watched as he tested it, nodded at her, took another spoonful, and said, "It's really, really good."

"Really?" She wanted to believe him, but her tone noted her doubt.

"I picked up some French bread as well," he added. "So, how about we turn it into garlic bread?"

She looked at him in delight. "That would be perfect." It took them a few more minutes to finish off the soup and to get the garlic bread ready. Before she knew it, she was sitting down to a hot meal. As she took several bites of the soup, she nodded. "It's really encouraging that I could make a soup from scratch," she said.

He smiled at her. "You're doing a wonderful job with your cooking. You know that, right?"

"No, *you're* doing a wonderful job with the cooking, with your patience while teaching me."

He laughed. "That has nothing to do with it. You're doing just fine. Remember that this isn't a race. It's a marathon."

She rolled her eyes at that.

"You have plenty of time to learn to cook and to do other things that you want," he noted. "You don't have to learn it all right now."

"Yet some people seem to just walk into a kitchen and make a hot meal, and it smells and tastes absolutely wonderful. However, I need recipes and time to figure out what I need and how to even do it," she complained. "And that's long before I ever get to the point of cooking."

"Lots of people are that way," he noted, with a shrug. "You will get to be a cook who can walk in and cook things after you've done it for ten years. But, until then, you need recipes, and some people always use recipes. Some people always measure. Some people never do."

"It would be nice to get there," she admitted.

"And you will," he said. "You're doing fine. Just remember that."

"So, this woman. Lynda Mahoney ..." she began, as she pushed away her empty soup bowl. He stiffened and glared at her, but she just shrugged and continued on. "She came to town because her father disappeared."

"What do you mean, her father disappeared?" Mack asked.

"The local gossip is that she came to town because her father disappeared somewhere in this region, and I will say that it's a really wide region and goes as far as Kamloops. Apparently he disappeared some twenty-odd years ago."

He stared at her. "Okay, but I'm not sure we have a cold case on it."

"I don't know whether you do or not," she pointed out. "Did the daughter say anything to you?"

"Nobody has told me anything about her being here for that. The woman we interviewed and who knew Lynda stated that she had asked if she could come up for a visit. They apparently used to be school friends. Anyway, while Lynda was here for a couple days, she was off exploring, as far as the friend knew. Then when Lynda returned to her friend's house, she was on the front step, looking down at her phone for something, and somebody shot her."

"Drive-by shooting?"

"There seems to be a little bit of confusion on that element, as nobody saw a vehicle."

"Then not a drive-by."

"Maybe," he replied. "The thing is, there is traffic at that hour of the day, and there was definitely traffic that day, but nobody could say that a vehicle pulled up, shot, and then took off. The house is, however, on a major road, so has lots of traffic."

"Ah." Doreen nodded. "That adds to the confusion."

"At that point in time, traffic was heavy with people who were coming and going from home to work. So finding a witness who knows something is a different story. Nobody that we have spoken to at this point," he shared, frowning at her, "has mentioned anything about her coming here to look for a missing father."

"Interesting."

"Do we know the story about why the father went missing?"

Doreen shook her head. "Not that I know of."

He groaned. "Sure would be nice if the people would talk to us and not to you and Nan."

"Nobody is talking to me," she pointed out. "This is a case of somebody at Rosemoor who knows the neighbor who was visited by the lady who got shot. So I'm not saying that the information I'm getting is clear and honest because I haven't had a chance to confirm it," she clarified, waving her garlic bread at him as she took a bite. She looked at it and smiled. "This is really good garlic toast."

"It is really good garlic toast," he agreed, "but that won't get you out of answering my questions."

She shook her head. "Of course not." She stuffed another piece of bread in her mouth. "It's just a reminder that you're a good cook."

He sighed. "You're really trying to distract me, *huh*?"

"No, of course not," she said. "I wouldn't do that."

He stared at her suspiciously, as she batted her eyes at him. He chuckled. "If this neighbor could be trusted, we would expect to see her coming down to the station and talking to us."

"Oh, that's not likely to happen," Doreen noted. "Of all the things I've come to understand about people right now, it's that nobody really wants to go to the police station and talk to the cops."

"But Crime Stoppers is always offering rewards and looking for information."

"But then the callers would have to give all their own personal contact information, and that is enough to stop people from speaking."

"And yet she's quite happy to speak to this neighbor friend of Nan's."

"Of course, and why not? It comes under the heading of gossip."

He studied her, while snagging a big piece of garlic bread, and nodded. "Apparently that's enough to make a difference, isn't it?"

"I think it makes all the difference. If they go down to the police, the cops will just say that they can't verify anything and that they can't say specifically for sure in a court of law, *blah, blah, blah*. But this 'between-friends' way, they get to tell their story, relish it a little bit and enjoy it, being a little part of this whole drama," she explained. "So, when you bring the police into it, it becomes official, and everybody's lips are sealed tight in case they're caught saying something wrong, and *they* get in trouble."

"And yet if people would at least tell us what they know without embellishment, we could probably put a stop to this pretty quickly."

"Maybe," she agreed cheerily, "but gossip is a popular activity for a lot of people. It doesn't matter what walk of life they come from. Loads of people just want to gossip."

He groaned. "It's not helpful," he muttered.

"Nope, it sure isn't." Then she got up, grabbed her bowl, and took it over to the sink, which she filled with hot soapy water.

Just as he walked over with his dishes, his phone rang.

He looked down at it and winced.

She turned to him and asked, "Something interesting?"

"No."

His short response was a complete and immediate give-away. "Oh, I'm so glad you don't lie well," she stated, with a big grin on her face.

He sighed, then kissed her gently. "It's a no, a no to you, a no to Nan, a no to anything. You just stay put."

"Wasn't planning on going anywhere," she said, "but you should know that Nan was talking about going to the hospital." He stopped and looked at her with a perplexed expression. She shrugged. "I told her that she shouldn't go, but I'm not sure she'll listen."

"Why would she go to the hospital? Does she have a friend there or something?"

"Ahm, no, not a friend." She winced. "She wanted to go see Lynda, the woman who was shot."

He closed his eyes, pinched his nose, and whispered, "Jesus, Nan."

"I did tell her that it wasn't a good idea and that you wouldn't be happy."

"But I bet she didn't listen, did she?"

"No, I don't think she did," Doreen agreed. "That's why I gave her a list of questions they could mull over at Rosemoor, hoping to distract her into chatting with the resident friend of a neighbor instead. Still, it's a long shot. It is possible that Nan calmed down a bit, but she was pretty excited."

Immediately his eyes popped open wide, and he looked at her in astonishment. "I'm sure you have noticed as much as I have that they seem to be getting way worse, if that is even possible."

She burst out into laughter. "Honest to God, if I could enjoy my old age as much as they are, it's hard to make a case for stealing their joy."

"Maybe," he grumbled, "but they are also a pain in the butt."

Chapter 8

LATER THE NEXT morning Doreen heard a soft rap on her front door. With one eyebrow raised, she noted that Mugs was wagging his tail like crazy at the door, not barking in any way. She opened it to see Nan standing there, looking around carefully. She was nicely dressed against the cold, and her bright red cheeks matched the bright inquisitive look in her gaze.

She bent closer to Doreen and whispered, "Is Mack here?"

"No, Mack's not here," she replied, opening the door wider. "Come on in."

Nan darted inside. "Oh, good, he's not here." She stopped to give all the animals a warm hug and a snuggle.

"Is there a reason you're avoiding Mack?"

Nan's eyebrows shot up, but then she quickly recovered. "We don't want him getting upset at our detective work, do we?" she asked in a calm and quiet tone.

"Our detective work, *huh*? I don't have a clue what you're even detecting."

Nan chuckled. "And that's why you're the boss because you can keep all this straight, whereas the rest of us have to write it down." With that, she pulled out a little black notebook.

Doreen frowned at the little hat on Nan's head. "What's with the hat?"

"Do you like it? We all got them."

"But they're like, it reminds me of ..." She stopped, unable to find the words.

Nan supplied them. "Sherlock caps, yeah. Houndstooth Sherlock caps. We ordered six, but, since then, we've had to do another order," she declared proudly, "because everybody wants them."

"But what's that on the front?"

"It's a *DD* logo." She patted Doreen's shoulder. "It's because of you, dear."

"What's because of me?" she asked suspiciously.

"All of this," Nan replied. "We're having so much fun that we decided to create the DD Club."

"DD Club? What is that? *Drop dead?*"

Nan stared at her, blinked several times, then noted, "Honestly, that is a great line but, no, dear. It stands for Doreen's Deputies."

Doreen opened her mouth, frozen.

"It's okay," Nan said. "You can do it, just try again. I know that brain fogs can start at your age, but I wasn't expecting it quite so soon."

Doreen sighed, her knees wanting to buckle, as she contemplated a whole group of Rosemoor residents wearing little houndstooth Sherlock caps with a *DD* emblem on the front. "Oh my," she whispered. "Mack won't believe this."

"He should. I'm pretty sure that he mentioned we should form a support club or something."

"I don't think he meant it in this way," she noted, unsure when that would have happened in the first place, or whether it was something Nan just pulled out of the air to make it seem more reasonable.

Nan shrugged. "Doesn't matter. Everybody looked pretty cute in them. Of course *some* people had to get *other* colors. Here we were trying for a nice sober respectable club, but you know how Maisie is. She decided she wanted to have one in purple of all things." Nan pulled off her cap, a black and gray Houndstooth. "Isn't it lovely?"

"It is," Doreen said, with a small smile. "And I'm glad you're having so much fun with all this."

Nan gave her a bright smile. "Oh my, you have no idea how much life you've brought to that home."

"I'm just not sure management would be all that happy about it."

"Oh, who cares." Nan gave a wave of her hand. "We're pretty harmless and easy to look after now. Everybody is doing so much better with a different gardener and wonderful cooks," she explained. "Of course, with all this attention turned toward the home, they really had to step up and mind their *P*s and *Q*s. So now we get much better service."

"Even though Richie keeps stealing all the kitchen goodies?"

"He hardly steals them, considering what we all pay monthly to live there."

Doreen had to admit the caps really were quite cute. As Nan walked around preening, her notebook in hand, Doreen couldn't help but chuckle. "All you're missing is the cape." At the sudden gleam in Nan's eyes, Doreen rushed to say, "Yet I don't think that would be very practical."

Nan narrowed her gaze, as she contemplated the idea. "It would also have to be fashionable. Otherwise it would look terrible."

Then barely suppressing a giggle, Doreen added, "Especially in purple."

Nan just frowned at her, not amused. "I'll think about it," she muttered, settling down into one of the two living room chairs. Meanwhile, Mugs jumped up in the chair with her, while Goliath stretched out on the back of the chair. Thaddeus came to join everyone and now sat on Nan's shoulder. "Anyway, what have you found out?" Nan asked, her little notebook out. Her pen at the ready, she turned to Doreen expectantly.

"Oh goodness," Doreen muttered, realizing Nan was getting into this role in a big, big way. "All I can tell you is that Mack was just called away, and it has to be something exciting because he refused to tell me about it and wouldn't even talk to me in terms of whether it *was* related or not."

Nan started writing. "We can find out pretty fast. I think Darren is visiting Richie right now." She pulled out her phone and quickly sent Richie a text message.

"I'm sure Darren won't want to get caught in the middle of that, not with Mack as his boss."

"Oh, hush," Nan said. "Richie, the silly fool, can't keep his mouth shut, so what will you do except use it?"

Doreen winced. "But we still need to be the same nice people we started out as," she reminded her grandmother. "And we certainly would never want to hurt our sources."

Nan's gaze widened, as she went quiet for a moment. "You are really good at this." She texted something again to Richie, but Doreen didn't even want to ask what it was about.

"As far as the DNA," Doreen began, "we don't have results yet from the dirt sample we got from Milford, and we haven't got any more news on the recent shooting."

"Oh my," Nan muttered in disappointment. "I started looking for any information on the missing father angle. I wondered," Nan added delicately, playing with the pen in her hand, "did you happen to check the files from Solomon?"

Doreen's eyes widened. "That's a good thought." She brought her laptop over and, sat in the chair beside Nan, brought up Doreen's duplicate file copies she had scanned in. "I digitized everything," she shared. "It's easier for searching."

"Oh, good."

Doreen added, "And I've learned to log in my own notes as well. Then I have an easy reference to search for, when pulling related files, should something become relevant later." Doreen moved her chair closer to Nan's, so her grandmother could see the screen better. Then the two of them went through the table of contents Doreen had created. There was a section on Missing Men.

"Why isn't there ever a Missing Women section?" Nan complained.

"There is. It's down below. See? There it is. … Missing Women." She tapped the screen.

"Oh my, Solomon really was thorough."

As Doreen opened the Missing Men section, several old articles and newspaper clippings were referenced. She pulled up the images and quickly scanned through them. "We've got somebody from, oh, fifty years ago, but it's barely a footnote."

"Oh, that's mighty interesting," Nan replied, looking at her expectantly. "But how much information will we find about that man?"

"It would be very challenging, I would think." She eyed Nan and asked, "You lived here back then, right?"

"Sure did. It was a small town at that point, though."

"Do you remember anybody going missing?"

Nan frowned at her, surprised. "I should, shouldn't I? I guess I would officially be one of those actual old-timers."

"Exactly, but if you don't remember—"

"I'll have to think about it," Nan said, as she wrote herself some notes. "Does it say anything about where this one went missing?"

"Two men are listed here. One went missing fifty years ago. He was Bartlet Jones, thirtysomething back then," Doreen read out loud. "Solomon's notes are pretty unclear, and even one saying that little-to-no information was available. The second missing man was Jack Mahoney, who had a cattle ranch and ran quarter horses too, went missing twenty-odd years ago, and he was about fortyish at the time, married, with a daughter, Lynda—that poor woman who was just recently shot," Doreen added.

"That's not helpful," Nan muttered, sounding upset.

"I know, but that's all right. We'll keep looking," she reminded her. "I'm really just getting started on this now. I'll make another trip to visit the archives at the library here soon."

Nan nodded. "It's always frustrating at the beginning, until we get some information."

"And remember, when we do get information, we'll have to toss away anything we can't confirm. Hopefully we'll get enough information to keep going forward from one little thread to the next little tip, then on to the next one."

"Exactly," Nan agreed, with a bright smile. "That's the way to do this." When her phone buzzed, she looked down at it. "A text from Richie. He just got back to me."

When she pulled up the text, Doreen was absolutely amazed and delighted that these two old-timers were capable of using cell phones in that way.

When she mentioned it, Nan nodded. "I like technology. But I've got to tell you, an awful lot of people in Rosemoor just won't learn anything new." She shook her head. "It's as if they're back in the '80s or something, and they're still looking for rotary phones. We gave those up a long time ago."

"Yeah, but they're nice to have too, during storms and such," Doreen pointed out. "And it seems as though anything retro is coming back around again."

Nan looked at her with interest. "Good, then some of that clothing you have should be coming back around again."

"Some, maybe. I kept a few pieces, but I also let go of a lot that I didn't think would suit me."

Nan nodded. "Oh, but the dress you wore to the party," she said, then made a kissing sound on her fingers, as if she was a crazy Frenchman, "it was beautiful."

Doreen's gaze misted over, as she smiled at her grandmother. "Thank you, Nan. Sometimes I feel like a different person, as if the one who used to know how to wear nice clothing is no longer me. I seem to have lost my sense of self-confidence on how to dress."

"It's not that you've lost your self-confidence, child," Nan clarified, looking at her in astonishment. "You just haven't gained the confidence in this new version of you. You knew how to dress the old you in that environment. Plus, you had old what's-his-name bossing you around with your every move, but this new you is younger and far more exciting, independent, and adventuresome. Naturally it'll take you a little bit to figure out what kind of clothing suits, especially as you find yourself needing to dress for different situations—but, for the party, you looked divine."

"Thank you."

When Nan's phone buzzed again, she looked down at it. "Okay, now Richie is finally getting somewhere. He's one of those people," she muttered crossly, "who can only do one sentence in a text, and then he has to send another one, then another and another. It's so darn annoying. You end up getting five buzzes on your phone, and he still hasn't got his point across."

Her phone buzzed yet again. "Okay, Darren is there, with an update. He's heading back to the station. Nobody really knows what's going on yet. Ooh, that's exciting." Nan clapped her hands but then frowned. "Richie shouldn't text everything. Too much work to text it all."

"It would be too much effort if he's texting instead of just calling you," Doreen noted. Then she frowned at her grandmother and suggested, "Maybe you should go check in with him in person."

Nan hopped up. "My thoughts exactly. That's a very good idea. I'll phone you when I hear the rest." And, with that, she hugged everybody goodbye and darted outside, exiting through the back door. She was generating so much energy that even Mugs wanted to run behind her in excitement.

Doreen smiled, as she watched her grandmother race down to the river and around the corner of the fence. Doreen walked outside. It was a beautiful sunny day, with no sign of the snow that had threatened earlier, but it was still cold out here. And yet her grandmother hadn't even seemed to notice.

Doreen stood on her patio, her face toward the sun, and let the moment seep in. She let the sun's heat soak into her face and smiled as she remembered how different her past year was from her last year as a married woman. She had a lot of firsts in this previous year and knew she would create a lot more. What was still so amazing to her was how much fun they had had last year, and how much good she had managed to do. She never wanted to be somebody in the limelight, who made their mark in the world, made millions, or created dozens of companies, or anything like that. She'd always just been the kind of person who was happy to help out where she could.

Nan had worried about Doreen in her marriage, but now, in this new life of hers, it seemed as if she had found a place in the world for herself, and that had changed Nan's attitude toward Doreen as well. It was a good thing. Enough was going on in the world where everybody was upset and full of judgment. Luckily, once the estates from her former life and the various pending court cases were settled, hopefully Doreen could finally put all that behind her and continue to carve out her new life, free of drama and trouble. Well, that kind of trouble, anyway.

Right on target was a phone call from Mack's brother. That also reminded her that she had promised Millicent that she would get over to her place. "Hey," she greeted him. "How are you doing?"

"I'm doing fine. How is our newest family member?"

She blushed at that. "Not quite a family member yet," she cautioned.

He laughed. "I know, and, according to Mack, he's not letting you get cold feet."

"I'm not getting cold feet," she declared, "but I am also determined to not get pushed into this before I'm ready."

"You might have a challenge with my mother then. She's intent to see Mack married off before she dies."

"That's fine," Doreen conceded, "as long as she lives to be ninety. That would suit me just fine."

He burst into laughter. "I have a hunch that nobody will let you put if off that long. Anyway, on another subject, I'm sending over more paperwork," Nick shared cheerfully. "I'll send it in an electronic signature format, so you can sign it digitally. Then send it back whenever you're ready." And, with that, he disconnected.

She smiled because, as part of the deal with agreeing to marry Mack, she quite liked both Mack's brother and his mother. As soon as she finished signing the documents, she picked up the phone and called Millicent, who was delighted to hear from Doreen. "I thought I would come over for a cup of tea, if you'll be home and open to visitors."

"I would love that," Millicent replied. "Come away."

"And the animals are okay to come along?"

"Oh, yes, please do bring them. They're such a joy to have around."

With that, Doreen smiled, packed up the animals, then looked outside and frowned for a moment, considering the weather. Should she drive or walk? She quickly decided that the cold wouldn't hurt her or them and that the fresh air would probably do them all some good. Then, corralling her animals, two on leashes, she opened the door, and she set out toward Millicent's place.

As she walked up the front walk of Millicent's house, Doreen looked critically at the grass and the flowers along the edges, poking through the snow.

Millicent opened the front door and said, "Come in. Come in. You must be freezing out there."

"It's beautiful," she murmured, as she took the front steps, the animals racing to greet Millicent. They seemed to love her almost as much as they loved Nan. Maybe it was the Mack connection. Doreen didn't know, but they'd come here many a time over the summer to garden.

As she walked inside, Doreen sniffed the air. "Have you been cooking?"

Millicent shrugged. "I was hoping you would come by, so a couple days ago I made cookies."

"I'm sure Mack loves the cookies too."

"Yeah, I sure hope so."

When Doreen was seated in the kitchen with a cup of tea and a cookie, she looked around and smiled. "You've had a lot of good years in this house, haven't you?"

"Oh my, yes. There was a time when I contemplated going into Rosemoor—or another of the homes around here—but it never seemed to be quite the right choice for me."

"I guess it depends on how lonely you are."

Millicent frowned at her. "That never came to mind. However, all I could think about was having all these restrictions and rules, having to eat the food they chose, never being able to cook what I wanted, plus the signing in and signing out whenever I wanted to go somewhere," she explained. "It just wasn't the right thing for me, at least not then. I want to keep my independence as long as I can, especially since I own this beautiful home."

"I get it." Doreen smiled. "I'm not suggesting you go there at all. I just know that they all seem to be having so much fun."

"And that would be the one reason I would consider it. They do look as if they're having fun," she replied wistfully. "Especially your grandmother."

"Ah, she is always leading the pack when it comes to creating fun," Doreen said, with half a laugh.

"She always was like that, even fifty years ago."

"Funny you should mention that. We are looking at a couple old cases."

Immediately Millicent's eyes gleamed. "Ooh, tell me more."

"I was wondering if you might even know anything about them," she began. "Two guys are listed in the files I got from Solomon, if you remember."

"Of course, of course. We're all dying to know what's in those files."

"Solomon made reference to a man who was in his early thirties when he went missing in this area, but that was some fifty years ago."

"Oh my." Millicent sat back in shock. "Fifty years ago. That's a long time to find any leads, much less evidence."

"I know," Doreen agreed. "It would be one of the oldest cases I've ever tried to solve.

"Plus, did you hear about Lynda Mahoney, the woman who was just shot in town recently? She's in the hospital, but I hear she's not doing well."

"A shooting? My goodness." Millicent blinked several times. "I didn't even hear about that."

"I don't imagine you listen to the news much, do you?"

"No, no, no, I don't. It's all very depressing. They never seem to say anything good about anything these days."

"You're right about that," Doreen noted, with a smile. "Yet it seems everybody rushes to read about the bad news."

"That's human nature, I suppose. … I seem to remember that Lynda found a long-lost brother or something." When Doreen cocked one eyebrow, Millicent shook her head. "Don't mind me. I'm an old woman with random memories wandering around my brain." She waved a hand toward the cookies. "Have another cookie, dear."

Doreen looked over at them, and she really did want one. Mugs putting his paw in her lap made her decide that maybe she could have a second one. As soon as she picked it up, Mugs gave a soft *woof*. She looked down at him. "I don't know if you're allowed oatmeal raisin cookies."

"Just give him a little bit of the oatmeal," Millicent urged, "and keep out the raisins. Obviously he needs to have something. I meant to buy some dog biscuits, but I never know what to get for the rest of the critters."

"Not that any of them need anything," Doreen added.

"No, but *need* is a very different thing, and, when you're my age, I don't think we need very much," she noted. "But we like to have company, and we like to have things just the way we want them. I think that's often one of the bigger challenges, you know? How we can no longer get everything we want."

There seemed to be a bit of melancholy to her tone, which surprised Doreen. "Is there something that you want and can't have?" she asked.

Millicent shrugged. "It's not that I can't have it. Eventually I'll get it, but I just want to see it happen earlier."

Doreen realized she should have seen that coming from a mile away, but she didn't and had walked right into it. "And what is that?" she asked. "You know if I can do something to help you, I will."

Millicent looked at her with a bright smile on her face,

as she replied, "Marry Mack while I'm still alive, please."

Doreen winced. "You know I do intend to marry Mack, right?"

"I know that, and I'm delighted, but, at my age, I could die any day."

Doreen gave her a small smile and pointed out, "So could I, Millicent."

She blinked at that and then nodded. "All the more reason to make it happen fast." She then laughed and laughed.

"I don't know about that," Doreen replied, "but I will take it into consideration. Trust me that an awful lot of people at Rosemoor are also hoping to attend the wedding," she shared, with an eye roll, "and I've already been given that lecture too."

Millicent chuckled. "I'm sure you have. I should have talked to your grandmother to see if we could apply some pressure to get you to make this wedding happen sooner."

"That was part of my agreement with Mack, you know? *No pressure*," she said gently. "And I have to admit, it's helpful to know that I won't be pressured into a certain time frame that I'm not comfortable with. And I get that everybody knows that my ex was a terrible person and believes that I should just be ready to move right in with Mack and to start my new life," she shared, "but Mathew was still my husband when I moved here, up until his death even. So a lot of things still need to be cleaned up, his estate and whatever, and I feel that I should sort that out before I can move on."

"That makes sense," Millicent agreed, nodding.

"That was one of the reasons I agreed to the engagement," she added, "because I know Mack will give me the time that I need. So, I'm asking you to give me a little time as well."

"*A little time*, absolutely," Millicent said, with a beaming smile.

"The question is, what's *a little time* to you versus *a little time* to me?" Doreen asked, with a half laugh.

"At your age, sweetie, a little time could be twenty years."

"No, no, no. I'm not guaranteeing I'll get married this year, but that is what we're talking about."

At that, Millicent brightened. "That helps, at least it gives me a date in mind."

"No dates," Doreen corrected. "Not a date. It gets you a time frame. I am working toward this year, but I won't promise it."

"No, no, that's all good. I'm definitely not trying to pressure you because I know Mack would be all over me if I did," she admitted, laughing.

"That's because he's afraid I'll back out if people put the pressure on me, and he's promised me that wouldn't happen," she shared.

"Oh my." Millicent stared at her in shock. "You wouldn't do that, would you?"

"I'm not planning on it, but that was our agreement, *no pressure*," she murmured. "With that in mind, I'll ask you to give me a chance to get clear of all these other things, and then we'll talk about the wedding."

"Perfect," she said. Then she hesitated. "Will I be allowed to be a part of it?"

Doreen looked at Millicent, and then realized the old lady just needed reassurance that she was loved and cared for and would be included.

She reached out her arms and wrapped her up in a warm hug. "Of course you will. I wouldn't have it any other way."

Chapter 9

MILLICENT BRUSHED AWAY happy tears, smiled at Doreen, and whispered, "I'm really glad to hear that. Now, are you sure you don't have something I can help you with on your cases, those two you mentioned earlier, while we await further wedding plans?"

Doreen instinctively wanted to say no, since she already had enough people dealing with these missing persons' cases. Then she sat back and frowned. "You and Nan might be some of the few people left in town who could remember this one missing person's case."

Millicent's eyes opened wide with an immediate gleam of delight. "Tell me more." Then she realized what she sounded like and added. "Oh dear, we shouldn't be quite so delighted that people are missing, should we?"

Doreen nodded. "I've had that thought cross my mind a couple times already today," she murmured. "On the other hand, if we could bring them home, that is obviously what we want to do."

"Of course, of course," Millicent agreed, with a more somber nod. "Does Mack know you're doing this, dear?"

"Mack knows about some of it," Doreen offered, with a

chuckle. "He's told me to butt out already."

Millicent nodded. "He does want to keep his job."

"Oh, don't worry." Doreen smiled. "I don't want anything to happen to Mack or to his job. I know how much this is his dream job."

"It really is, you know? He wanted to be a cop from a very young age, and his work is so important to him. I certainly won't be the one to tell him otherwise."

"Admittedly I haven't been at it all that long," Doreen said, with a chuckle, "but, in my experience, so far, telling Mack anything otherwise doesn't work very well."

Millicent grew misty-eyed. "I have to admit you're right there. He was always so determined to do whatever he wanted to do. We couldn't talk him out of it, no way, no how."

"Did it bother you that police work was what he wanted to do?"

"Oh no, yet I can't say we thought the police force was in his future. You look at your babies and dream that they'll grow up to be a doctor or a lawyer or something safer," she shared, with a smile.

"Ah, you mean like his brother."

Millicent rolled her eyes, chuckling. "Mack has used that against us a time or two, saying that we already had a lawyer, so he could go off and do what he wanted."

"He has a point there," Doreen noted, her smile brightening. "Anyway, back to these cases." She stopped to think about the best way to present it. "As I mentioned before, I have two missing person's cases."

"Oh, tell me more."

She then told her about a guy in his thirties, who went missing fifty years ago with no leads. But Jack Mahoney, who went missing some twenty-odd years ago, was the father to the victim of this current shooting case, Lynda Mahoney. That poor young woman had come up looking for her father and had subsequently been shot outside of a friend's house, where she had been visiting. Now she was fighting for her life in the hospital.

"Oh my." Millicent stared at her in horror. "That's so terrible."

"That is absolutely terrible," Doreen agreed. "On the other hand, that's why we do what we do, so we can help solve some of these cases, and people don't have to get hurt doing it."

"No, of course not." She stared at Doreen worriedly. "I wouldn't want you to get hurt doing it either."

"No, I don't intend to. And you know Mack'll keep an eye on me."

Immediately she relaxed. "That he will. I've never seen him this happy before. I'm so glad you moved to town."

Doreen chuckled. "For that, you'll have to thank my grandmother."

"If I ever see her again, I'll be sure to do so."

That comment made Doreen pause. "I guess you don't get down there very much, do you?"

"I don't get out much at all these days," she stated, with a shrug. "I do catch a bus and go get groceries, but that's happening less and less. When my boys are nearby, they come take me shopping, when I need to go, and the odd outing for lunch. I won't be here much longer," she murmured, "and I would really like ... *Uh-oh*, I promised I wouldn't say that."

Doreen sighed. "You do know that saying it halfway is the same thing as saying it."

She laughed. "But I'm really not trying to pressure you."

"I appreciate that, though, from my position, it looks exactly like that."

Millicent shook her head. "Nope, definitely not."

"Glad to hear it," Doreen murmured, shaking her head. She then spoke out loud, almost to herself. "Solomon's files were never updated to reflect whether the missing man from fifty years ago was ever found. And Mack always tells me that we have to be careful with that assumption, since it's quite possible that he has been found, and maybe the files I have are old news, so to speak."

"Oh, I hadn't considered that." Millicent frowned at her. "I guess that is a problem, isn't it?"

"It can be, yes, since they simply reflect what was compiled, and nothing since then has happened, until I came along." Doreen sent a wry look in Millicent's direction. "And we do want to keep notes nicely updated with information as it comes in. I certainly don't want to create more problems."

"You'll have to, or Mack will get on you if you don't."

At that, she burst out laughing. "You are so right on that."

While Doreen fussed around, pouring more tea, Millicent sat back and closed her eyes, as if thinking back fifty years, trying to recall what things would have been like back then. "I do remember something about Jones disappearing," she murmured.

"What is it?" Doreen raised her eyebrows. She intentionally hadn't mentioned the name on Solomon's file. "Bartlet Jones," she murmured, "that was his name."

That convinced Doreen that Millicent was on the right case. "Do you remember anything about it?"

"The problem is, my memories are already so dicey."

"They can be, indeed," Doreen agreed, with a smile. "It's one of the reasons for always questioning what people see versus what they think they see, plus interviewing more than one witness."

"Is my memory important?" she asked, looking at Doreen.

"It could be, yes, because we don't know if Bartlet was ever found. And if he wasn't, I should keep looking for him."

"Oh my." Millicent eyed her oddly. "I guess you can pick and choose what you want to look at, can't you?"

"Only to a certain extent, and only if I have some information to follow. I can't just create information without something concrete that we can verify," she pointed out. "So, if nobody can remember any of the details, we're stuck until a body shows up." Doreen pondered that angle for a few minutes and asked, "Do you know anybody up in Joe Rich area?"

"Joe Rich," Millicent repeated. "*Hmm.* I've certainly known lots of people up there over the years, though I'm not sure that I know anyone up there now."

"Right." Doreen nodded. "That makes sense."

"There was Biddy and … I can't remember his name. It was Biddy and maybe Duff or something weird like that."

Doreen frowned at her. "Okay, and what do you remember about them?"

"I don't know that I remember them specifically, but I do remember how they lived farther out, more by choice of course. That was always a big thing with them, not wanting to be around people. Town was too crowded for them, even back then. But I think she's passed on now."

"How would you ever have heard about her passing?" Doreen asked curiously.

"Oh, sometimes I read the obituaries," she noted, with a wave of her hand. "At my age, it's about the only way I can keep tabs on friends anymore."

Doreen stared at her, fascinated and repelled at the same time. "Seriously?"

"Absolutely," she muttered. "It's not as if you can go around asking if certain people are still alive or not. So reading the obituaries is just a way to help me stay in touch."

"I hadn't considered that," Doreen admitted, studying her.

"No, a lot of people your age probably wouldn't even think of it, but it's something that a lot of us do. Ask your grandmother. I'm sure she does the same thing." Silence fell then as Millicent added in a sad tone, "It's a shock when you see somebody listed on those pages, but it is a way to find out who's dead and who's alive," she muttered. "I suppose that does sound gruesome, though."

"Not at all," Doreen replied. "If you don't get around town anymore, and you're not big on technology or even the internet, and don't know the phone numbers of the people to call, it seems to be a sensible solution."

Millicent smiled at her. "And, even if it's not," she teased, "you'll make it all sound good because that's who you are."

Doreen flushed. "I'm really not a crazy do-gooder, you know?"

"Ah, surely not." She shook her head and laughed. "I wonder how Mack would see it."

"Let's hope I don't have to ask him and find out," Doreen quipped, "because I may not like the answer."

Millicent burst out laughing. "Oh, my dear, you need to understand that you can do nothing wrong. Mack would forgive it all."

"I wonder," she muttered, "because I do keep getting involved in his cases."

"Yes, but he hasn't done anything about it yet, has he?"

"Not sure what he can do."

"Oh, you would be surprised." Millicent beamed at her. "Believe me, if he really wanted you out, he would ensure you were out."

"I guess that's possible." Doreen wasn't sure what to say at that point.

Millicent promised to think more about the missing man case from fifty or so years ago and to get back to Doreen with any further insights. At that, Doreen gathered her animals and headed home again.

Chapter 10

BACK HOME, ALMOST the minute Doreen walked in the door, Mack called. "Hey," she greeted him. "Are your ears burning?"

"No. Why?" he asked.

"I was just at your mom's."

"Ah, how's she doing?" he asked, but he seemed a little distracted.

"She's doing fine, just reminiscing about you as a little boy."

"*Ugh*," he said, with a groan.

Doreen laughed. "It's cute."

"Glad you think so," he muttered.

"So, what's happening? You sound distracted."

"I am, but I just wanted to check in and to ensure you're staying out of trouble."

She laughed. "Since when do you call to see if I'm staying out of trouble, when I don't even have a case or anything to work on?"

"Are you sure you don't have a case to work on?" he asked, with a note of humor. "You have a whole group of cronies looking to cash in on your latest hobby."

"I don't think *cash in* is quite the right phrase," she noted.

"It is if it means keeping themselves from dying of boredom."

"Okay, maybe," she muttered. "But, outside of going to your mom's, I haven't really been too involved yet today."

"She's okay though, isn't she?" His tone sharpened with worry.

"Yes, she's okay."

"Good. She's just, … you know, at that age."

"I know," she murmured. "Hopefully, we will have a lot more time with her yet."

"Did she hassle you about the wedding?"

"Yep, she sure did, until I told her to back off, or else I would back off."

"Ooh, ouch," he muttered. "I hope that's not really part of your argument for *no pressure allowed.*"

"I did try to make it clear to everyone," she stated, "that I would not be pushed."

"And I don't want you to feel pushed," he confirmed. "So, you do whatever you feel you need to do."

Although that's what she wanted him to say, and she appreciated that he said it, she still felt a little odd to have him say it was okay if she decided they weren't getting married. She figured she was just being contrary and quickly changed the topic. "How's the hunt going for your shooter?"

"Not very well," he muttered.

When he hesitated to say more, she asked, "Did you contact the neighbor who was talking to the victim?"

"We did a canvass of all the neighbors, but nobody had anything to say," he replied in frustration.

"Yeah, that's a problem."

"Part of the problem is you," Mack pointed out, his voice gentle. "They want to talk to you versus anybody else."

"Which is silly because, if they have any information, they should be talking to whoever comes to their door."

"Apparently people think it would be a whole lot better if you were the one who came to their door," he explained, with that same note of humor in his tone.

"That's too bad though. You're the police, and you're the ones out there canvassing and talking to everybody."

"Yeah, we sure are, not that it's getting us much."

She suggested, "I can phone Nan, if you like, and see if the neighbor came up with any more information."

"Or you could tell me who Nan's been talking to, and I can go talk to them."

"I don't even know who that is, and you know that Nan won't tell you because nobody else would ever share with her again."

"I do know that," he said in frustration, "which is why I haven't asked yet."

"I am sorry. It's sad to think that so many people don't want to talk to the police, but, after all the things I've been through, I get it." Then came silence for a long moment.

Mack finally spoke. "Getting people to talk is one thing, yet obstructing or withholding information that we need to solve cases is a completely different story."

"I know. By the way, per Solomon's files, he had one on Jack Mahoney, who went missing twenty-odd years ago, the father to your shooting victim. Jack still seems to be missing." When Mack didn't reply, she continued. "Do you have a file on him?" When Mack remained silent, she knew she was pushing it, but she added, "If you have a file on Jack that you could share with me, then I could start working on finding Lynda's missing father."

Mack sighed. "I'll see if we have a file on Jack." Then he clammed up again.

"Solomon also listed somebody who went missing about fifty years ago," she began.

"Oh?"

"I don't know if it's still a missing person's case or not. It's possible that he was found and that Solomon just never updated it."

"What was the guy's name?"

She gave him the name that she had in the files, which was also the same name that Millicent had come up with.

Mack replied, "*Huh*, Bartlet Jones. I don't think I've even heard that name before. I'll have to do a scan in the database and see if anything matches."

"It would give me another cold case to work on," she said cheerfully. "And then I would be out of your hair."

"Oh, don't worry. I've already got the benefit of that stuck in my head," he noted, chuckling. "However, I do have other things to do, so checking that on Bartlet Jones and also Jack Mahoney will have to wait until I get back to my computer."

After he disconnected, she sat down and brought out the few notes that she had—not really much to go on. Not much on Bartlet and not much on Jack. Her own files were depressingly slim. What she really needed was to get out to the crime scene area for Lynda's shooting and talk to somebody herself. Mack probably wouldn't be very happy if she did, especially when the people started opening up to her. Regardless, she wasn't sure what she was supposed to do about that. It could end up helping Mack on his current case. Plus, she had a related cold case with no leads, so she had to resort to talking to the locals.

If people wanted to talk to her and not the police, why not? She would share what she found out regardless. So she pondered that, then decided she should head back to the library, now that she had names to search for, and find out whether any other information existed on Bartlet Jones or Jack Mahoney that Solomon had missed. She sighed. That could be a waste of time, especially since Mack hadn't called back and confirmed that both these guys were still missing. Dithering back and forth, not sure which way to go, she decided to go for a walk, which would take her mind off the rest of this stuff.

So, with the animals in tow and knowing that they'd already gone over to Millicent's, Doreen headed them up the river. She hadn't gone very far when she saw a bunch of boys throwing rocks in the river. Mugs woofed at them several times, but the boys just looked at her, then at her dog. One of them picked up a rock, then went into pitcher mode, as if to throw it at Mugs. One of them called out to his buddy, "Hey, you can't do that."

The boy with the rock looked at him and asked, "Why not?" His tone was surly and ugly.

"She's the lady who does all the detecting work, and that dog is special."

At the word *detecting*, the boy with the rock turned to look at her. "But she's old."

Doreen winced. "I guess to you I'm old."

"You're old to anybody," he declared, with a sneer.

She frowned at him and nodded. "Had a rough day, *huh*?"

"Rough life," he muttered.

"Sorry about that. It goes along with being young sometimes."

"Why? Does it get better when you're old?"

She barely held back another wince because, for the longest time, her life really hadn't gotten any better. But now, well, it was lovely. "I definitely had times when it wasn't good," she shared calmly, "but then there are times when it's great."

"What? You mean, when you close a case?"

"Yeah, those are great times. Those are times when I feel as if I've accomplished something and as if there was a point to getting out of bed."

"The whole point of getting out of bed," he stated, "is to eat the food you want and to do things you like."

"I like helping people," she added. "What's your name?"

"It doesn't matter what my name is," he snapped, sneering at her again.

She nodded. "You've got a whole lot of hate for the world, *huh*?" He just shrugged and didn't say anything. She looked over at the other boy. "And how do you know about me?"

He laughed. "You're everywhere, and people are always talking about you and all the different cases you've been solving," he replied enthusiastically. "Like, wait. Are you involved in that shooting case?"

"Nope, it's an active case, so the police handle it."

"Oh, right. You do cold cases, don't you? What about that old man who disappeared? I heard my grandpa talking about it a while back."

"Which old man?" she asked, testing his knowledge.

And sure enough, he said, "Bartlet Jones."

"That is fascinating. I was just talking to somebody about that case."

"Yeah? My grandpa really wants it solved. He can't believe the old guy never showed up."

"I don't think he was all that old."

"Are you kidding? He was thirty."

Doreen barely held back a laugh because apparently, to some, thirty was absolutely ancient. "Where is your grandpa? I wouldn't mind talking to him about it."

"Ah, he's in a home."

"Yeah, which one?" she asked.

"The one close to here," he said. "Rosemoor or something."

"What's your grandpa's name?"

"Lynon, but I don't know what his other name is. We just call him Grandpa Lynon."

"Good enough. Maybe I'll go chat with him." And, with that, she turned to the other kid with the rock and said, "You must have something better to do with your life than throwing rocks at dogs."

He glared at her. "I didn't throw a rock at your dog."

"No, but you would have, right before your friend here told you not to."

"Yeah, I don't listen to him."

"Maybe you should," she suggested, "because, although you want to be tough, anybody who hurts animals is just picking on something that can't protect itself. That doesn't make you tough. It makes you a bully." And, with that, she waved at the two of them, heading in Nan's direction. She pulled out her phone and called her. "Hey, Nan."

"Ooh, are you coming to visit?"

"Maybe. Do you know somebody down there named Lynon?"

"Oh, sure. I'm not certain anybody ever listens to him

though."

"Why is that?" she asked.

"Because he's always making up stories."

"Making up stories or telling stories about things and places and people who you don't know?"

At that, Nan gasped. "Does he have information?"

"I don't know. Any chance I could come down and talk to him?"

"Sure, come straight away. I'll expect you soon."

Doreen was already heading that way along the river, and she just kept on going toward Rosemoor. The animals were more than happy with that routine and didn't put up a fuss, once they realized they weren't going home just yet. As soon as they reached Rosemoor, the main door opened. Doreen wondered if she should go in that direction or head over to Nan's patio.

But the stranger held the door for her, a big smile on his face. "Anybody coming with that number of animals has got to be Doreen."

She laughed as she walked inside, more accustomed to being recognized now, but still feeling weird about it all. She nodded. "That's me."

"Are you here sleuthing, or have you come for social reasons?"

"My grandmother is here."

"Ah, that's a difficult stage in life, isn't it?"

She raised an eyebrow. "Honestly, they get into an awful lot of trouble here, but they really seem to enjoy every moment of it."

He burst out laughing. "I think you're right there. I can't believe the things I get called in about, and they all seem to think that you're responsible."

She frowned at him. "I don't think I'm responsible, but I have to admit that my grandmother could be."

"Now that's possible too," he agreed. "They did say that they had somebody here who was a bit of a troublemaker and always got everybody going."

Doreen winced. "Yeah, that would probably be Nan."

Chapter 11

DOREEN WALKED INTO Nan's apartment after a brief knock. Nan and Richie sat there with Maisie. They looked up expectantly at Doreen, and it was all she could do to hold back her chuckle. They all had on their Sherlock caps, with the initials *DD* on the front. She just smiled, looked at Nan, and stated, "I gather you guys are looking for your next assignments."

Richie brightened and nodded, leaning forward. "Have you got one for us?"

"Maybe, but I was hoping to talk to this Lynon guy."

"He's here, but … are you sure you want to speak with him?" Nan asked.

"Is there a reason I wouldn't want to?"

"Yes, because you can't necessarily trust what he says."

"Is he just old and lonely?" Doreen asked.

"Probably," Nan said crossly, "but he's also a little too forward."

Doreen frowned at her. "Meaning he's made a move on you that you didn't want made?"

"Something like that." She shrugged. "Most people accept a simple no."

"Ah, and he didn't."

"I didn't really give him a chance to explain," Nan added.

"Maybe he didn't know how to take a no. Maybe he had no experience with accepting no. Or maybe he's just lonely."

At that, Nan rolled her eyes. "Maybe, maybe, maybe, whatever. Yet, for a cold case, I would talk to him if I must."

"But can I talk to him? That's the question," Doreen asked.

"I think so. I did ask one of the family who was visiting, and he seemed to think it would be fine."

"Good, let's go do that now, and then we can talk details afterward."

Everybody hopped up. Nan looked at them and shook her head. "I don't think everybody going is a good idea. We don't want Lynon to feel as if he's being interrogated."

"He might want the attention," Richie noted, looking at Nan pointedly. "If he's just lonely, this would give him some attention."

"Maybe," Nan conceded, but her tone was a little cross. She fluffed her hair up, looked at Doreen, and muttered, "The decision is up to you."

"How about I go talk to him alone?" Doreen asked.

Nan frowned at first. Then her eyes widened, and she beamed. "That sounds perfect. I'll take you down and introduce you. Then I'll leave you there." She looked at the others. "Agreed?"

They all nodded. "Agreed." And that's what they did.

Nan led Doreen to Lynon's apartment, and, as they got closer, Doreen asked her, "So, what's really bothering you?"

Nan shrugged. "I've never really got a good feeling off this one."

"We've always learned to trust your feelings," Doreen noted, "so let's try to keep the contact between the two of you to a minimum."

"Yes, I would like that."

"You're sure it's not just a case of his being enamored with you?"

"Of course he's enamored with me," Nan stated, then laughed. "I still wouldn't want to go out with him."

"And has he asked you out?"

"Sure, he always wants to have coffee in the garden. He's asked me several times, but just nothing is there."

"If you say so," Doreen said, holding back her smile.

"Don't you laugh at me," Nan snapped, a warning in her tone. "Otherwise I'll start hassling you about your wedding."

"Oh no you won't," Doreen declared.

At that point they had reached the door in question. Nan knocked smartly, and a frail voice called them to come in. She rolled her eyes and repeated, "Remember that you brought this on yourself."

Surprised at that, but willing to take it in whatever direction she needed to, Doreen pushed open the door and walked into the room. And there was the man she'd met at the main entrance.

He smiled at her. "I thought it would be you."

"You have the advantage on me," she said, as she held out a hand. "I'm Doreen."

"And I'm Nate," he replied, reaching back. "Nice to meet you. I understand you have some questions for my father?"

"I met a couple boys down at the river. Are they yours?"

"My nephews," he said, with a wince.

"One is definitely struggling."

"I keep getting on his case, but it's not helping. What did he do to you?"

"It's not what he did to me, but what he was looking to do." She pointed down at Mugs at her side. Goliath at this point was stretched out in the hallway and refusing to go any farther into the apartment. As she tugged on the door so they could close it, Goliath looked at her with a sullen look, then slunk inside but stayed close to her legs.

"You even have a cat on a leash," Nate noted in bemusement.

"I do, and sometimes the cat is cooperative, and sometimes he's just not."

At that, Nate laughed. "I can see that." He turned and introduced her to the old man nearby. "And this is my father, Lynon."

"Hi, Lynon," she replied, walking forward to give him a handshake.

He held her hand just a little too long, as he looked up at her in delight. "Well, well, it's a fine time when you come calling to my door."

"I was hoping you might have a little information for me."

"But first, what about my nephew?" Nate asked.

"He wanted to throw rocks at my dog," she said, pointing down to Mugs, who was staring up at him with a narrowed gaze.

"Seriously?"

She nodded. "The other boy told him not to, and he did stop, but I got the impression he only stopped because the other boy recognized me."

"Good Lord," he muttered. "I'm at a loss as to what to do with him."

"Apparently he's having a tough time," she shared.

"Yeah, he's heading for trouble right now, but I keep hoping he'll find something to turn himself around."

"It's pretty frozen down there at the river, so throwing rocks there probably wasn't giving him the satisfaction he was looking for. So, when we appeared, my dog seemed to be a more likely prospect."

He just shook his head. "I'll have a talk with him."

"You can do that, but, if you tell him it was me who told you, it'll just make it that much harder the next time I see them."

"Do you think you'll see them again?"

"I walk the river all the time," she shared. "Depends on if you let them back out again."

"His mother passed away not very long ago," he explained. "And he's not adjusting very well."

"Of course not," she murmured. "Children need their mothers, and, when they don't have them, it's tough. I'm sorry for your loss."

"Thank you. My sister was many things, one of which was a speed demon on the road. She died in a car accident a while back."

"I'm sorry. Something sudden is hard to handle as well, with no time to adjust, no time to adapt."

"I'm not sure adapting is something any of us do when it comes to death," Nate replied. He turned and looked at his father. "Pa, she has some questions for you."

He nodded. "I was waiting for you guys to stop your yapping about that useless grandson of mine and get around to me."

Doreen looked at him. "You don't like your grandchild?"

"He's trouble, and, when someone is trouble, they make trouble for everybody else," he stated in a brisk tone. "I don't have time for trouble."

"Right." She looked back at Nate. "Sorry if I brought up tough times for you."

"It is tough. I'm not married, and Pa's looking for a firm hand, but apparently what I'm doing isn't working," he explained. "So, we're still at odds."

"Keep working at it," she suggested. "The boy is not a lost cause."

He smiled. "Thank you for that. Already the teachers are telling me how he needs therapy and extra help, and he needs an attitude change and on and on." He gave a wave of his hand.

"And I imagine they're quite right," she noted, "but that doesn't make it any easier on you." He just smiled, as she looked over at Lynon. "Lynon, a man went missing around here a good fifty-odd years ago."

"Bartlet Jones," he stated triumphantly. "I was just talking to some people about that, thinking it was high time somebody solved the case." He looked at her in delight. "Did you solve it?"

"No, but I am looking into it. It depends on whether or not I can find and confirm enough information to get anything new going."

"Right, right, right. That's always a big problem, I'm sure."

"It is," she agreed, with a smile. "Nothing easy about tracking down information that's fifty years old."

"I can't even imagine," he murmured. "What can I help you with then?"

"You can tell me what you know about the case."

He shrugged. "I don't know much. I just remember it."

"And what do you remember?"

"As far as I can remember—" He stopped to take a few minutes to collect his thoughts.

However, when he didn't say anything further, Nate stepped forward and tapped his shoulder. "Pa?"

Lynon shook his head. "Sorry, I tend to drift off these days."

"That's all right," she said. "I'm sure you deserve the rest."

He laughed. "I don't know about *deserving* it, but it seems as if I'll get it before long no matter what."

"We all do," she replied, with a smile. "It's just a matter of the time frame." Then remembering that Nate had just lost his sister, she realized that probably wasn't something she should have mentioned. Looking over at him, she whispered, "Sorry."

He just shrugged helplessly, as if he didn't quite know how to handle it either.

"So, this person, Bartlet Jones. Was he someone you knew?" Doreen asked Lynon.

"I used to know him, yep," he replied. "Don't know that I knew him all that well, but, as soon as somebody dies or goes missing, it seems as if everybody knows him."

She smiled in agreement. "That is something that I have found to be true."

"Is it really?" Nate asked.

She nodded. "Not everybody, but a lot of people tend to want to be associated somehow, or to have something to do with it," she shared. "So, all of a sudden, little bits and pieces come out of the woodwork. The problem is, not everybody understands whether what they know and are saying is even valuable or not. So I listen to all of it, then try to figure out what is useful."

"That has got to be frustrating," Nate said, staring at her.

"It can be. It definitely can be," she agreed. "Yet it can also be very rewarding when I do solve something, and either we bring somebody home or we figure out what happened to them."

"Nobody should go through life without answers," Lynon declared, staring at her intently. "If you do find out something, you'll let me know, won't you?"

"Of course I will," she agreed. "I'm sure the gang here at Rosemoor will be more than happy to keep you updated on any news as it happens."

"That gang of yours?" he muttered, lifting a hand. "They sure don't let anybody join in."

"I don't know that it's a case of not wanting anybody to join in," she clarified, with a smile at him, "as much as they want to be involved in the case. So they prefer to keep matters close so they get more for themselves."

"Ha." He nodded. "Can't say I blame them. It would be nice to have something to keep me active."

"I'll keep that it in mind, but no promises," she said. "I do most of my work alone."

"Of course you do. It's the only way to do these things. Now, that man," he began as his fingers tapped the edge of his wheelchair. "I'm pretty sure—I'm not sure of her name, but Bartlet had a wife, and I think he had a set of twins. I might be wrong about the twins. One of them may have passed on, but I can't quite remember."

She pulled out a little notebook, thinking Nan had been spot on. This man wasn't a reliable witness. Still, Doreen was here, so she would keep asking questions. She should ask him about Jack too. Noticing that both Mugs and Goliath had refused to move any farther inside, she was a little worried about what had happened to them on that visit out to Joe Rich. They certainly hadn't been their best ever since meeting Milford and now hadn't taken a liking to this old man either. She tried to take down a few notes. "Okay, do you know what Bartlet did for a living?"

He frowned. "I think he did what the rest of us did back then, worked the farms. I don't think he had a business of his own, like some of them. Seems as if he may have had a place in Southeast Kelowna, but it might have been in Joe Rich."

She looked at him and nodded. "It's a lot more wintery up there. Seems the farms would be more vulnerable up there."

"Oh, sure, but, now that I think about it, he may have been one with cows and horses. I don't know how much of it was commercial." He pondered that, and she just waited. Finally he shrugged. "I'm not sure about what he did or what he didn't do. It seemed as if he had some hard times back then, and he might have ended up doing a lot of things for a while in order to stay alive."

"Right. It's not as if there were as many options back then."

"No, there sure wasn't. There was just lots of hard work," he said. "And those of us who made it, well, we're glad we made it, but it wasn't easy. So many of the young kids these days, they just don't seem to appreciate what we went through."

She gave him a smile. "And I'm pretty sure those kids would also say that we old farts have no idea what they're going through."

He looked at her and burst out laughing. "Oh my, isn't that the truth."

Chapter 12

DOREEN SAT HERE, visiting with Lynon a bit longer, trying to get any more information she could possibly get. He did give her some, but it wasn't much more than what she already had, or he just contradicted himself.

"Bartlet was a ladies' man. I don't know how he had the money to date women. I really think he was looking for a sugar mama to support him."

Doreen nodded. "What about a man named Jack Mahoney? He went missing twenty-odd years ago. Do you remember him?"

When Lynon went into a deep stare and didn't speak, Nate stood up again to pat his father's shoulder. "Pa?" This time Lynon didn't respond.

Nate apologized. "Sorry. I should get Pa to bed. Was nice to meet you."

Doreen thanked them both and got up and gathered her animals to head back to Nan's apartment, only to open Lynon's door and find all three of them standing there outside Lynon's door, expectant looks on their faces. She rolled her eyes and shooed them all ahead of her, calling back, "Thank you, Nate. Thanks, Lynon." She shut the door and turned to Nan.

"Nate and Lynon," Nan repeated, frowning at her. "Who's Nate?"

"Lynon's son, and I met his grandson down at the river today." Doreen explained about that encounter from earlier this morning. "I only just found out from Nate," she added, "that the boy lost his mother recently and is living with his uncle Nate now, and the boy's not handling the adjustment well."

"Of course not," Nan agreed, as she looked back toward Lynon's door with a frown. "I had no idea."

"And that's part of the problem. We need to be open and honest with others."

Nan reached out a hand and stroked her granddaughter's cheek. "You are a lovely girl."

Doreen laughed. "You guys only came down here to see if I got any information out of him."

"And did you?" Maisie asked at her side.

"Nan, you were right. He was telling stories, but I think somewhere in all that gossip was some truth. Lynon appears to know more about Bartlet's last day than anybody so far. Apparently he went to work and basically never came home again."

"That seems to be such a common theme that you would think people would stop going to work," Maisie declared in a perfectly nonchalant voice.

Doreen winced at her, then looked over at Nan, who just rolled her eyes and shook her head. "That may be," Doreen conceded, "but most people need to work to get a paycheck to keep food on the table."

Maisie just blinked at her, then shrugged. "It seems as if they should get danger pay if that's what they're doing."

"And I think some companies do have danger pay," Doreen admitted, "but, in this case, Lynon thought Bartlet was living in the Joe Rich area and had horses and cows on his place."

"Mighty slim businesses up in the Joe Rich area," Maisie noted.

"But not all of that part because, as you head farther down, it gets better."

"It sure does."

"It's beautiful country up there."

"*Hmm.*" At that, Maisie didn't say anything more.

As they got back to Nan's apartment, Nan nudged Doreen. "What are you thinking?"

"I'm thinking that I have another case in Joe Rich, the Bartlet Jones one," she stated. "Yet he went missing fifty years ago, and Milford said his bloody garden bed showed up about twenty-five years ago. So I don't see how those two tie together. Yet Jack Mahoney went missing twenty-odd years ago, so that might connect in some way with Milford's bloody garden bed. Those two timelines are much closer, and Milford may have been off a year or two on his recollection. Then they could match up."

"Oh, that would be way too easy though."

"I know," she agreed, "and it wouldn't make a lick of sense either."

"Not making a lick of sense is normal, until you put all the pieces together. Then it all matches perfectly," Nan described, with a strong vote of confidence for her granddaughter.

Doreen smiled. "Thank you for that."

"It's the truth."

Even Richie was nodding. "Yep, it's the truth. I keep

asking Darren why the police department doesn't hire you. I think the last time he mentioned something about you couldn't bring the animals to work, but I thought that was really an outrageous reason."

Doreen smiled at him. "Pretty sure there are other reasons as well," she replied, "but that would be a big one."

"Yeah, and you're not about to leave the animals alone."

"No, I'm not. And thankfully I no longer have to work for a living."

"But you're still doing cases, right?" Richie asked, stopping in his tracks.

"Yes," Doreen replied. "I will still be helping people as I can."

"Right," Richie agreed, "because money shouldn't change who you are. Not at the core. You should still be you."

"Oh, I intend to still be me," Doreen stated, with a bright smile. "Don't you worry about that. So clearly we need a few more answers for all our questions, before I can go farther."

Chapter 13

BACK HOME AGAIN, Doreen warmed up the last of her leftover soup and sat down to an early dinner. She didn't know when to expect Mack or if to expect him at all. He'd seemed quite distracted earlier, and, since they didn't have a set plan as to where they would eat on a day-to-day basis, everything was still very free flowing in their developing relationship. She wasn't really expecting to see him.

After she finished eating and all the animals were fed, she sat down and did a little bit of research on her animals' recent behavior. Something was definitely off, and it had started when they had gone to Joe Rich and had met with Milford, who had that very large feral cat. In fact, her animals had all reacted in their different ways as soon as they reached the old homestead—before meeting Milford and definitely before learning of the huge predator cat. Doreen didn't understand what had happened with her pets that day and wished she could do something to give them back their peace of mind. Something about that trip, that whole visit, had really bothered them, and now her.

Thinking about it, and particularly Thaddeus, she phoned Jerry, who had Big Guy. When he recognized her voice, his laughter boomed through the phone.

"Doreen, how are you? Are you coming down with Thaddeus for a visit?"

"Maybe. I had a couple animal husbandry questions that I hoped you could shed some light on."

"Sure. How does tomorrow sound? Or what works for you?"

She thought about it, then said, "If you're okay, maybe we'll come down tomorrow for a visit."

"I think that's an awesome idea. Big Guy will be happy."

"I know Thaddeus will be too." She chuckled as she got off the phone, writing down the time and the date, then looked over at Thaddeus. "That should help, right, buddy?"

He just looked at her, walked closer, and murmured, "Thaddeus loves Doreen."

"I'm really glad you do," she replied, touched by the sentiment. Normally he was all about *Thaddeus loves Nan*, but this time he was definitely not feeling well. She picked him up and put him on her shoulder. It was too cold to sit outside, even if she really wanted to. Instead she kept herself busy around the house, as she changed the bedding and put on laundry, just doing some general housekeeping. All the while she looked forward to soaking in the bathtub before heading to bed for the night.

When a knock came at her back door, she frowned over at Thaddeus. "Do we know who that is?" He looked at her and didn't say anything, just waited for her to do whatever. She headed downstairs, and Mugs was there, sniffing away at the back door.

"Are you okay, Mugs?" she asked him. He sniffed but didn't bark. Not sure what to make of that, she opened up the door a little bit, so she could see out. "Hello," she said to the two boys she'd seen at the creek. She opened the door wider and asked, "How are you doing?"

"Did you go see my grandpa?" one kid asked.

"I did," she confirmed. "He was telling me all about that poor man who disappeared many years ago. Why don't you boys come inside out of the cold?"

They frowned at each other but hesitantly stood inside just enough for Doreen to close the door.

"And did you tell my uncle anything?" asked the same boy.

"Sure," she admitted. "When you threaten to throw rocks at my dog, you can expect repercussions."

"I didn't threaten," he argued, staring at her glumly.

"But you did," she countered, "and I, for one, will always call the truth as I see it."

He snorted. "Everybody has a variation of truth."

"Maybe," she conceded, with a nod. "I will agree with that. What are you guys doing here?"

The other boy spoke up. "He wanted to see if you had tattled on him."

"Did you get in trouble?" she asked the boy, looking at him with one eyebrow raised.

"He told me not to do it, but other than that he doesn't care."

"I think he does care, but maybe he just doesn't know what to do with you. He doesn't have any kids, does he?"

The young boy shook his head. "No, he doesn't."

"And, of course, you're missing your mom."

"I don't care," he blustered. "She wasn't there much for me anyway."

"Whether she was or wasn't, it's a big change in circumstances for you, and it's hard to adjust."

Again he shook his head and just stared around the area.

"You boys been home for dinner?" she asked them.

"I don't think there will be any dinner," the one said glumly, kicking the little bit of the snow off his shoe and onto Doreen's kitchen floor.

"I'm sure food is there for you," she replied.

He looked at her and shook his head. "I don't know that there is."

"If there isn't, then you need to tell people, tell the adults, so they can ensure you get food."

"I'm not telling anybody," he grumbled. "I would likely end up in foster care if I do that."

She just nodded, not sure how that system would work, but having had enough cases that had dubious relationships involving foster care, she knew she needed to watch her step on what she told the boys. "I don't really know how to cook yet, some hot and fast, but I can make you boys some peanut butter and jelly sandwiches. How does that sound?" When they just shrugged and acted like they didn't care one way or the other, she set about making four sandwiches, figuring growing boys ate more than she did. She motioned for them to sit at her kitchen table.

"I'm sorry life is so tough for you right now," she murmured. "Yet I'm sure, if you found something constructive to do, it would help you move forward."

"Yeah, and what does *constructive* mean?" he asked, staring at her.

"Something to help you or to help others." She could see the anger, but she could also see the wounding in his gaze. "You guys got any hobbies?" she asked, looking from one to the other. She looked at the second boy and asked, "What about you? Don't you have a family to go to?"

He shrugged. "They're out."

"Out?" she repeated.

"Yeah, out." At that, his tone turned a little defensive.

"So, let me get this straight. You both have places to be, but you don't want to be there. Is that it?" They both nodded. "Right, at least I kind of understand that." She set a plate with two sandwiches before each boy, then poured them each a glass of milk.

They just shrugged, then looked at the food and back at her. "It just isn't a whole lot of fun at our homes."

"Right, I'm not sure what I can do to help you with that," she shared, "but I certainly understand." She waited for the boys to finally eat something.

"Yeah, but like everything else," the first boy declared, "understanding doesn't change it."

"No, it really doesn't," she agreed, nodding at him. "As much as we might want it to, the change doesn't happen easily." Mugs stepped out, sniffing the boy, but he didn't seem to be too bothered.

"You could say hi to him," she suggested. "If you really want to be nice to him, you can give him a small piece of your sandwich."

The boys looked down at Mugs and glared, but one boy did offer a corner off of his first sandwich.

Doreen sat down with the boys at the table. "His name is Mugs. He's got all kinds of tricks at the ready, whenever we get into trouble."

One boy looked at her with interest. "What do you mean by tricks?"

She laughed. "He has this tendency to trip up people who are attacking me." He looked at her and laughed, as if she was joking. She nodded. "I'm not kidding. All of them have saved my life many times."

"Seriously?" Both boys looked down at Mugs and shook their heads.

"I know that he doesn't seem very scary," she began, "and he probably wouldn't take it personally if you mentioned something along that line to him, but he has been a godsend for me."

"Maybe if you weren't getting into trouble all the time," the first boy offered, "it wouldn't be such an issue."

"Mack would agree with you."

"Who's Mack?"

"He's a friend of mine," she replied, with a big smile. "He's a police detective in town."

"A police detective?" one boy repeated.

She nodded. "I have to work with the police with a lot of my cases."

"Wow." It seemed as if that had somehow earned her some respect. She wasn't exactly sure though, as the expressions on their faces were quick to fall away.

"I did see your grandfather. He's nice. Have you spent any time with him?"

The one boy just shrugged and mumbled, "He's old, older than you even."

She laughed. "He is old, but he seems to have a lot of stories."

"That's all he does is tell stories. It's boring in there."

"Do you ever go and just sit and enjoy?"

"There isn't anything to enjoy," he stated, looking at her.

"What about your games? Don't you have any of those computer games you could play?"

"Sure, but we just play on our phones most of the time."

"And who pays for your phone?"

The taller boy frowned at her and then shrugged. "I don't know."

"Your uncle?"

"Maybe. I don't know."

"Okay, that's interesting."

"Why? Are you stopping that too?"

"No, I've got no intention or interest in trying to stop your phone plans," she said, with half a smile in his direction. "As a matter of fact, I think, in this instance, that's probably something that's keeping you connected to your friends."

"I don't have any friends," he grumbled, staring at her.

"And what about you?" she asked, turning to look at the other boy. "What are your names?" But the hurt boy spoke up instead.

"I'm Gavin, and he's Randy," Gavin replied. "He's my friend, but we don't have other friends. We're also cousins."

"Ah." Doreen nodded. "Sometimes it's hard to make friends, isn't it? Particularly after a loss."

"Why is that?" he asked, staring at her.

"Because they don't know how to act around you. They might want to be friends or to at least reach out and be friendly, but they don't know how to do it without getting into a discussion that they don't want to get into."

Gavin grumbled, "That just makes them cowards."

"No, it doesn't at all," she said. "It's not as if you'll say anything mean to a friend who lost a parent, would you?"

"No, I wouldn't," he replied.

"And sometimes that's just the way it is. So they may want to be friends with you, but, if you're acting ugly, angry, or whatever, they'll probably just want to avoid you until you get over it."

Gavin sighed. "It's not something you get over."

She reached out and stroked his head. When he reared back and glared at her, she smiled. "You're right. It isn't something you get over. It's something you get past."

He blinked several times. "Just words."

"Sometimes words count," she said, "but I get it. Life sucks right now, and you don't want anything to do with it, but this is the hand you have to deal with. Yet, despite how you're feeling right now, it's a better hand than you may realize. You have an uncle who has provided you with a home and food and all that other stuff you need, like a phone with minutes to play your games on. So now it's up to you to make the most of it. I get that you might not enjoy his food or his rules, but at least he cares enough to try. You might also keep in mind that he suffered a loss too, losing his sister, and he may be just as mixed up as you are."

When Gavin started to bluster, she interrupted him. "Sure, it would be much nicer if you still had your mom with you, and a dad for that matter, and all that lovely stuff that goes along with it," she explained, "but it's still no guarantee that you would have a happy family."

"Yeah, that's for sure," Randy muttered.

She studied him and nodded. "You don't have a happy family?"

"Not really," he muttered. "That's because my dad took off a while back."

"Sorry to hear that. An awful lot of single parenting is happening nowadays."

"Yeah, a friend of ours has got a single dad, and here I've got a single mom." Randy laughed. "We should put them together."

"Or not," she said. "I'm not sure either one of them would take kindly to your matchmaking."

"Maybe not," Randy noted, gulping down the last of his sandwiches and the remaining milk. Then, as if disinterested, he said, "Come on, Gavin. Time to go. You got the answers you wanted."

"Yeah, I don't want her interfering in our lives."

She smiled to see that both boys had eaten both sandwiches. "I'm not planning to," she told them, "unless you're threatening my animals or you've got anything to do with my cold cases."

"What cold cases?" Gavin asked, turning to look at her.

"Like Bartlet, who went missing, the one I went and talked to your grandpa about."

"Oh, you mean the one about that old guy who disappeared ages ago."

"Yeah, that one. That's one of them anyway," she replied. "I'm just taking a look to see if anyone out there has information I can use to find out what happened."

"You won't find anything. That was a long time ago."

"I know that can happen. That's one of the reasons why I take a look and see what I can dig up. If I can't find more clues, then I can't move forward."

"I remember Grandpa saying the old guy was a hound dog and probably got what he deserved a long time ago."

"Interesting."

"It might be interesting to you, not so much to me," Gavin muttered, as he opened the back door and turned to walk out onto the deck.

"Go home and get some real dinner, *huh*? I know it's a trite thing to say, but life does look a little better when you have a full tummy."

"Yeah, I don't really care about food right now."

"Neither did I," she muttered, "not for a long time."

He stopped and looked at her. "Did you lose somebody?"

"I did, not the same scenario as yours and not in the same way," she shared, "but it still sent me into a tailspin. Yet there is life afterward."

He just snorted and walked away.

Mugs gave a solid *woof* and ran behind the boys, as if wanting something.

Gavin looked down at him and back at her, then bent down and awkwardly petted Mugs, as if he'd never had a pet before.

She smiled. "He really is a good dog."

Gavin just nodded and then quickly disappeared down the pathway with his cousin Randy.

Mugs came racing back to Doreen, looking happy, as if he'd made a new friend.

"Don't know what that was all about," she noted, looking down at him. "However, I don't think he'll be throwing rocks at you again." He hadn't thrown any rocks, but he surely made it seem as if he was willing to. Either way, she was glad he'd had a change of heart over hurting her dog. Mugs might be a lot of things, but he wasn't mean or dangerous, and he certainly wasn't a nasty dog that people needed to even think about treating in a bad way.

She headed back into the kitchen, then realized how late it was and that the boys were out all alone. She frowned at that, wondering if she should follow them home. Now she wished she had a way to contact their uncle. If she stepped up and said something, her inquiry might not be very welcome. Still, she'd never been afraid of interfering in things before, so why start now?

She quickly phoned Nan and asked for Lynon's phone number. Nan was a little cross about it.

She asked, "What do you want his number for?"

"It's Nate's number that I need. I had his nephews here just a bit ago, and I think he needs to know."

"He probably won't appreciate it."

"Maybe not," she said, "but I didn't get the feeling that Nate was heartless. I think he's just lost and doesn't quite know how to deal with the boys."

"Oh, that could be true," Nan conceded. "Let me go see." Then she ended the call. When she phoned back, she just said, "Hang on," as she handed over the phone. A younger man than she was expecting answered.

"Doreen, this is Nate, Lynon's son."

"Oh, good. I wanted to talk to you. Your nephews were just here, not very long ago."

"Oh no. Gavin's supposed to be home, doing home-work."

"He came to see if I'd tattled on him."

There was a pause. "Oops, I guess I let it slip, didn't I?"

"Doesn't matter," she said, "but the thing is, he's hurt-ing."

"I know. I just don't know what to do about it."

"I'm certainly not a psychologist or in any way the per-son with answers, but I do think he could use some help of some kind."

"Yeah, if you can tell me how to make it happen and in what way it'll make a difference, I'll be happy to do it," he stated. "He won't talk to a counselor, and it seems as if he doesn't care one whit about anything."

"I know this will sound strange and probably not a responsibility that you want to take on, but one of the last things he did before he left was pet my dog, Mugs."

"So, you think I should get him a dog now? Just from that?"

"No, not necessarily, but I am thinking that he needs something to love," she suggested. "Something that's his, that won't be taken away, like his mom."

"Ouch, that hits a little close to home."

"I don't know about you, but I think all of this hits a little close to home for him. Anyway, I just thought I should let you know that he was out and about. I told him to go straight home, but he just shrugged and said that home sucks."

"Great," he muttered, "now he's telling everybody I'm a terrible parent."

"I don't think he's telling everybody you're a terrible parent. I think he's just telling the world that he doesn't like his life right now." And, on that note, she disconnected.

Chapter 14

DOREEN WOKE UP to the ring of an early morning telephone call. Groggy, she reached for her cell. Nan's excited voice hit her hard. "Nan, what's the matter?" she asked, trying to prop herself up and to get her bearings.

"She died. That woman died!" she cried out.

"What woman? Who are we talking about?" Doreen asked, rubbing her eyes. "Who died, Nan?"

"Lynda Mahoney, the woman who was shot."

"Oh, ouch," she muttered, feeling sorrow in every bone. "That poor woman. I am so sorry for her family."

"Exactly, but now," she explained, "it's a murder inquiry, so it's definitely Mack's case."

"Yeah, it'll be Mack's case, not my case," she pointed out.

"But the cold case on her missing father," Nan suggested, "is still there. So you need to get your deputies on that. I've already talked to Mary here, and she gave me the 4-1-1 on the neighbor. Now tell us what to do next."

Doreen sat up straighter. "So, did Mary speak to the neighbor about any other information regarding the circumstances surrounding Lynda's missing father? Do we have the neighbor's name? Do we have anything?"

"I have it. Somewhere I have it. I have it." Then she started reading off all kinds of information.

Doreen groaned. "Whoa, whoa, whoa. Hang on now. I'm not even out of bed yet."

"Why aren't you out of bed? It's 5:30 in the morning."

Doreen looked at her phone. "What? Why on earth are you calling me so early?"

"This is important, Doreen. You know that we're off and running to the races now on the cold case of Jack Mahoney."

"If you say so," Doreen muttered. She reached for a pen and paper beside her bed and said, "Okay, give me that neighbor's name again."

"Right." Then Nan repeated all the info she had gathered from Mary, her fellow Rosemoor resident. "And Jack Mahoney *is* a name connected to Kelowna."

Doreen scribbled down the last note, asking, "How's that? I thought he was traveling for hundreds of miles, related to selling his cattle or his quarter horses, and just happened to meet his daughter in Merritt, before he took off down the road."

"Because he had one home here—and probably more residences in other places too. Anyway, Lynda, the daughter, last saw her father at Merritt, where they met for coffee because she was working on a big ranch out of that area. Her father was coming to see a friend nearby. Or wait, maybe that wasn't the reason. I can't remember."

"Why would Lynda work for another ranch when her father has one in the family?"

Nan shrugged. "Too bad we can't ask her. Doesn't seem she was estranged from her father. Maybe Lynda had a boyfriend who worked there in Merritt, and so she hired on there too, just to be close to him."

Doreen snorted. Leave it to her eightysomething grandmother to have sex on her mind. Doreen sighed and got back down to business. "So, how old was this woman, Lynda, who died? I thought we were talking about someone who was younger, so how could her father have disappeared some two decades ago?"

"She is young compared to me," Nan noted. "I think she's fortysomething, and she supposedly last saw her father about twenty years ago."

"And now we can't ask her to confirm that. ... So tragic that she passed on," muttered Doreen.

"Yes, of course," Nan replied. "And goodness knows that could happen to me any day."

Doreen pinched the bridge of her nose. "Yes, it could, but, then again, it could also happen to me."

"And that's why we have to do everything we can to help this poor woman in her quest to find her father. Apparently she never regained consciousness."

"Oh boy," Doreen muttered. "Okay, so does anybody else have information on her father?"

"That's the trouble. Apparently Lynda last saw her father in Merritt some twenty or so years ago. When he missed a scheduled call to her a couple days later, she looked all over this area but never found him. She reported him missing to the local police, who have been looking for him too. So this was an active current case at the time. Yet still nothing has come to light, even after twenty some years. So Lynda came back up again just the other day to try to find something out herself."

"Hmm. She must have had some new information to

prod her into coming up here. ... And now she's dead," muttered Doreen.

Nan asked, "Didn't you say you might have a body?"

"No, I did not say I have a body," Doreen clarified. "The farmer Milford out in the Joe Rich area thought a person might have died in one of his garden beds many, many years ago because he saw so much blood in the bed. But we need confirmation from the lab that the dirt contains human blood, not like a deer died there or whatever. And yet everyone I've talked to says the chances of anyone being able to tell is nonexistant as too much time has passed."

"That would not help us," Nan muttered.

"But back to Lynda, we do need to find out who shot her and to figure out what happened to her father. And, if we figure out what happened to her father, chances are, we'll figure out what happened to her—or vice versa."

There was a moment of silence, and then Nan continued. "Ooh, you're right. You're so good at this. We expect you down here for coffee in thirty minutes—or forty-five, so you can brush your teeth and get dressed and can walk over here." And, with that, Nan disconnected.

Doreen groaned, flopped back onto her bed, and muttered, "What on earth?" She'd created monsters. She knew that. Although it might make them all feel good at Rosemoor to have a meeting, this was way too early for Doreen. She got up, dragged herself into a hot shower to shake the cobwebs from her brain. As soon as she got downstairs to the kitchen, she made a small pot of coffee and poured a cup as soon as she could.

She wasn't even sure what she was supposed to do with this news and was struck by the fact that Lynda's family had just had another major loss, and nobody should forget that.

That poor woman had died trying to find her father. Somebody needed to find him and to pick up the threads, particularly if it had anything to do with the daughter's death. In her mind, Doreen couldn't imagine how it *wouldn't* be connected, one way or another.

But why after all this time did Lynda return here? Unless she had come to some enlightened answer as to what had happened and then decided to contact someone herself. What if her contact person was the same one who shot her? Then her father going missing might explain why she'd been shot, but Mack wouldn't like Doreen's assumptions because they were just that, assumptions. She looked down at Mugs.

"Assumptions they may be, and, if that's the case, we need to do something to get some proof. No way this poor woman should have died, just trying to find answers regarding her missing father, who she loved."

Armed with caffeine in her system, a notepad in her pocket, and bundled up against the cold, she apologized to her animals for leaving them behind, then headed down to Nan's, hoping for answers. She expected nothing but some overly excited elders, with little hope of verifiable information. So, as soon as Doreen was done visiting with them, she planned to head to the library to see what she could dredge up there.

She arrived at Nan's apartment to find Nan, Richie, and Maisie all sitting there, waiting for her impatiently. Richie appeared to have gone to the main kitchen area and had stolen at least a dozen treats. She looked at the treats, frowned at him, and he beamed.

"Hey, we need to get our brain cells firing."

"And sugar does that for you, does it?" she asked in a dry tone.

He grinned. "I'm far too old to worry about the damaging effects of sugar," he declared. "I get to eat whatever I want to now."

"Personally I think that's a good idea no matter what age we are," Doreen added, with a laugh. When she sat down, Nan poured her a cup of coffee, then shoved the basket of goodies toward her.

"Eat something," Nan ordered. "We don't want you fainting from hunger."

Doreen nodded. "I didn't have any breakfast."

They all gasped, and the basket was up-ended onto her plate.

"You have to eat," Maisie scolded.

Doreen looked at the three of them and sighed. "You do know that I'm old enough to take care of myself, right?"

They looked at each other, then back at her and shook their heads. "We know that, but that doesn't mean you're doing it."

Doreen groaned. "Okay, let's change the subject and turn our attention to this poor woman who died." With her notepad out, she began, "So let's make sure all four of us are on the same page and go over the facts here. What's her name?"

"Lynda Mahoney," Nan replied.

"Lynda Mahoney." Doreen put a checkmark by her name in her own notepad. "And her father?"

"Jack Mahoney."

"Jack Mahoney." Another name checked off. "And he was in Kelowna when?" she asked, turning to look at them.

They looked at each other, then at her. "When what?"

"When did the father go missing?" Doreen repeated.

Nan nodded, searching through her notepad. "We don't

know that exactly, but more than twenty years ago," she stated. "And we don't know exactly where he went missing from."

"We'll hopefully find that out from Mack's files," Doreen muttered and made a note of that. "Has anybody talked directly to this neighbor about the shooting?"

"Nope, not yet."

"Okay, do we have a number, so I can go talk to her?"

"Oh, that's a good idea," Nan stated. She pulled out her phone and started texting.

"Who are you texting?" Doreen asked.

"I'm texting Mary, the resident here, who knows the neighbor."

Before long a knock came on the door, and a woman with a walker made her way inside.

"Mary," Nan said, "this is Doreen."

"Of course, Doreen," Mary replied, with a bright smile. "I'm so excited to be invited into this group." She beamed with joy, as she faced Nan. "You promised me a hat, you know?"

"You promised information," Nan replied craftily. Doreen, her gaze going from one to the other, opened her mouth, but Nan shook her head. "Don't you worry about that now," she said, with a wave of her hand in the air. "Mary has information about the neighbor."

"Okay, let's start with that," Doreen began, knowing that getting sidetracked wouldn't be helpful right now. "So, who is this neighbor?"

"Her name is Shirley, … Shirley." Mary stopped and frowned. "I don't remember the last name."

Doreen nodded. "That's okay. I'll find it."

"Oh, good," Mary said. "You're really good at that stuff,

aren't you?"

"I would like to think so, but it seems to be a lot harder these days."

"Ooh, I'm sure it is. Criminals are getting much smarter."

Nan grimaced. "If they get any smarter, we will all lose out."

Doreen asked Mary, "Now, what did Shirley say, and what's her phone number? Do you have her address? I'll need a heads-up as to what she told you happened."

"I already contacted her this morning and told her that Lynda Mahoney passed away early this morning. Shirley is pretty scared to go outside right now."

Doreen frowned. "I thought the police considered it a targeted shooting, so she and her neighbors should all be safe."

"Yes, but that's a *should*, and nobody wants to listen to a *should*."

"Right, that's a fair point," Doreen conceded. "Okay, so I need to make a trip up to see her." Doreen frowned as she looked down at her notepad. "So, she's saying Lynda Mahoney was here, looking for her father, Jack Mahoney. Do we know anything else about her father? Does Shirley know anything about what Lynda was looking for and why Lynda's father may have gone missing?"

"I don't know any of that," Mary admitted. "The neighbor Shirley was a little cagey on the phone, as if she didn't really want to say too much."

Doreen frowned at Mary and asked, "Does Shirley live with someone?"

"She lives with Old Man Simmons," she shared, with a grin. "And he's cranky."

"So maybe he wasn't letting her talk."

"Oh, I can see that," Mary agreed. "He's cranky."

"Okay, when people are cranky, they usually have a reason of some kind."

"Yeah, but he's always been that way," Mary noted. "I don't think he needs a reason."

"Okay then, I'll go see if I can talk to her and this cranky old person."

"Good luck," Mary offered. "I really admire that you'll do that."

"Is he dangerous?" Doreen asked, looking at Mary.

The woman frowned back at her and shrugged. "Don't know. I don't think he's killed anybody."

"Do you know if he works?"

"Yes, he does."

"Perfect. Let's hope I can get there while he's at work then, shall we?"

"That's a very good idea," Nan agreed. "I think we should come with you."

"No, I will take my team, the animal team," Doreen butted in. "We all know how much the animals break the ice for everybody."

"That's true," Nan confirmed. "Very true."

As soon as Doreen left, she headed home to get her car and her animals and then sent Mack a text about her plan to talk to the neighbor.

He called her and asked, "Why?"

"Because we heard that the woman died this morning—Lynda Mahoney—after being shot while looking for her father. So, of course, the gang thinks I should now look for the father."

"Of course they do. You do know that we are looking

into that as well?"

"Good," she replied. "I'm not sure I can do this one on my own. Anyway, I'm just letting you know that I'm going to talk to Shirley today."

"Good enough. Go ahead and talk to the neighbor. We've already talked to everybody, but you'll share any information you get, right?"

"Of course. Just be prepared that it'll probably *not* be information that you particularly like."

"It never is," he muttered, with a groan.

She laughed. "Do you know anything about that area?"

"Not particularly. Why?" he asked.

"Supposedly this woman's husband is cranky."

"Cranky how?" he asked, his tone sharp.

"I asked Nan's source if he was dangerous, and the woman told me that, as far as she knew, he'd never killed anybody."

"Good Lord," he grumbled.

"Yeah, that's what I thought you would say," she teased.

"Keep out of trouble today, will you?" he admonished.

"Plan to," she added, with a bright smile, even though he couldn't see it. "Hey, give me kudos for calling and letting you know."

"Yeah, *great*. If I get a phone call about some woman harassing the locals," he pointed out, "I'll know just who that is, won't I?"

"I never harass anybody," Doreen declared.

"Ah, I'm not so sure about that."

"Of course you aren't," she replied, "but it's really *not* what I do." And, with that, she disconnected.

Just as she went to load up her animals in her vehicle, a knock came at her back door. She walked over and opened it to see the two boys standing there, a soaking wet lump in their arms. "Goodness," she gasped, as she stepped back to let them into the house. "What are you guys doing here? Aren't you supposed to be in school?"

"Yes," Gavin began, "but then we found this." And they held out a wet mop.

She looked at the mop and realized eyes glowed up at her. Then it whined. "Oh, my goodness," she exclaimed. She dropped her purse and keys and looked down. Mugs was sniffing all over it. "This is a puppy. Where did you find this puppy?"

"Up the river," Gavin moaned painfully. "Somebody just dumped it."

"People will be people, and a lot of people," she began, as she turned and looked at them, "seem to hurt animals."

Gavin flushed and shook his head. "I never would have hurt him."

"Please," Randy spoke up, "can't you help this one?"

"I don't know. It looks as if he needs to see a vet. He's really, really cold."

Gavin nodded. "We need you to help."

Randy added, "Please, you help the other animals. Can't you help this one?"

"I don't even have a vet," she muttered. "That reminds me that I need to make an appointment for Mugs to get his shots again." Mugs, hearing *vet* and *shots*, turned around and raced away from her, deeper inside the house.

The boys frowned at her, while watching Mugs's reaction, and asked, "Did he understand what you said?"

"Probably. That dog is nothing if not supersmart."

"Wow, it's as if he really did know what you said," Randy muttered.

"Yeah, he sure did," Gavin added.

She accepted the wet mop and became concerned when she felt how cold the little dog really was. "Look, boys. I will get him to a vet, but you guys need to get to school. Do you hear me? Who knows? You might want to become a vet one day so you could help these animals."

"Do you think we could though?" Gavin asked, eyeing her.

"Why not?" she asked. "You'll need some kind of job, and you might as well do something with your life that you enjoy. And, if it makes you feel good to help animals, that would be a great thing to do."

"I don't think I have the smarts for it," Gavin admitted. "He might," he added, pointing to his friend, "but not me."

She studied Gavin and suggested, "You absolutely have the smarts for it."

"Maybe, but I don't have any money for college or whatever."

"Those are all things you can work out later," she suggested. "First off, get your butts to school, and you do your very best as a student, while you think about this puppy all day. I'll get him to the vet, and we will see what happens. I'll probably have to drop him off and leave him there overnight or so, as it will take time to warm him up. I've got to go out myself right now. If you come by after school, I'll let you know what the vet told me, okay?"

And, with that, she shooed them off, hoping that they would go to school. She looked down at the poor little guy in her arms, still shivering. She wrapped him up in several dry towels, pulled out her phone, and called the office of the vet she'd already checked out for getting Mugs's shots when the time came. As soon as someone answered, she explained what had happened.

"Oh my," the receptionist replied, "bring him right in. He's probably hypothermic, and we'll need to get him warmed up."

"Thank you. I'll be there as soon as I can." She loaded up the animals, and, with the puppy half on her lap and half not—knowing that, if she were pulled over, she would be in trouble—she quickly made her way down to the local vet. As she parked in front of the building, Mugs hunkered down in the back seat.

"I know," she told him. "You're all concerned about *you* today, but not everything is about you," she explained. She headed inside, leaving Mugs, Goliath, and Thaddeus in the car. As soon as she and the puppy got inside, one of the receptionists looked up. Doreen explained who she was and held out the puppy she had wrapped up in towels.

Taking one look, the woman exclaimed, "Oh, what a sweetheart."

"Can you please check him over and see what can be done for him?" Doreen asked. "The little boys who found him are quite distraught. I think I persuaded them to get to school, but they were pretty upset about this little guy."

"Of course we will," the woman stated. "I'm really glad they brought him to someone who could help."

Doreen shrugged, then laughed. "They brought it to me, so they must have known I wouldn't leave the poor thing to suffer."

"Of course not," the receptionist agreed. "We'll get him warm and dry, then do a full check-up. Let me get your name and number, and we'll get back to you."

Hating to leave the poor little thing, Doreen looked back several times as she walked out, and the woman called back to her.

"We'll look after him. I promise."

With a sigh, Doreen nodded. "I know. I'm just being foolish."

"It's all right. It just shows you've got heart," the woman replied. "We'll take good care of him and will be in touch soon."

Doreen headed back to her car with mixed emotions.

She didn't know what she would do if she ever lost Mugs, but she hoped that, if he ever got lost, somebody would have the compassion to look after him until they could find his home. She didn't know whether this poor little guy the boys had found had a home or not. It was hard to say what had happened, but Doreen was supposed to be heading out to talk to Shirley, when she got a phone call from Jerry.

As soon as she saw the number, she groaned, "Hey," she greeted him. "Am I late?"

"No, not at all. I was just checking to see if you were still coming."

"On my way right now," she stated, embarrassed she had forgotten. "Be there in five."

Chapter 15

N OW BEGINNING TO feel stressed with everything going on around her, Doreen quickly raced to Big Guy's house. As soon as they pulled up, Thaddeus started squawking, "Big Guy, Big Guy, Big Guy."

"Absolutely, buddy. If nothing else, let's see if we can get you cheered up." With all the animals in tow, she headed up to the front door, which opened immediately, and there was Jerry with Big Guy on his shoulder. Thaddeus started squawking and hopped onto Jerry's shoulder.

He laughed. "I know that you have this one at your home, and I've got mine here, but, man, they sure do get along for two birds living apart."

"They do, but only as long as Thaddeus agrees to get along," she said, with an eye roll.

Jerry led the way to the kitchen and a fresh pot of coffee. She sat down gratefully, poured herself a cup, and muttered, "Boy, I tell you, sometimes these animals ..."

"Yeah, *sometimes*, I agree. Now what's going on with yours? You mentioned you had some husbandry questions."

"I just don't know what's going on," she began, "but I am concerned."

"Okay, *concerned* is definitely worrisome."

"Yeah, definitely worrisome," she agreed, with a sigh. Then she explained about what had happened with Thaddeus at Milford's farm and how all her animals had not been quite themselves ever since.

He nodded. "It does happen. I hate to say it, but I have seen that before."

"What do you think happened?" she asked.

"It seems they got a smell of somebody who didn't like them, and they made a judgment based on what they saw, what they felt. It sounds to me as if they didn't like anything about this person, plus that cat of Milford's, skulking around too."

"Yes," she agreed, "nobody liked that cat."

"Because that cat was more of a hunter, the dog probably wouldn't have been an issue, but Thaddeus would have been for sure. Plus, this feral cat might have picked a good fight with Goliath." He eyed Goliath for a moment. "He does seem to be a little off."

"They're all a little off," she declared, "and I'm quite frustrated and down about it all because I don't know what I'm supposed to do. It's the first time we've ever had something like that happen. Mack was with me, and it should have been fine, but … I don't know."

"But?" he urged.

"It didn't seem to be fine at all. They all went really quiet."

"And yet they've been to crime scenes before."

"Yes," she agreed, "they've been to all kinds of different places before, but never with that reaction."

Jerry nodded. "All I can suggest is that something about that location bothered them. Something about what may have happened or about the people there that your animals didn't like. They didn't like that spot or something about it. They will recover from it, but it may change how they react to other situations too."

"Goodness," Doreen muttered. "I don't want to take them out if they'll get so upset over what they see."

"It's not even so much what they see," he pointed out. "It's what they feel—or smell. The old man up there, Milford, do you think he was the kind to treat an animal badly?"

She turned to him and winced. "You and I would call it *badly*, but I don't think Milford would."

"Exactly," Jerry confirmed. "So I'm sure Mugs picked up on that. Thaddeus was already picking up on the cat, and Goliath probably felt out of his depths and maybe threatened because of the other cat. It's not uncommon for people to not really like you," he explained pointedly, "but generally they have nothing against the animals—or it's all of you at odds with someone."

"Now that's true," Doreen muttered.

"And, in this case, I think everything was against them and not you, which was a different experience for your animals, and probably confusing."

She sat back and stared at him. "I hadn't considered that."

"So, in a way, it's their first time being rejected—in a big and confusing way."

"Wow."

"And maybe that rejection," he pointed out, "was just because of what was going on there." He hesitated before asking, "I don't know why you were there, or what was exactly going on, but was it criminal in any way? Was it bad news, as in something you need to go back to, so you can try and figure out what's happening?"

"I don't know yet, but definitely something weird was going on."

"Definitely weird," Jerry repeated, "particularly the way the animals reacted, but that doesn't mean *criminal* weird."

"No, it doesn't," she admitted, staring at him with a nod. "I was just hoping that maybe a visit here would cheer them up and maybe would put them back to normal again."

"They will go back to normal," Jerry noted. "This definitely isn't something that won't be resolved, but clearly they were unsettled and lost their confidence in that encounter."

"That makes sense," she noted.

Jerry continued. "So, if you do have to go back up there, maybe don't take them with you."

"Right," she said, with a nod. "That's probably a smart idea. It's a hard one to absorb, but good advice."

He chuckled. "This guy seems to be doing better."

And, in truth, Thaddeus kept up a steady conversation with Big Guy, who just looked at him, cleaning his beak every once in a while. That seemed to be enough for Thaddeus, continuing his storm of discussion.

"He's not even slowing down," Jerry said, with another chuckle.

"The amount of conversation he can maintain just blows me away," she muttered. "He really is something."

"He's wonderful," Jerry confirmed.

"Speaking of animals," Doreen began, "this morning I had two young boys come by my place. I say young, but they were probably … eleven or twelve. They brought me a puppy they found in the river this morning. It was soaked and chilled to the bone."

"Really?"

She told him a little bit about dropping off the puppy at the vet to figure out what he needed. "They're supposed to call me with the results," she added, "and I'm a little worried. I'm not sure what we do with puppies."

"You can drop him off at some animal rescues in town, if nobody owns it," Jerry suggested, "though they're all strapped for money these days. Honestly, I think all animal rescues are strapped for money."

"Right," she muttered, with a sigh. "It seems to be a regular refrain."

"Even when people do have money, they don't necessarily share it."

She nodded. "I've known lots of people with big money," she shared, "and so many of them were fairly superficial in how much they gave away and to whom."

"Exactly. And sometimes they do it as a tax break, and then, when the tax break's done, they don't do it anymore," he said. "They don't do it from the heart."

"Right," she noted, frowning. "This is embarrassing, but I wasn't even aware most of these charities even needed people to support them."

"Of course," he said, "you've been one of those blessed people, living in the dark."

She shook her head. "I was, but I can assure you that I'm not any longer," she clarified.

"So, does that mean you'll be helping out various places?"

"Yeah, I sure will, as soon as I get my finances sorted out," she stated. "Then I'll have to figure out how best to help some of these charities."

"Keep Big Guy in mind," Jerry noted. "We are a registered charity, or at least it's in the works for birds," he added, "like this one."

"Interesting," she replied, making a mental note to look into this further. "What would you suggest I do with the puppy?"

"You could see if the boys' family would take it in for one," Jerry suggested, "particularly if the kid is struggling. It would be a really good thing for him to focus on and to have something to love that would love him back."

"I was wondering about that," she replied, "though I'm not sure if the uncle could handle it."

"Uncle?"

"Yes, the boy lost his mom, and now he's living with his childless uncle, and, of course, that's not ideal either, particularly given the boy's rebellious behavior at the moment."

Jerry winced. "No, it sure isn't. So, that would be one option, but, if not, we do have several shelters that take in animals, and, once the animals are fixed, they'll be adopted out."

"Okay, that would be a good alternative."

"First off is to see what the vet has to say about whether the puppy will make it," Jerry explained. "No telling how long he'd been in the river or what shape he was in to begin with. Even in our modern world, the doctors can't save everybody. If the puppy's hypothermic, they'll need to keep him, and that will add to his bill."

"Right, and, for so many people, it's the cost of pets that can be a major and unexpected expense, and they end up giving away the animal because they can't afford to keep them any longer."

"I know that, for you, based on what I've been hearing,

your financial situation is looking up, and you're doing okay, but a lot of people out there simply can't afford to look after their animals."

"Yes, that is so true."

"So, what about your cold cases?" he asked, looking at her with a bright expression. "What case are you involved in now?"

"Looking at possibly a missing person's case from about twenty-five years ago. I was up in the Joe Rich area, speaking to Milford, a farmer up there, because apparently one morning years ago he found an insane amount of blood all over one of his garden beds. He supposedly contacted law enforcement back then."

Jerry snorted at that. "He might have made a phone call, but I highly doubt anybody did much about it. If there was no body and no proof that it was human blood," he began, "then nobody would have been concerned enough to make the trip, especially if nobody turned up missing."

Doreen grimaced. "That seems to be what happened, but Milford lost his wife recently, and one of her last orders was that he sort it out."

"And this is the same guy who caused all your animals to react differently?"

She nodded.

"So, you started thinking that maybe *he* killed somebody," Jerry suggested, with a laugh, "just because the animals don't like him?"

"I have to admit that I was struck with that very thought," she acknowledged, with a shrug, "which isn't fair to Milford at all."

"Or to his wife, who he's trying to honor," Jerry noted, with a smile. "On the other hand, it's just the way that life works sometimes."

She explained about the other two missing men, how Bartlet Jones went missing fifty years ago and Jack Mahoney around twenty years or so ago. She stayed and visited for a little bit longer. While Jerry had heard about the recent shooting in town, he didn't have any information about any of the missing person cases she had shared.

"I didn't realize that the poor woman was up here looking for her father who'd gone missing so many years ago. Good God. I don't know how you do it, Doreen. I work with the animals every day, and while they bring me a lot of peace and joy, it's still tough and can get me down," he shared. "But to deal with broken people every day? No way," he declared. "That's more than I could do."

She smiled up at him. "I wouldn't have thought that I would be happy or comfortable working these cases either, but that's where I'm at, and it's something I can do, at least for now." And, with that, she took her leave, as Thaddeus called out all the way to the car, "Bye, bye, Big Guy. Bye, bye, Big Guy." She laughed when they got into the car, as he seemed to be much more his usual self. "Was that a good visit, buddy?" she asked him.

He nuzzled up against her neck as she drove toward Shirley's home, finally getting to what she had been meaning to do all morning.

Chapter 16

DOREEN HOPED THAT she would still get there in time to talk to Shirley before her husband came home from work. As it was, just as Doreen and her animals walked up to the front porch, the door opened, and a woman stepped out, looking as though she was leaving. Doreen stopped her and introduced herself. "Hi, I'm Doreen. I was speaking with Mary down at Rosemoor earlier."

"Oh my," Shirley replied, "I certainly didn't expect to see you."

"I just wanted to confirm a few things."

"Sure," she said, then frowned. "I have to leave soon."

"I don't need very long," Doreen promised. "I just want to verify some of the details, as Mary is getting on in years."

"Oh my, yes," she agreed but grimaced afterward. "Will I have to sign a statement or anything?"

"Nope," Doreen replied, "I'm not the police. I work with the police, of course, but I am not employed by them."

"Oh good," she muttered, "because my husband really won't like it if I get myself involved in something like that."

"Understood," Doreen agreed brightly. She quickly went over the information Mary had provided, and Shirley confirmed every bit. "And you didn't see anybody on the street? Any cars? You didn't see who shot Lynda? You didn't hear the shot?"

"No, I didn't see or hear it," Shirley stated. "Yet, now that I know a shot was fired, then maybe I probably did hear it, but I didn't necessarily hear it, if you know what I mean."

"Meaning that you heard a weird sound and that you wondered what it was?"

"Exactly. There was this little *pop, pop* thing," she shared, "but I didn't recognize it for what it was. I was outside, but I didn't see a vehicle or anything. I saw a man walking, and he seemed to walk a little bit faster, but I didn't mention it to the police. Besides, for all I know, the poor guy was just out having a Sunday stroll."

"Exactly," Doreen noted. "Any description on him?"

"Oh, I know who it was," Shirley stated. "He's Clive from the corner store. Just up around the corner here, in that little shopping mall. It's not much, but he has the corner store there."

"And his last name?" Doreen asked.

Shirley frowned. "Now why can't I remember that? He was adopted by a local—not a founding family or anything like that. Just one of us, you know? And my mind is still blank. Can I call you when it comes to me?"

"Sure." Doreen nodded, handing her a card with her number on it. "Were you surprised to see him here?" Doreen asked.

"No, he lives close by. … Well, he used to live close by. I'm really not sure where he lives now." She frowned. "I guess maybe I should have been surprised to see him but, then again, maybe not. I think he's probably got a ladylove around here or something," she suggested, turning to look around the neighborhood. "Not sure which one it would be though."

"Have the police come by and asked you any questions?"

"Oh my, yes, but every time my husband is in the back of the house, yelling at me to not say nothing. He doesn't want to get involved, doesn't want to get in trouble, all that good stuff."

"Of course," Doreen agreed, with a bright smile. "Understood."

Shirley smiled at Doreen's animals and added, "You sure do have such nicely behaved pets."

Doreen almost snorted. Instead she just smiled and nodded. "Thank you. I do love my animals."

Chapter 17

DOREEN WALKED BACK to her car, her animals in tow. She walked slowly, her mind contemplating so many random events, with nothing really checking the boxes as to what was going on. Just as she reached the car, her phone rang. She looked down to see it was Mack. Buoyed and always happy to hear from him, she answered the call with a cheerful "Hello." When all she heard in response was silence from the other side, she asked, "Mack? What's up?"

"That was an awfully cheery hello from you," he asked, his tone sharpening. "Where are you?"

She groaned. "Nowhere."

"Which just means you're getting into trouble," he declared. "So, fess up. Where are you, and what have you been up to?"

She snickered. "I'm out in Glenmore."

He stopped, then asked, "Seriously?"

"Yeah, why not?" she asked. "I told you that visiting Shirley was my plan. You've already talked to everybody, so it's not a big deal. Did you guys talk to a Clive about the shooting?"

"Who?" Mack asked.

She smiled, knowing her diversion had worked. "A man named Clive. Apparently he was walking by here at the same time as the shooting. Shirley fleetingly wondered if it was related, just because he was here."

"And he shouldn't have been there?" Mack asked, his tone quiet.

She heard paperwork shuffling and then the sound of a keyboard clacking on the other end of the phone. "He works at the corner store and used to live nearby," she replied, "but doesn't anymore. Originally Shirley didn't give it a thought, thinking it made sense that he would be in the neighborhood, as he used to live here. Then Shirley realized it didn't make that much sense that he would be here, since he didn't live in the area anymore."

"*Hmm*, do we have a last name for this Clive?"

"Nope, but he's at the corner store."

Mack sighed. "*Doreen.*"

"I know. I know, but I could just be asking questions about the cold case. About Lynda's missing father, you know?" She tried to make it sound encouraging, hoping he would take the hint. However, he took one leap too far.

"Right, the cold case where *maybe* somebody connected was shot at point-blank range for asking questions?"

She winced. "Yeah, okay, so maybe I'm jumping to conclusions."

"*Not* the brightest idea," he declared, his temper building. "Have you at least got the animals with you?"

"Yes, I do," she replied brightly, as she opened up the car door to let Mugs hop in. "They've been good as gold."

"Did you get Thaddeus over to visit with Big Guy?"

"Yes, and it went well. I thought I would pop down to the corner store and see if this Clive knows anything about the shooting. And, of course, you've likely already talked to him, so—"

"As long as it's got nothing to do with *my* case," he warned.

"No, and, of course, if he were to volunteer anything, I would share."

He groaned. "Everybody does seem to prefer to talk to you than anybody else. Makes my job harder, you know?"

"So, you agree that it's a good thing what I'm doing?" she asked cheerfully.

"I don't know about that." He then changed the topic. "Did you take anything out for dinner?"

"Nope, I sure didn't," she said. "Why?"

"I just thought maybe we could have dinner together tonight."

"I would love that," she replied warmly. "I'll let you know how I make out with Clive."

"You be careful," he muttered. "We don't know what's going on here. Someone was murdered, remember? You could be walking into something very dangerous."

"I get it," she murmured. "I assure you that I'm not suicidal in any way."

"No, but you're also not the most cautious person around."

Such a wry tone filled his words that she had to laugh. "And I get it, but I did bring the animals."

"But they won't save you every time," he fretted.

"And I won't be silly all the time either."

"No," he muttered, "just enough of the time that it causes trouble."

She burst out laughing. "It's nice to know you care."

"You know I do," he stated, "but I need to ensure you

live long enough to marry me."

In the background of the call, she heard somebody yelling.

"I've got to go," Mack said, then disconnected quickly.

With the animals in tow, Doreen hopped back into her vehicle and drove to the corner store. She hadn't been to this one before, and it was an interesting little place. She pulled up in front, looked at the animals, and decided they probably needed to stay where they were this time, even though they wouldn't like it much.

She hopped out, walked into the store, and looked around to see who was on staff. One man was here, maybe thirty-ish, though she found herself struggling to determine ages, especially when people like Nan acted and appeared so much younger than she was. Walking to the cooler, Doreen picked up a cold iced tea and headed to the checkout stand. She looked up at the cashier and smiled. "Hopefully all that excitement has died down by now."

He frowned at her, then nodded. "You mean, the shooting?"

"Yeah, it's scary to think of it happening right here."

"It wasn't really right here," he clarified, with a wave. "Apparently I was nearby at the time, but I never even heard anything about it," he shared, with a noncommittal shrug.

"Really?" she asked, studying him. "How is that possible?"

"Just busy heading to work," he replied. He pointed at the iced tea and asked, "Anything else?"

She shook her head. "No, I just find the cold cases around this town fascinating and was trying to figure out how there could be so many in Kelowna."

"What do you mean, cold cases?" he asked, turning to

her, as he swiped the iced tea across the scanner. When it buzzed, she held out her card and paid for it.

"Unsolved police matters. We've got one here, concerning the woman's father who disappeared. That's why Lynda Mahoney was here and how absolutely awful that she was killed because of it," Doreen shared, with a heavy sigh. "I think her father disappeared at least twenty years ago. Then we have another person missing, maybe from twenty-five years ago, and he's still not been found, you know, the one in the Joe Rich area." She leaned forward and whispered, "I think the police are onto that one."

Clive's gaze narrowed as he stared at her. "I don't think I've heard of these," he noted, his tone deep, almost glaring at her.

She nodded. "I just started looking into them. It's a hobby of mine."

He shook his head. "Considering Lynda just got shot, it seems to be a dangerous hobby."

"The only reason she would have gotten shot was if she were close to finding something," Doreen suggested. "So, with all the information the police found, I can't imagine it will be very long until they find the culprit."

He glanced at her, then, in a flat tone, asked if she needed anything else.

At that point, she realized she was being dismissed. She shook her head. "No, that's all, thank you." She gave him a bright smile. "It's exciting that you were practically there on the spot."

"Nope, I wasn't. I wasn't there on the spot, and I didn't see nothing."

"Oh, I thought you said you just walked past."

"No, I didn't," he snapped, turning to glare at her with a

bored look, as if to say, *Lady, are you done yet?*

Of course she wasn't done, but she didn't dare tell him that. She smiled and nodded. "What is the Joe Rich area like?" she asked. "Do you know?"

He frowned at her. "How would I know?"

She shrugged. "I just thought, if you were a local, you would have some experience with it. I heard it's pretty wintery up there."

He snorted. "It's not wintery up there," he argued. "If you go on up the mountain, then it's wintery, but it's hardly wintery anywhere around here. This is Kelowna, and we don't get much winter. We used to, but not for a long time."

"Oh, interesting," she replied, studying him. "*Used to* as in five years ago or *used to* as in fifty years ago?"

"Fifty years ago," he stated. "At least according to the old timers around here."

"I can understand that too," she muttered, while she stared around at the area. "It's hard to see how quickly time is flying by."

"Yeah. It is what it is." Clive waved her out the door, almost shushing her.

"Maybe I'll take a drive up and see what I can find out about this poor missing guy," she shared.

"Drive up where?" he asked, astonished.

"The Joe Rich area, of course," she said. "I told you that's where one person went missing from."

"How long ago?" Clive asked.

"Oh, quite a while ago, some twenty-plus years," she replied. "I figure it's connected somehow to the missing father of that poor woman who just got shot."

"Whatever," Clive muttered, aiming for a bored tone, but missing the point completely.

In fact, his entire demeanor changed as soon as she discussed the two cold cases and suggested they might be connected. She just nodded.

Clive frowned. "Yeah, whatever, have a nice day."

And, with that, she waved and walked outside.

As she turned to look behind her, he stood at the window, watching her. She gave him a bright, beaming smile and continued on. Not sure if he was still watching or not, she walked past her car and went around the corner of the building. She didn't want him to connect her to the animals. For some reason, at this point in time, it seemed important to keep that to herself.

Just something was off about the way Clive was acting. It would be way too obvious if he had been there at the scene, but, as she thought about it, all he really had to do was hide the weapon and carry on to work. Under that scenario, it could easily have been him. Since she didn't like anything about him from this first meeting, she was more than willing to cast him in that villain light. Jumping to assumptions would get Mack riled up, and he would have her head over it.

She continued on around the corner and waited. After a minute or two, she poked her head around, and, sure enough, Clive was outside, talking on the phone. Her eyebrows shot up at that. She hadn't really considered that somebody else would be involved. Or he could be calling the cops to report a suspicious woman at his corner store. Doreen groaned. It was also completely possible that Clive could be having a completely innocent conversation, but she didn't think so. It didn't go along with the scenario that was trying to work out in her head.

When he got off the phone and returned inside the

store, she quickly walked around to her car and slid into the driver's seat. Mugs woofed at her and gave her a nuzzle. She had the iced tea in her hand and quickly popped the top on it and took a long drink, putting the car in Reverse and exiting before Clive saw it was her behind the wheel. She needed to figure out what could be happening next. The idea that Clive was involved wasn't confirmed, but he was definitely suspicious.

She frowned at the thought because, if the cops hadn't talked to him, they probably needed to. And, if they had talked to Clive, they should have picked up some data on him, which Mack may or may not know—and may or may not have shared with her. That was always possible concerning his current cases.

Chapter 18

WONDERING ABOUT THIS Clive guy still, Doreen drove slowly toward her house, her mind occupied, as she considered all the potential scenarios that could be going on. To think that someone here potentially took out that poor woman who was involved in a heartfelt search for her long-missing father was very disturbing. As Doreen pulled up to her home, she hopped out and released the animals, all converging on the front steps.

Richard stepped out of his house at the same time, as if to go shopping.

In all the time that she'd been living next door to him, she had yet to meet his wife, but she'd heard voices, just fairly strange voices. Doreen looked over at him and asked, "Hey, you were here twenty to thirty years ago, weren't you, Richard?" When he stopped and glared at her, she shrugged. "Do you remember any of the missing persons from back then?"

His brows drew together. "You've got another case?" he asked in astonishment.

"Maybe, we've got a couple people missing, plus a bloody garden bed where a third person may have been killed. I'm looking into all three, but clues are hard to find, as they go back as far as fifty years, twenty-five years, and then twenty-or-so years. I was thinking that I could potentially help bring some closure to the families."

He nodded, yet frowned. "I've got to admit that it felt good for my brother to get that closure."

"Exactly," she agreed, "and he wasn't alone in that. Other people are still suffering."

"*Hmm.*" Richard came closer, still staying on his side of the property line. "Who went missing?"

"We've got Jack Mahoney from twenty-or-so years ago," she replied. "And you heard about the woman who was recently shot in Glenmore?"

He nodded. "I heard briefly, but what about it?"

"That was Lynda, Lynda Mahoney, daughter to Jack. She was here looking for her father again. She last saw him in Merritt some twenty-odd years ago."

Richard stared at her. "Seriously?"

"Yeah." Doreen sighed. "Apparently Lynda had seen him there, but he'd left and went on his way. She thought he went missing from Kelowna, but it could also be as far up as Kamloops."

"That would be good if it was Kamloops," Richard muttered, frowning at her. "The last thing we need is more bad press about people going missing from here."

"Oh, I agree," she replied. "You'll get absolutely no argument from me on that."

He snorted at that. "You're just happy to have another case."

"No, not necessarily. The oldest one of the three I'm focusing on was Bartlet Jones, who went missing fifty years ago. Both Mahoney and Jones were referenced in Solomon's files."

"Oh," Richard said, as if that changed things completely. He shook his head. "Solomon was a good man," he stated.

Just something about that change in his tone made her realize how much validity Richard felt because the information came from Solomon. Doreen agreed. "He was, indeed, and I consider it such an honor that he gave me his files."

"He must have trusted you," Richard noted, sounding grumpy now. He glanced at her. "I do remember something about Bartlet. He went to work one day and disappeared. Or was that the other case you just did?"

"Yeah, you're right about both. One of my previous cold cases had a married man going to work and never returning. Plus, I heard the same thing said about Bartlet Jones, although he didn't seem to be married."

"Maybe it ended the same way too."

"That's possible—deep-sixed by a family member. I need to figure out exactly where Jack Mahoney's home was. I understand he did live here, did have a residence way back when, even though he must have stayed long periods of time at his ranch too."

"Wasn't that local address in the files?" he asked.

"It was, but the street no longer exists, or I can't read Solomon's handwriting enough to understand where the street was."

Richard snickered at that. "I'm not surprised. He probably had his own form of shorthand. He was really something. He used to cover all the trials and everything and kept us all in the loop. And then he got older, and it was just hard for everybody to keep up with the brand-new technology, and it took over everything," he muttered.

"Yeah, that's what happens in life," she agreed. "Change comes, and either we move forward or we fight it and fall behind."

"I'm all about fighting it and falling behind," Richard teased.

"But, if you do that, you get lost in the process," she replied, with half a smile. "So, do you remember anything else about Bartlet Jones?"

"Other than he was a womanizer? Maybe," he added, "I'll have to think about it." And, with that, he got into his vehicle and drove away.

That's exactly what Millicent had told her as well, that she needed to think on it some more, which wasn't helpful. On the other hand, it made sense that some people couldn't dredge up the information that easily, not when it called for fifty-year-old memories. Doreen had also planned on going to the library and seeing if she could come up with any information there.

For now, she went inside her home, back to Solomon's files, and pulled the records in question on Bartlet Jones. With that in front of her, she put on the teakettle and sat down to read. It was just cold enough outside that she wanted to warm up before she dashed off again. Besides, the library wasn't exactly a place where she could bring the animals. Unfortunately they still prohibited having animals in there. As she went through the Bartlet Jones file, she jotted down a few notes. There was an address, but it was up in the Joe Rich area and basically a P.O. Box on Highway 97, along with some weird numbers.

She frowned at that and wondered how she was supposed to figure out an address from that. Way back then they didn't exactly have house numbers or even street names. It was just a *turn here* type thing. And maybe he had a sign on the highway where you were supposed to know the turnoff. Back then, people talked to each other instead of the typical *leave me alone message* that she had to deal with most of the time now.

As soon as her tea was done and she had written up her notes, she got up and decided there was no time like the present. She might as well go deal with whatever was available at the library. She had two names of the three possibly missing persons, so that should at least help save her time and get to whatever information there was to go forward with—or not. If she didn't come up with more than what she had at the moment, it was clearly a case of *not* when it came to Bartlet Jones.

Leaving the animals at home, Doreen headed to the library. As soon as she walked in, the librarian looked up and smiled.

"*Uh-oh*, this must mean that Doreen has a new case," she teased.

"Does not," Doreen protested.

"It does too," she corrected. "You only ever come here when you're on the hunt."

Doreen winced at the phrase. "I guess that's what it seems like to everybody, doesn't it?"

"Yep. *When Doreen's off on a hunt, them criminals had better go dark*," she quoted, laughing.

Doreen smiled. "I guess there are worse things for people to see me as."

"There are, indeed," the librarian agreed. "Now, what can I help you with?"

"I'm a little confused," Doreen began. "I've got an old address in the Joe Rich area from one of Solomon's files, but it doesn't really match an address, not per my Google Maps online search."

"That's probably off the highway," the librarian suggested. "It will just have a number that corresponds to where the highway markers are. Who are you talking about?"

"Bartlet Jones," she replied.

The librarian raised both eyebrows. "Oh, that's a name I haven't heard in a very long time."

"Did you know Bartlet?"

"No, I'm not old enough, but my dad used to know Bartlet."

"Any idea what happened to the man?"

She frowned at Doreen and nodded. "Oh, that's right. I had forgotten all about that," she murmured, staring off in the distance. "My dad used to say that no good would come of him."

"And why is that?"

She winced. "I hate to tell tales about the dead—or the missing—but he was a womanizer and not always too careful about whose woman he chose to womanize with."

"Meaning, married women?"

"Yes. Apparently, in his mind, married women were even better because they couldn't lock him into marriage."

"But that just makes him a marriage breaker," Doreen murmured.

"Exactly, and my father used to tell Bartlet all the time how he would get in trouble, but that was a long time ago. I only ever heard about him after somebody tried to bring up the cold case file," the librarian added, turning to look at Doreen. "And that might have been Solomon."

"And it could have been," Doreen agreed. "He has it down as a cold case still to be solved, and it looks as if he opened it several times and never really managed to get any answers for it."

"I'm not surprised," the librarian murmured. "There was just nothing to go on. Bartlet just up and disappeared one day."

"And yet," Doreen asked, "where on earth would he go?"

"That's the thing. He ran the town in many ways. He was one of those guys who was all over the place. Everybody knew him, and he was friendly to everyone, too friendly to some." She hesitated. "Honestly, chances are he got a little bit too frisky with the wrong wife, and some husband probably popped him and left him where he lay."

"I wouldn't be at all surprised," Doreen admitted, with a nod. "We've certainly seen that happen."

"We have, haven't we?" she replied, with a headshake. "Let's go see if we can find anything in the archives."

Doreen asked, "Would your father be interested in speaking to me about Bartlet?"

The librarian gave her a sad smile. "My father passed on about five years ago."

Doreen put her hand to her heart. "I'm so sorry."

The librarian nodded. "He had been fighting heart disease for many years, and we were told to expect it, but you're never ready for it regardless."

"How true," Doreen muttered. "Did you know anything about Lynda Mahoney, who was just murdered?"

"No, what about her?" The librarian turned to her.

"She was here looking for her father, who went missing twenty-odd years ago. She met him for lunch in Merritt back then, and he was on his way to Kelowna. She did speak to him when he called from Kelowna, so she knows he arrived at least that far, and then she never heard from him again.

Her father was forty-something years old back then."

The librarian looked at her and shook her head. "I don't think I even heard about his daughter."

"Lynda came here just after he first went missing, and, when she came back up just days ago, she was shot in front of her friend's house, where she was staying."

"Good God, that's terrible."

"I know, and then, of course, I had yet another case."

The librarian stopped and frowned. "*Another* case? So you have three cold cases of different missing people?"

"Yeah, but this is the opposite though, although maybe it ties together somehow. I don't know. However, many years ago, maybe twenty-five, somebody found a significant quantity of what they believed or assumed to be human blood out in their zucchini patch."

"Zucchini patch," she repeated, putting her hands on her hips. "You're making that up."

"Nope, I'm not making it up, and, in this case, we're talking about the Joe Rich area."

"Right," the librarian noted. "Maybe that was Jack Mahoney's blood. Maybe someone hit him over the head and got rid of him. Lord knows he never showed up again."

"And that's possible," Doreen noted. "It happened on Milford's farm out there. Milford's wife passed away about a year ago. One of the things that she wanted Milford to do was to get that sorted out, so that they could find peace about the whole issue before Milford died. The police had been called all those years ago, but nobody opened up a file because they had no proof it was human blood."

"Right," the librarian muttered, "and honestly, you can't really blame them. What looks like blood in that corner could really be almost anything."

"That's what Milford told the police too. That blood could be a deer or coyote or whatever. So, nobody made a big deal about it."

The librarian nodded. "Oh, the things we get ourselves into. So, now what? Milford's called you?"

"Yeah, exactly," she confirmed, with a wry look at the librarian. "He called me, asking me to solve it."

"Good Lord," she muttered. "Good luck with these because you'll need it. If nobody has found any answers so far, it seems unlikely that you'll find anything now."

"I know. Believe me that I know. It's troublesome with these super old cases, especially since I have absolutely no idea what is going on with them. I very much want to solve the missing father case that cost this poor woman her life. Lynda Mahoney died trying to get answers about her father's disappearance, which is so sad."

"Agreed." The librarian sat down at the microfiche and started clicking through dates and years. When she found something, she pointed. "Here you go. I wish I could stay and help but …"

"It's all right, go," Doreen said. "I know you're busy, and you have other people to deal with."

"Sure do," she agreed cheerfully. And she took off to the front counter, where a line already had formed.

As soon as Doreen got into the files, she completely lost track of time, as she went down the newspaper articles rabbit hole, tracing every mention of Jack Mahoney or Bartlet Jones. It was amazing how much information was to be found in these old articles. Not necessarily helpful information, but fascinating nonetheless. When a tap on her shoulder interrupted her focus, she jumped and looked up to see Mack, gazing down at her. She beamed up at him. "Hi," she said.

"What're you looking for?" he asked, as he sat down beside her.

"Any information I can come across on the three missing persons cases."

He looked at her, puzzled. "Three?" She quickly reiterated the three of them—Bartlet Jones, Jack Mahoney and the one unnamed man. "Who knows? One of these may lead me to the body that bled out in Milford's garden bed."

"*Huh*," he replied. "I still don't remember hearing about Bartlet Jones, but you say it was one from Solomon's files?"

"So you didn't have time to check your database yet?"

"Not yet."

Doreen sighed. "That's the thing. If the locals don't have any information on them, what can I do?" she pointed out. "It just becomes another cold case, gathering dust."

"It's not as if we aren't looking at the cold cases too," he told her, "but we're a little limited on manpower, particularly when we got so busy all of a sudden." He gave her a pointed look specifically.

She winced. "I know, and I'm more than happy to have you guys take all the credit," she muttered. "But we also need to know that, if more cases need to be solved, they get the same amount of attention."

He sighed. "You just have to be a pain about all this, don't you?"

"I'm not being a pain," she argued. "I just want to know that everybody gets the same treatment, the same care they deserve."

"We aren't trying to ignore them, honey."

"I know," she muttered, teary-eyed, as she looked over at him. "But even thinking about that zucchini patch is keeping me quite distracted."

"Ah." An odd expression came on his face.

"What?" she asked, turning to look at him. "What's going on?"

"Nothing," he said.

She shook her head. "No, no, no, you don't get to say that."

He sighed. "I heard back from forensics."

"Yeah?" she asked, staring at him expectantly. "And?" she pushed on.

Reluctantly he replied, "They said the sample is too degraded. So nothing definite that it's blood.'

She sagged back into her chair and stared at him. It's what she'd half expected but still there'd been a little sliver of hope.

"Considering that and assuming there was a lot of blood, what we don't know is whether someone died, whether someone was taken to the hospital with a severe injury, if a large animal died there, or," he hesitated, then added, "if old man Milford is lying."

She winced at that. "Got to love how that automatically becomes a possibility, doesn't it?"

"We have to use common sense about this," Mack pointed out. "And, if that much blood was there, and some evidence that somebody was killed there," he explained, "the only two people living there were that couple, Milford and his wife, Rose."

She frowned, not liking where he was going with this. "And what is your theory as to why he would have called out of the blue on something like that?"

"I don't know why he called, but what I can tell you is that sample was definitely human blood."

"What will the captain do about it?"

"That's under discussion right now," he shared, with a smile. "But it's definitely not a case of *Hey, thanks, Doreen, for bringing this to our attention.* I would say his position is more like *Oh, good heavens, another one?*"

She chuckled at that. "I'm sure that's exactly how it is for him, but, if I can do anything to help, I'm in," she offered. "Oh, and this Clive character is very dodgy."

Mack looked at her and blinked several times. "I hate to ask," he replied, "but *what Clive character?*"

She looked at him expectantly. "Remember? I told you about him, the one at the corner store."

"Right," he muttered and gave her a headshake. "How could I have forgotten?"

"Exactly. How could you have forgotten?" Then she went off in peals of laughter. "We do seem to be coming up with cases fairly quickly. This one's definitely a bit more bizarre than some of the others."

"No," he countered, "it's not more bizarre at all. It's just amazing that still this many cold cases need to be dealt with in town. I had no clue about this one, until you told me about Milford," Mack admitted, as he stared around. "To think somebody was possibly murdered on that property and nobody knew is pretty amazing."

"And that's why I'm looking into that death myself," she muttered.

"Are you're thinking the husband did it or not?"

"I'm not thinking anything," she acknowledged, "at least not yet. I just don't know why Milford would have called and brought us there if he was the killer, you know? That makes no sense to me," she noted. Her phone vibrated, and she'd just missed a call from the vet. She gasped. "Oh no, those poor boys."

He jumped up at her alarm and asked, "What boys? What are you even talking about?"

She winced. "I guess I didn't have a chance to tell you about that."

"Tell me about what?" he asked, looking at her with a narrowed gaze.

She quickly told him about the puppy the two boys had found in the river. "I took it to the vet, but I was supposed to contact the boys and give them an update. I hadn't even heard back from the vet yet. Of course I put my phone on Silent when I came in the library. Wonder what else I missed."

"Why don't we run down to the vet before they close," Mack suggested quickly.

She smiled at him, then realized how late in the day it had gotten. "Oh my," she murmured, "how did it get to be so late?"

"It doesn't take long when you're having fun," he noted, with a chuckle. "Come on. Let's get you home, and we'll stop at the vet on the way."

"My vehicle is here," she pointed out, "so we'll both have to drive."

"That's fine," he murmured. "Let's get you moving." And, with that, he helped her gather her things, and they both moved out to their vehicles, hopped in, and drove to the veterinary clinic. As soon as she got there, the receptionist looked up and smiled.

"Oh good, we were hoping to connect before the end of the day."

Doreen nodded. "Sorry. I was at the library and got distracted. Plus, I had my phone silenced, of course."

"Hello," said the vet, as she came up to the counter. "That pup was very cold and dehydrated and still needs more fluids to get stabilized. Has a couple deep scratches as well. Definitely had a hard time," she explained, "but sure is adorable."

"So, what is the plan for the puppy?"

"I want to keep her overnight for sure, and then we'll see how she's doing tomorrow," she murmured. "By the time we're done, she should go off to a new family, but I just can't be sure when that'll be. She's very thin, so I want to see her fattened up a little bit and to see that everything is working correctly, just to ensure she's recovered from the hypothermia."

"Sounds good," Doreen replied. "I promised the boys who found her that I would follow up with them."

"Oh good," the receptionist added, with a smile. "Maybe tomorrow, if she's better, they could come down and take a look at her."

"Oh, that would be lovely," Doreen murmured. "Thank you." As soon as they got back outside, she turned to Mack. "I wonder what it would take to have Gavin be allowed to keep the puppy."

"I wouldn't go there," Mack suggested. "If the family is already struggling just to look after themselves and to adapt to the loss of the boy's mother, I don't imagine looking after a puppy right now would be an easy thing."

"No, it wouldn't be easy," she agreed, "but it might really help that young man."

"Maybe, but it's also a responsibility that the uncle or father or whoever it is would have to take on," he pointed out.

"True." She thought about it and nodded. "I guess it's a

decision that they would have to make."

"Absolutely," he said, with a smile. "Now, let's get you home." It was another ten minutes before they were home. No sooner were they inside when a knock came at her back door.

She looked over at Mack. "That'll be the boys."

"I want to meet these boys," he said.

With Mack at her side, she opened the door to see Gavin there. "Hey, Gavin. I just came from the vet. The puppy is still recovering from hypothermia and dehydration, but she's doing a lot better."

"Oh good," he said, with obvious relief on his face.

"They did say that, depending on her condition tomorrow, I could take you down there to see her," she shared. "If you want to, that is."

His face lit up. "Do you really think I could see her?" he asked. "That would be great."

"Let's see, tomorrow is …" She stopped, as she thought about it.

"Wednesday," he replied helpfully.

"Okay, so Wednesday it is. But again, it will ultimately be up to the vet, depending on how the puppy's doing," she pointed out.

"Right." He smiled at Doreen. When he looked at Mack, his face fell.

"Mack, this is Gavin. Gavin, this is Mack."

Gavin just looked at him and nodded. It was obvious that he didn't trust Mack at all.

"How was school today, Gavin?" Doreen asked him.

"It was okay," he said solemnly. "I don't like school much."

"No, but remember, if you want to be a vet or something and help more puppies, you'll have to get through school somehow."

He just nodded and didn't say anything, but he was starting to back up.

"I'll see you here after school tomorrow then, okay?"

He looked at her, as if trying to figure out why, and then remembered and nodded. "Okay," he said, a grin slowly spreading across his face as he took off.

Chapter 19

DOREEN KNEW MACK was dying to ask a ton of questions, but only so many she had answers for. So, as he cooked, she explained the little bit she knew about Gavin's family.

"You did tell me about them before," he noted, "and I'm telling you again. It won't be that easy to convince his uncle that Gavin should have a puppy."

"Maybe not, but you know it wouldn't be a bad idea."

Just then Mugs started to bark hysterically at the front door. Mack took one look at her, shut off the burner, and headed there. She was right behind him, but nobody was on the porch. A vehicle drove past, going out of the cul-de-sac, but that was it. As she watched the vehicle disappear, something was nagging at her, as if she'd seen it before.

"Do you know it?" he asked her.

She frowned. "I don't think so. … I was just trying to place it."

"Of course you were," he muttered.

She shook her head. "I don't really have any reason to know that vehicle," she said.

"I'm not sure anybody needs a reason when it comes to

you."

She sighed. "Do you really think I'm in trouble again?"

"I have no reason to think so," he replied. "It would sure be nice if you weren't."

"Agreed," she murmured. "Though it is weird." She turned to him and asked, "How is the investigation going into poor Lynda's shooting?"

He shrugged. "Slow."

"You never told me. Did you talk to Clive?"

He stared at her silently obviously busy thinking about something else.

"The corner store guy, who walked past the shooting scene shortly thereafter, per Shirley," Doreen explained, wondering if Mack was being deliberately obtuse.

"No, I'm heading down there tonight. That's when he's supposed to be back on shift."

"Really?" she asked. "That's interesting because he was there on shift earlier today, when I spoke with him."

"And what was your take on him?"

"Shifty," she stated.

He burst out laughing. "Now is that because he was really shifty or because you want him to be shifty?"

"Because I want him to be shifty," she declared, wearing a grin of her own. "Still, he is definitely an odd character."

"Odd in what way?" he asked curiously.

She frowned as she thought about it. "He seemed interested but didn't want me to know he was interested," she said finally. "What a weird visit. I went outside, after I bought an iced tea. And then I guess I knew instinctively to avoid my car. You would probably say it was just me trying to fit the evidence into my hypothesis," she acknowledged, "but, instead of going to my car, I went around the corner and waited."

His eyebrows shot up at that. "And then what?"

She laughed. "Clive came out and talked to somebody on the phone, as he paced around the parking area."

"Did he see your car?"

"I don't think so. It was right there, but he didn't appear to see anything. He seemed focused on the call." She shrugged. "Obviously I was around the corner, and I did see him and wondered what he was so upset about."

"I'll talk to him tomorrow," he said.

"I thought you said tonight."

"Yeah, but that was before you had a strange vehicle driving past your house."

She looked at him in astonishment. "That was nothing," she stated. "For all you know, that was just a new group trying to figure out if it's worth putting us on the Japanese tour bus system in the spring again."

He looked at her and then burst out laughing. "Oh boy, I can't argue with that."

Chapter 20

THE NEXT MORNING, Doreen woke to her phone ringing near her ear. Still groggy, she answered to find it was Nan.

"You up yet, lazy bones?"

"I'm not up," Doreen muttered. "I'm only just now awake."

"Ah, well, we had another talk with somebody else in this place."

"And?" she asked, shifting herself up and pulling the covers back from Mugs, who was on his back, all four feet in the air. snoring softly.

Nan stopped and asked, "Is that Mugs?"

"Yes," Doreen noted, laughing. "He's snoring gently."

"I don't know about *gently*," Nan corrected, "but he's definitely snoring. I didn't realize he was so noisy."

"Yes, he's definitely noisy," Doreen noted calmly. "So, what do you mean in terms of who you talked to?"

Nan replied, "You talked to Nate and his father, Lynon, and then we talked to him ourselves. Apparently he had a little more information on the man, Bartlet Jones, who went missing all those years ago. He told us how Bartlet was a real ladies' man."

"Right, and he played around a lot and got into trouble with the husbands."

Obviously disappointed, Nan muttered, "You already knew this, and you didn't tell me?"

"I just found out, and I haven't had a chance to phone you yet." And darn if she wasn't apologetic. She shook her head. "Besides, that still doesn't tell us who he was having an affair with lately."

"It might have something to do with a woman on staff down at the medical clinic."

"The staff at the medical clinic?" Doreen repeated, pausing as she thought about it.

"Yeah, it's the old clinic that was down on Bernard Street."

"Okay. Do we have a name?"

"Yeah, her name was Rose."

"*Rose,*" Doreen repeated, bolting upright. "Are you sure?"

"Yeah, I'm sure," Nan stated. "Does that name mean something to you?"

"Oh Lord," Doreen muttered, "it sure does. Look, Nan. I've got to get going. I'll call you in a little bit." Doreen quickly disconnected, hopped out of bed, got dressed, and raced down to her notes. It was Milford's beautiful Rose, who he had looked after all these years, who had an affair with Bartlet? She called Mack, and his voice was brisk and all business.

"I'm going into a meeting, Doreen. Is it important?"

"We just found out through Lynon, Nate's father, Gavin's grandfather, that the man who went missing fifty years ago, Bartlet Jones, was likely having an affair with somebody in the medical center downtown."

"And?" he asked, a note of impatience in his voice. "That was a long time ago."

"It was a very long time ago, … and her name was Rose." There was dead silence on the other end for a moment, and then it must have clicked in his mind.

"Oh boy," he muttered.

"Yeah, I agree," she replied.

"I'll call you back when I'm out of the meeting. Don't do anything." And, with that, he was gone.

With a chuckle, she made coffee, almost wanting to dance around the room. She was enjoying the moment, that feeling when she finally got a break in a case. It seemed as if it had taken a long time, although she hadn't had to do very much. She had asked a few questions, had pushed a couple people to remember, and that was it. But then again, she had to remember that, while this could be a break in the case, it also didn't mean all that much. Doreen would need to come up with something more substantial than this, which wouldn't be a walk in the park on a case this old.

Frowning, she went back to her notes, looking to see if anything from Solomon's files helped on this other cold case on Jack Mahoney. Outside of the fact that he'd gone missing some twenty-odd years ago, there didn't appear to be anything in Solomon's notes that she hadn't already found, and that was frustrating. She went back over everything she had discovered at the library, and again there wasn't a whole lot. It would come down to old-timers remembering details, or someone with a guilty conscience. At that, she had to stop and wonder. Mack had told her not to, but, boy, did she want to race back up to Milford's farm in the Joe Rich area. In the meantime, she was supposed to stay put. Easy for

Mack to say, not so easy for her.

She frowned at the whole concept, then realized she needed groceries, so maybe she would head out and take care of that now. And, if she was lucky, enlightenment would strike, and Mack would get back to her. With the animals nicely tucked up in the house, she drove to the grocery store and parked. She only walked halfway through the parking lot when she was stopped by several people, wanting to take pictures with her. Not at all sure how that was supposed to work, she felt a little odd, as everybody was desperately grabbing photos.

Finally, when they were all done, she went into the grocery store, only to have people laughing at the antics outside. Doreen groaned. "I just came to get groceries, people."

"Yes, but we want to know what case you're on."

Doreen sighed and took advantage of their curiosity. "Anybody know anything about a man named Bartlet Jones, who went missing fifty years ago?" At that, everybody chimed in, and pretty soon Doreen talked to everyone about it. Figuring it wouldn't hurt anything, though knowing that Mack wouldn't appreciate it if he had to do anything with this, she kept up the conversations with people, but nobody seemed to have very much.

Then she asked, "Does anybody remember Rose who used to work at the medical clinic?"

At that, an old man at the back laughed. "Oh my, that's a name from the past." Then he frowned. "Didn't she die?"

"Yes," Doreen replied. "I believe it was from breast cancer last year."

Several people clucked in sympathy right beside her. Something about telling people about a death like that initiated a universal reaction that had everybody going into that same zone. Doreen didn't even know what happened, but it was almost instinctive to have everybody react that way. "Anybody know anything about her?"

One woman said, "She was a good nurse."

The old man nodded. "She retired quite a number of years ago, long before her diagnosis I would imagine," the old geezer added. "She and that husband of hers, they stayed up in the middle of nowhere all their lives."

"How come she was a nurse down here for so long then?" Doreen asked.

"She was independent, liked making her own money—until he convinced her to move into the boondocks with him and to get away from people," he said, with a laugh. "And of course he kept her out of trouble."

"Was she trouble?" Doreen asked.

"She was a beautiful woman."

"Right, but she married him, correct?" Doreen asked.

One woman nodded. "Yeah, many years ago."

"Not all that many years ago," the old guy countered, frowning. "Maybe fifteen years ago or so."

Doreen's head tilted to the side. "I thought they were together close to fifty years."

The old guy shrugged. "Oh, they probably were together that long, but I'm certain that they married much later. It all happened very quickly as I recall, and she wasn't a big fan at the time."

"Interesting," Doreen muttered.

"Yeah, they were both interesting. After the big blow-up, we didn't hear or see much of her," he shared. "She quit her job and stayed in the Joe Rich area."

Doreen stared at him. "And exactly what was that big blow-up over?"

He snorted. "She had an affair with Bartlet Jones, one of our local lotharios. Yet he wasn't married. However, Rose had affairs with two more men at the time, both married," he stated, chuckling. "Plus, it didn't go down so well with Milford either."

"You mean, her soon-to-be husband didn't like it?" Doreen asked.

"Yeah, and I don't think it went down so well with the wives who Rose was skirting around either. You know, a pretty lady like that, she didn't have any strings and lived a good life on her own terms."

"Interesting," Doreen repeated, staring at him. "You got any names I can follow up on?"

He looked at her and nodded. "I've got two, Lily Dale and Sandra Brown."

"And who are they?"

"The wives of two of the men who had relationships with Rose."

Doreen wrote down the names and asked, "Any idea if they're still in town?"

"They're both still in town," he replied, "but neither one of them will take kindly to having any of that mess brought up again."

"Of course not," Doreen agreed, with a gentle smile, "but, if it crosses some *T*s and dots some *I*s and brings closure to another family, it might be worth upsetting them by bringing back some memories they would just as soon forget."

"I'm right with you there," the old guy said, "but, in order to get them to talk, you'll probably have to tell them that John sent you."

"Good enough," Doreen replied. "I presume that you're

John."

He cackled. "I am, indeed."

"And did you have affairs with these ladies too?" Doreen teased.

He looked at her, a twinkle in his eyes, and shared, "One, maybe, but I ain't telling you which. One more thing. Bartlet Jones left town to pursue another woman. He probably cut ties and started a new life." And, with that, the old geezer walked out of the grocery store, chuckling to himself.

Doreen called out, "Hang on, John. I'll need your number too."

When he looked back at her, the twinkle was still there. "That's something I haven't heard a lady ask for in a very long time."

That set off the entire store full of people into gales of laughter. All in good fun, Doreen waited until it died down, then got John's number and watched as he walked away.

The clerk grinned at Doreen. "You really do have a fun life, don't you?"

"Sometimes things end up on the uglier side." With that, she frowned, as she began her own grocery shopping.

She was starting to get a good idea of what was going on here, and it would be an unfortunate event at the end of the day, but maybe it would pan out to be a whole lot more helpful than what it seemed to be right now. The concern was that it still didn't answer any questions about Lynda's father. And that was something she would have to sort out. Or not … not everything was solvable. …

The lack of definitive dates for when these two men went missing caused problems. For the captain or anybody else in the department to take on these cases, they would need details. Particularly to open up their budgets and to get things moving further along. She finally grabbed some groceries and then left, stepping outside, noting somebody standing there, with a grim look on his face.

She walked closer, and one of the women nearby whispered, "Look out. That's Rose's husband."

With a surprised look, Doreen turned, and, sure enough, there was Milford, the man she'd seen up on his farm property. He was better dressed today, and just being in town made him appear different.

Chapter 21

DOREEN WALKED OVER to Milford. "Hello. How are you doing?"

He looked at her glumly. "I think it was a mistake to bring you into the case of my bloody garden patch."

"Was it? Why is that?" she asked.

"Because I don't want you poking around into Rose's life."

She nodded. "Meaning that her life was a little less than spotless and that will become evident when it's put under a microscope?"

He stared at her. "You could say that."

"Rose has been gone a short time," Doreen said, "and I wouldn't do anything to besmirch her reputation."

"Not anything you could do that Rose hadn't already done herself."

Doreen just listened to details about this woman that she hadn't really expected to hear.

"She was still a good woman," Milford stated.

"I didn't say she wasn't," Doreen noted gently. "And whether she lived a life that a lot of other people wouldn't agree with is not ours to judge."

He looked at her, tears collecting in his eyes. "I really miss her," he whispered.

"I know you do," she said, "and I'm so sorry. Loss, no matter who it is and how it comes about, is very hard, and, in your case, I'm sure you didn't want to be left behind."

"No, I sure didn't," he admitted, rubbing his shoulder.

"You came into town for groceries?" she asked.

"Yeah, I don't come in much," he muttered. "It's just not a place I want to be."

"But you need food."

"I don't even need food," he argued. "I've got lots, but that darn cat of mine."

She chuckled. "That darn cat that you love?"

"I ain't telling it that though. That'll just make it more arrogant, and it already thinks it owns the place as it is," he muttered.

She smiled. "So, you came to get cat food. I thought he hunted."

"Probably hunts a little too much. He's very good at it, you know?"

"Yeah, I got that impression when I was there. My animals were pretty uncertain about him."

"Oh, I don't know about that. The dog looked as if he was ready to go on the jump."

"Maybe," she conceded, "but I can't have him going around picking fights either."

He laughed. "Cats are a law unto themselves."

"They think they are anyway," she agreed, with a smile. "You want me to come in and do some grocery shopping with you?"

He looked at her. "Whatever for?"

She shrugged. "In case you're lonely."

He shook his head. "I'll never tell anybody I'm lonely. That just makes me sound as if I'm some weak, old, pathetic geezer."

"No, it makes you sound as if you're human."

That stopped him in his tracks, just as he'd been about to step away. "Good Lord, I really hadn't considered that."

"Of course not," she said, with a laugh. "It's always about trying to maintain the status quo, isn't it?"

"For some people there is nothing else, and, in my life, you know, I loved her dearly, but she was definitely somebody who didn't always play the same as everybody else."

"Did she break up relationships?"

"Sometimes, yes. Definitely some people in town were probably happy to see the breast cancer take her," he noted, "and I surely wouldn't want to be talking to them."

"Of course not," she agreed. "You loved her, and love is never wrong."

"Are you sure?" he asked. "It seems as if, for so many of us, it's never quite right either."

She nodded, not sure what else to say. "I'm sorry it's been so tough dealing with losing her."

"It's more than just losing her. It's thinking of all those years we spent together, and, at the end of the day, it's still just you, all by yourself," he muttered. "Nobody even remembers her, and, if they do, it's not fondly."

"What they remember has nothing to do with it," she stated pointedly. "It's all about how *you* remember her because you're the one who loved her. Did she have family?"

He shrugged. "Everybody had family at one point in time, but we never had much of any contact with hers."

"Interesting," Doreen said, "because a lot of people turn to family when they get sick."

"No, she turned to me, and honestly, I was grateful because she could have turned to so many other people."

"Even then though?" she asked. "She was up there all alone with you for a very long time, wasn't she?"

He nodded. "And I didn't force it either," he declared. "No matter what some of these people might say."

"I'm not too bothered about what they might say," she acknowledged. "I'm more concerned about you."

He snorted. "Don't know why," he muttered. "All of our days have come and gone. We're just in the waiting room now, waiting for that final trip home."

"Did Rose have any regrets at the end of her life?"

Milford sighed. "She did. She had a lot of them. She didn't say much about a lot of what she saw as she looked backward. I kept telling her not to look back but to look forward, but she got very melancholy there for a while."

"Of course," Doreen agreed, "and I'm sure that's not unusual. When we get to that final boarding gate, I think a lot of people look back on life and have regrets."

He nodded. "She was a good woman."

"Glad to hear that," she replied. "And I have no intention of ever saying anything against that," she added. "But other people are also entitled to have their opinion, though it doesn't matter."

"Exactly," he declared, with a firm nod. "You're better off going home and not gossiping about my wife either."

"Not gossiping," she clarified. "I'm still trying to figure out what's going on."

"What's going on about what?"

Doreen hesitated, and then decided to just say it. "One of the men that Rose may have had an affair with some fifty years ago, a Bartlet Jones, has been missing for a very long time," she explained. 'And I'm pretty sure his family would very much like to have some closure."

He just looked at her and shook his head. "Ain't got nothing to do with me and ain't got nothing to do with her. Any man Rose had an affair with a long time ago, who was an adult, could make his own decisions."

"Absolutely," Doreen agreed. "It's certainly got nothing to do with that. I'm not worried about that in any way right now, but Bartlet's been missing for fifty years."

"Fifty years?" he asked, his eyebrows shooting up in astonishment.

She nodded. "Yeah, fifty years."

"Good God," he muttered. "She was seventy-seven when she died one year ago," he noted. "So that would have made her twenty-eight back then." He paused, then winced. "Honestly, she was quite the going concern back then too."

Doreen laughed. "That's okay. She was entitled to live her life as she wanted to."

"Oh, she lived it all right," he said, with half a smile.

"When did she marry you?"

"She didn't marry me until, oh, I don't know, a dozen years or so ago, maybe not even that much. I never could keep the dates in my head," he muttered.

"And why so late?"

"She said that marriage wasn't for her." He snorted. "I wanted it to be a legal thing. I wanted her to be mine. I was a little desperate for that, but she wasn't willing to give it to me until the end, until she had passed a certain point in life. And then she was all about getting married," he shared, shrugging.

"She came to me one day, and that was it. She wanted to get married. She was pretty hot about it too. I never really understood, but I wouldn't say no. I just ended up marrying her right away. We came down to the registry, got a license, and got married," he said, with a smile. "We had just the clerks in the office as the witnesses." He looked back at Doreen's car, as if suddenly realizing she didn't have the animals with her. "How come you don't travel with the animals?"

"I do whenever I can. And I need to get back to them," she added, with a smile.

"That's for sure. Go," he urged. "And, if you want to come back out to visit me in Joe Rich and take another look at that garden plot, feel free."

"I might have to," she declared, staring at him. "It is human blood."

The color faded from his skin, and he winced. "*Great.* I should have just waited until I died and left you a note. The last thing I want is people poking around up there."

"I don't know about people poking around," she admitted, "as I have no idea what the police will do about it right now."

"Not a whole lot," he muttered, "and, if you're thinking anything different, you have more faith in law enforcement than I do. I did contact them long ago, but they sure weren't too bothered."

"Of course not," she said, with a smile. "And maybe that's just life."

He nodded, then headed into the grocery store.

Chapter 22

"YOU TOLD HIM it was human?" Mack asked Doreen, when she called to update him.

"I wasn't sure whether you wanted to tell him yourself or not, but, with the information I had already discussed with him, it needed to be said."

"And was he surprised?"

"I think in a way he was, yet, in another way, he wasn't, as if he was half resigned. However, after all this time, maybe surprised that it was confirmed."

"And, from what I'm hearing, you're thinking Rose had something to do with the missing man from fifty years ago, that Bartlet Jones she had an affair with," Mack stated. "That makes no sense at all. You know that, right?"

"I understand. I get it. It makes absolutely no sense, and I'm not sure that's what I'm really thinking. So don't go putting that thought into my mind."

He snorted. "Are you telling me that you hadn't already considered it?"

"Oh, I considered it, but it didn't mean a whole lot at the time," she muttered. "I've just been trying to figure out how all of this fits together. And, so far, it doesn't."

"That's the thing about our job, isn't it?" he asked, with a smile in his tone. "We try to fit random pieces into some rational explanation, but it doesn't always work. That's why it's important to have evidence."

She groaned. "I hear you. Got it. Point taken. And, yes, I do know it's all about evidence."

"Good to hear. Stay out of trouble. I need to finish up here at the office," he added, "so I don't know whether I'll make it back to your place or not. I've got to go over to my mom's."

"Is she okay?" Doreen asked. "I know she seemed a little stressed when I was there."

"I think she's stressed as well. I just don't know why."

"Oh, I know part of the reason, but I don't want to be pressured into anything."

"Ah, if that's the reason, I'll tell her to chill out," Mack offered, "because I promised you no stress."

"You may have promised that, but I can see that your promise doesn't preclude your family from pressuring me."

"No, and you've got the same problem with your own relative," he pointed out, "because you also know how much your grandmother wants this to happen too."

"I know," she muttered, with a wistful tone to her voice. "And I am getting there."

"Good, take your time, and it'll all work out." And, with that, he added, "I've got to go. The captain is calling me." And he ended the call.

She looked down at her animals, quickly dished up their food, and poured herself a cup of tea. When her phone rang again, it was Nan. "Hey, Nan," she answered.

"So, what's happened? The whole town's abuzz."

"Abuzz about what?"

"You and that old man in the parking lot," Nan replied. Then, as if she had no time to listen to Doreen's answer, Nan continued. "And what about the woman in Glenmore? Shirley? Did you speak to her?"

"Right, I did. … It's been a long day."

"Come down and have tea," Nan urged. "We need to have an update." Doreen looked down at the cup of tea in her hand, then outside at the freezing cold, and groaned.

"Oh, posh," Nan declared. "You'll be fine. It's just a little bit of cold."

"Yeah, a little bit cold to you," Doreen pointed out, even while laughing. "Fine, fine, fine," she muttered, as she moved to bundle up the animals. Thaddeus squawked until he nestled into her hair, and they headed down the creek toward Rosemoor. As soon as they turned in that direction, Mugs and Goliath raced ahead, almost tripping over each other with their antics. She swore to God that Mugs was even trying to trip up Goliath as they moved. She watched as Goliath jumped over her dog and then appeared to jump right in front of Mugs. It was almost a game of leapfrog. She enjoyed their antics, all the way down the path, until finally she made it to Nan's little apartment patio and called out for her.

The patio door opened, and Nan said, "You should be coming in through the front."

"I know, but the animals …"

"I understand," Nan replied. "Come on in, child. Hurry up."

As Doreen made her way inside, she saw at least six seniors gathered here and this time they all were smiling and looking more like themselves. "Oh goodness," Doreen muttered, as she stared at them all.

Richie hopped up and announced, "I brought you treats."

She smiled at him. "And thank you for that," she murmured, "but you'll make me fat."

"This won't make you fat," he argued. "Besides, we need to get a little more weight on you before the wedding."

She rolled her eyes at that. "You do know that most people tell the bride that they need to lose weight before the wedding."

"Not you," he declared. "You've got to get some meat on your bones."

"Thank you for that," she replied, with half a laugh. Just something about this entire scenario always brought tears of joy and in some ways, not quite humiliation, but a sense of what else could they possibly do to her. Doreen didn't want to say it out loud, just in case they came up with something. As she walked in and sat down on the chair obviously intended for her, she looked over at them. "You all look as if you have something to say."

"Oh, we do, we do, we do," Maisie exclaimed, bouncing up and down in her seat. "We found out some information too."

"Good," Doreen said. "You first."

Not giving Nan a chance to interrupt, Maisie lunged into a tirade about how the old guy from fifty years ago used to have affairs all around town.

Doreen nodded. "And do you have any names of any of the women?"

"Yes!" And they gave Doreen the same two names she already had.

"Interesting," she noted. "Do you know either of them?"

"Lily Dale lives in the *other* home," Maisie replied, with

a sniff, as if the other retirement home was definitely not as good as Rosemoor was.

"Okay, so I may need to go over there and talk to her." Doreen turned to Nan. "What about you? Anything on this other lady, Sandra Brown?"

"I don't know her," Nan admitted. "I've been here in Kelowna all these years, and I don't think I know either of these ladies."

Nan seemed almost affronted that they could exist without Nan knowing them. It was all Doreen could do to hide her smile. Then she looked over at Richie. "What about you?"

"Oh dear," he muttered, flushed now. "I was hoping you wouldn't put me on the spot. I didn't find out a single thing, which is why I brought the treats." When Doreen burst out laughing at that, he grinned at her. "See? Treats have always been the way to get out of trouble," he explained. "You bring some treat for the teacher, and then, if you're lucky, she doesn't put you on the spot while the class is being questioned."

Doreen shook her head at him. "Oh my, that brings back memories."

"Right," he agreed. "These are the little tricks you learn when you are young to get out of trouble."

"You're not in trouble," she confirmed, with a bright smile. "Absolutely no way doing this job should put anybody in trouble."

"*Ha*, not sure Mack would agree with you though," Nan pointed out, apparently a little miffed that she hadn't been the one to provide the great news.

Doreen got up, walked over, and gave her grandmother a hug. "Maybe not," she noted. "You've sure done a wonderful job of keeping track of all of our various team members."

"Oh, I have, haven't I?" Nan nodded, now with a beaming smile. "And you do need to go talk to that woman."

"Which woman is that?" Doreen asked her.

"That Lily Dale woman," Nan stated.

"Why is that? You told me that you didn't know her."

"Oh, I don't know her personally," Nan clarified, "but I do know of her, and she has a reputation of her own."

"What about Rose?" Doreen asked, looking around at the others. "Anybody remember a Rose from the medical center?"

At that, Richie let out an audible gasp. They all turned to look at him, and he turned an impressive variety of shades of red. They all burst out in laughter.

Doreen noted, "Richie, it looks as if you won't get out of this one quite so easily."

He flushed again. "That is a name I haven't heard for a long time, but I do remember her," he admitted with a smile, and then a cheerfully bright chuckle.

"*Aha,*" Doreen replied. "Am I correct in presuming you may have, shall we say, *intimate knowledge* of this Rose woman?"

He shrugged. "In our day they called it *biblical knowledge.*"

Nan rolled her eyes. "Good God, Richie. Really?"

"Why not?" he asked. "I was pretty young back then."

"Fifty years ago, you were still old enough to know better," Nan said in a droll voice.

"So, was this before or after Rose hooked up with her husband?" Doreen asked.

"Oh, before," he replied. "And, for the record, she wouldn't marry any of us. I did ask."

"Seriously?" Nan looked at him.

"Yes," he muttered, "but it was a very long time ago."

"And did she give you a reason for turning you down?" Doreen asked.

He sighed and shrugged. "She had no intention of marrying anybody. I'm surprised to hear you say she got married, though I guess people change over time. However, I don't know why she would have done it in the end. She was really adamant on the matter."

"Interesting," Doreen murmured. "What I heard was Rose got married ten or twelve years ago, out of the blue, but to Milford, the man she had been living with for like five decades. I think he told me that they married twelve years ago."

Richie frowned. "Wonder what brought that on because Rose always said she would have to be on her deathbed in order to marry anybody."

"Considering the fact that she died of breast cancer, maybe there was another incident of a cancer scare before that," Doreen suggested. "Or maybe Rose simply changed her mind."

Richie snorted. "You could be right, but, at the time, I was devastated. Yet, then again," he added, with a groan, "so were another dozen men around town. She dated rich and poor and usually married, but she preferred the good-looking ones with money."

Doreen smirked. "I did hear that Rose was beautiful and led a fairly active social life."

"Yep, she sure did. But then she up and disappeared a numbers of years back. I think she got pregnant, though I really don't know what happened, and I'm not even sure who the father was. Then the gossip was that she ended up with that Milford guy, and she moved to be with him in the Joe Rich area. I might have seen her around town once, maybe twice over the ensuing years, but it wasn't much more than that."

"Rose did end up at Milford's place. I hadn't heard anything about a pregnancy, but who knows?" Doreen stated. "All that fun she was having, back when birth control wasn't so readily available, could certainly have had some side effects." As it was, Doreen had to wonder about whether she'd had any children with Milford over the years. She smiled at them. "It sounds as if you've all been having a wonderful time, while sleuthing out all kinds of information."

"We have," Maisie declared. "So, will you talk to the Lily Dale woman?"

"I will, tomorrow. Now I didn't ask Mack if I could tell you this, but, if you don't pass it around, I think I could share it."

They all leaned forward.

"The soil samples that we tested up at Rose and Milford's place came back but they weren't able to determine human blood."

"Ooh," they all exclaimed in disappointment and sat back.

Doreen looked at the two new people in the room. "Now, I don't know you two as well as the others, but I do need this to be strictly confidential as so far we have nothing evidential to go on. Heresay can be so hard to work with and in this we only have Milford's word."

"Of course, of course," they promised.

Doreen knew—the minute they went out that door—everybody would know. Doreen sighed, then looked over at

Nan, whose eyes were twinkling. "Please don't tell me that you've put a bet on this one."

"Of course not," Nan replied, with an offended expression. "I didn't place any bets. Richie did."

Doreen winced, then looked over at Richie. "Seriously?"

He chuckled. "We have to pay for our little games one way or another," he said, with a big smile in her direction. "And you do keep us entertained."

"Keeping you entertained is one thing," Doreen noted, with a smile, "but remember that I could get in trouble with Mack, and that could change things totally."

"Oh, we can't have that happening."

All of them nodded.

"We'll keep quiet for Mack's sake," they agreed, "because it's way too much fun to be a part of this to lose it."

"Exactly," Doreen agreed, "and, therefore, we have to honor what Mack requires."

"Of course, of course."

On that note, Doreen realized it would be completely useless to expect this much from this group regardless. She quickly sent Mack a text, telling him that she'd told the Rosemoor gang that there was no evidence of human blood in the sample they brought back from Milford's farm in the Joe Rich area. He sent back a response with several question marks, a sequence of dots, then a resigned **Whatever**. She snickered at that because it was almost as if he knew exactly what she was like, in addition to what these sleuthing seniors were like, making the sharing of information almost a foregone conclusion.

Doreen continued. "Okay, I'm off to see these two women tomorrow, if I can find an address for the second one, that is, and then we'll have to sort out what exactly happened to Rose during her *missing period*."

"I wouldn't be surprised if you need to go to her sister for that," Richie muttered.

Doreen turned to face Richie and said, "Nobody has mentioned a sister yet."

He nodded. "She had a sister, though I'm not exactly sure if she's still alive. We are all growing older. So this Bartlet case will have you fighting even harder to find witnesses."

"Was the sister younger or older?"

"She was younger, so that's in your favor. If she was older than Rose, I wouldn't give you a glimmer of hope in finding her," he muttered.

"Okay, so any suggestions on where I might start?"

"At the other home," Nan suggested. "Check it out while you're there visiting with Lily."

"Do we have a name for the sister?" Doreen asked the group.

Richie thought about it for a long moment and nodded. "Poppy."

"Poppy?" Doreen repeated, looking at him.

He nodded. "Poppy. Their father named them after flowers."

"I guess it could be worse," Doreen quipped, with half a smile in his direction. "They could have named her Crocus."

Chapter 23

As Doreen walked home with her animals, she remembered the boys and the poor little puppy they had found and saved. Groaning, she raced back up the river, and, as soon as she got home, she phoned the vet.

"If you want to bring the boys down," she said, "you are welcome to."

"That would be lovely. How late are you open?" She had no sooner disconnected the phone, when she heard a knock. There stood the two boys, standing at her doorway, waiting for her. "Okay," she said, "hop in the car and let's go before they close." Then she drove them to the vet clinic, where they spent a wonderful twenty minutes with the puppy, and she could see how much of a heartbreak it was for Gavin to leave her. "It'll take some time to fix up the puppy," Doreen told him.

"And then what?" he asked, staring at her, tears in his eyes.

"And then we'll find a home for her."

"It's a her?" he asked, staring at her.

She nodded. "It's a little girl puppy." She could see his face melt. "Did you ask your uncle?"

He nodded grimly. "He said no way."

"Of course he did," she muttered. "He's already struggling to handle you, so you and the puppy would be a much harder proposition for him."

He looked at her and his shoulders sagged. "I didn't think about that."

"Of course not. You were reacting to your own feelings about that puppy," she noted, "plus reacting to a circumstance and a situation that for you is untenable, the loss of your mother. But you've got to remember that it is all very difficult for your uncle, as well. You're not the only one who lost someone they loved. He lost his sister."

Gavin just nodded, his shoulders sagging farther.

"Anyway, maybe offer to take care of the puppy, to be responsible for her. You may have to give your uncle some time to adjust to that. Let's not worry about it right now. We should be happy that the puppy will be fine, and she has you boys to thank for it."

Gavin smiled and nodded, but he was pretty sad all the drive home. His cousin had been silent the whole time. Gavin grimaced as he got out of her car, having to head home to his uncle's house.

She looked at his cousin and friend Randy and said, "Try to keep him cheerful."

He nodded and whispered, "He really, really wants to keep the puppy."

"I can talk to his uncle, but no guarantees." As soon as they were gone, she wondered what she had promised.

Chapter 24

DOREEN WALKED INTO the old folks' home out in Glenmore called Sunnyside. It had an interesting winery-estate feel, making her think that they would all be in their cups. With half a smile she dismissed the thought, then walked in, introduced herself to the woman at the front desk and asked to speak to Lily Dale.

The woman nodded and stood up. "Let me see if she is doing okay and if she is up for a visitor." When the woman returned, she seemed surprised. "She is quite excited to see you. I will take you to her."

"Good," Doreen replied, with a bright smile. She followed the receptionist to see Lily Dale, who was sitting at a small bench, looking out a window. The receptionist left them alone without another word.

As soon as Doreen came into view, the other woman turned, looked at her, and nodded. "Oh, you look exactly as I expected you to."

Doreen chuckled. "Normally I would have the animals with me, but I understand they are quite restricted in this home."

"I know," Lily replied, "though you could probably get

away with one, if they were therapy animals." As she mentioned that angle, she looked inquiringly at Doreen.

She shook her head. "No, they don't fall into that category at all."

"Too bad," Lily murmured, "because I know most of the people here would absolutely love to see them."

"I could consider bringing them down sometime, maybe to meet everyone outside," she mentioned, looking around. "I do know that pets or animals are allowed in other homes, like Rosemoor."

"Yes, but it's got to be on management's time frame, the management's rules, and all that good stuff," Lily stated, with a headshake, as Doreen pulled up a chair nearby. Lily spoke up as soon as Doreen was seated. "So, I heard through the grapevine that you're looking for answers to some questions."

Doreen nodded, wondering which of the Rosemoor crew had somehow gotten to Lily first. "I do have some questions, and I'm hoping they aren't painful for you."

Lily Dale looked at her and snorted. "At my age, the only thing painful is not being able to go to the bathroom," she muttered. "I've been through so much in my life that I really don't care about the past anymore. I'm happy to go when I'm called home, and I will leave nobody behind."

"You don't have any family?" Doreen asked.

"Not left alive anymore," she replied. "They all went before me, and it really sucks to be the last one."

"I am so sorry," Doreen whispered and meant it because it would be rough to be the only one left.

"So, who is it you want to ask me about?"

She hesitated a second, then said, "Rose."

Lily's face pinched. "Good God, now that's a name I

haven't wanted to think about in a very long time."

"I'm sorry, and I understand it was a difficult time for you back then."

"Sure, it was, but I can't really blame Rose. She was beautiful, and the men were all over her. So, as much as it's easy to blame her for having an affair with my husband, the real betrayal was by my husband, who had an affair with her."

Lily had such a calm and matter-of-fact approach that Doreen had to appreciate how far this woman had come from that time of betrayal in her life. "I do understand that," Doreen acknowledged. "I'm really very happy that you've come to a point in time of finding peace with it all."

"You're not really given a lot of choice in these matters," Lily declared, looking at Doreen. "Didn't you have something similar?"

"I did," Doreen confirmed, not surprised, knowing that the gossip touched everyone.

"Did you kill him?" Lily asked, obviously hearing of Mathew's murder.

Doreen chuckled. "No, I surely did not." Wow, the gossip in this town was brutal.

"But you wanted to though, right?" Lily asked.

"I never really got to that point," Doreen admitted. "I was so shocked and flummoxed, trying to figure out this change in my own life that I wasn't too worried about ending his," she shared, with a smile. "And because I had quite a mess of things to adjust to, I really had no time or energy to hate anyone."

"That would have been a lovely option," Lily noted. "*Hate*, I mean. Because I did, to be honest. I hated Rose for a long time, but not as much as I hated my husband. He's the one who ultimately betrayed me. Rose betrayed basically everyone, but not with a mean spirit. She just didn't care. She was out for a good time, not a long time, and nothing involving commitment. That just wasn't her thing."

"Interesting," Doreen replied. "I don't know that much about her, only the bits and pieces people have shared."

"Is she still alive?" Lily asked, eyeing Doreen intently.

"No, she's not."

"See? Some satisfaction can still be had here." Then she chuckled. "Maybe that is reality telling me how I haven't dealt with all that mess as thoroughly as I thought I had."

"Nothing like having a trigger out of the blue to bring back memories you would just as soon do without."

"I never did remarry, you know? I couldn't really trust anybody after what happened."

They shared a comfortable silence between them for a moment. Doreen could certainly understand the other woman's position.

"What happened to Rose?" Lily asked, turning sideways to face Doreen.

"Breast cancer. She died about a year ago."

"Only a year ago? Wow." Lily appeared deep in thought for a few moments. "She disappeared, you know? And then she was out of sight, out of mind. I tiptoed around town for the longest time, afraid I would see her, afraid I would see them together," she shared. "It was really hard because I just didn't want to run into her. Eventually I realized that it was controlling my life, and I needed to get a handle on it.

"So, at some point, I just decided I didn't need that thought process in my world. I decided that, if I saw her, fine, and, if I didn't see her, whatever. I would be the casual one with the *Who cares, I didn't love him anyway* attitude.

Yet, on the inside, I was dying. The good news is, I eventually got over it," she stated, "and I did end up having another relationship with a wonderful man."

Doreen smiled, happy to hear it. "But you never married him?"

"No, I sure didn't, and he understood. He told me that he didn't need to be married to me to be loyal and committed to me. If it was something I felt strongly about, he didn't want to push it." She stopped and looked at Doreen. "Eventually I came to realize that not remarrying because of that betrayal meant that I had given away far more power than was deserved."

"To her or to him?"

"Both of them," she snapped. "Good Lord, that came out far sharper than I intended. The woman is dead and gone, so why do I feel this way?"

"Love is a complicated thing," Doreen said. "One of life's mysteries, I guess."

"Speaking of mysteries," she asked, "why are you going to all this effort asking about her now?"

"I'm trying to find a man, Bartlet Jones."

"Oh my, he was another married man who Rose had an affair with, wasn't he?"

"I'm not sure he was married, but, yes, Rose had an affair with him too," Doreen confirmed. "And he disappeared about fifty-odd years ago."

"Fascinating," she murmured. "What happened?"

"That's unknown. For all I know he committed suicide, or had an accident, or just moved away and started a whole new life. Nobody seems to know."

"Several men were interested in Rose back then. She was just one of those femme fatale types," she burst out. "You knew you were in the presence of something unbelievable when she walked by, and she's the only person I've ever met who was like that."

Doreen kept quiet, just letting the woman talk.

"And yet I'm sure many others are in the world with that same presence, but Rose was the only one I ever met with that aura," she shared. "It was just bizarre. Because of who she was, the way she acted, and the way she carried on with men, she created lots of talk, and everybody was always talking about her."

"I can imagine," Doreen muttered, not wanting to interrupt.

"We had all kinds of names for her back then," Lily noted. "And honestly, I think she reveled in it. She didn't seem to mind being called those names. She would just laugh and say it wasn't her fault that the men liked her. The trouble was, Rose liked the men back, and there didn't appear to be any boundaries. Back then especially, it was quite something to have a woman to be so carefree about it all."

"So, I have a question for you," Doreen began. "Do you think Rose charged these men for her time?"

Lily looked at her, caught completely off guard, then burst out laughing. "Oh my, that's a thought I've never had, but, if she did charge, she would have made a freaking fortune because the men just couldn't leave Rose alone." She giggled again. "I never considered for a moment that maybe she was in the industry."

"But wouldn't that have been perfect? If you think about it," Doreen noted, with half a smile, "maybe it was a business opportunity for her."

That sent the other woman off into gales of laughter. "Oh my, I am so glad you came to visit. I really hadn't even considered that."

"Now that she's passed and her affairs are out in the open, maybe it's something that should be considered. If she had that attractiveness to men, maybe she put it to good use."

"Wow," Lily exclaimed, and then she giggled again. "I don't know what to say. As far as I know, she gave it away freely, but what do I know? … Apparently I was the last to know about her and my husband, so I wasn't nearly as aware as people thought I should have been."

"Everybody thought you should have known?" Doreen asked.

"Yes, how about you?"

"Oh, yeah, same thing. Everybody thought I should have known or assumed I did know. Everybody thought that I should have expected it because, in that world of affluence, men were men and, as such, were entitled to do whatever they wanted," Doreen repeated, with a wave of her hand, "particularly rich men."

"Oh goodness," Lily muttered in disgust.

Doreen nodded. "As if it was just nothing, you know? As if vows and promises are meaningless." Doreen smiled. "As we both found out, they don't mean much to a lot of other people."

"That's true," Lily agreed, "very true. But now I can't keep thinking about what you asked. Never for a moment had I considered that she was charging these men. I don't think she was, but you have definitely given me something to consider," she said, with a smile.

Doreen added, "It just was something that occurred to me. With so many different men spending time with her back then, I still think it could be a valid question."

"I don't think so, but I really don't know," Lily murmured. "If she was getting money from all those men, then why did she work?"

Doreen shook her head. "Do you know what happened when she disappeared and dropped out of sight or whatever?"

"I always thought she got pregnant," Lily replied. "And honestly, back then, that was to be expected. It's not as if birth control was accessible everywhere, and, if she did get pregnant, it would have been that much harder for her."

"True," Doreen replied. "I only know of her husband, Milford, the man she was married to when she died, and they don't have any children. Maybe Rose had a child out of wedlock but the child died or maybe it wasn't an easy pregnancy and she miscarried. Or maybe she came close to losing her life, and that's even what caused her to change. I don't know," Doreen said, looking back at Lily.

"You've definitely brought up some ideas I hadn't considered," Lily noted. "It would be an interesting trip down memory lane to give it all some thought though."

"Maybe you should," Doreen agreed, with a smile. "You appear to be well adjusted to everything that happened."

"It was a long time ago," she stated, looking at her. "I'm just grateful I found the new relationship I did." Then she laughed. "And maybe you don't know this, but my husband did come around at one point, hoping I would take him back."

"Oh, now that's interesting," Doreen said, giving her a smile. "And I gather you declined?"

"That's a nicer way of describing how that went." Lily laughed. "By that point in time, I had already met up with the partner I stayed with for the rest of his life. Gordon died a few years back, … and life hasn't been the same ever since. Not the same at all." And, with that, she returned to the melancholy tone she'd had when Doreen first arrived.

"Of course not," Doreen agreed, "but at least you found one true love."

"And I think that was the trick too. If my ex-husband hadn't had the affair and hadn't hooked up with Rose and hadn't made my life so very painful and so very difficult," she began, "I probably wouldn't ever have found Gordon. So, for that …" She stopped and shook her head. "I guess for that I owe Rose my thanks, and that is something I didn't think I would ever say."

"Yet I can see that," Doreen noted. "It's a good place to come to now."

"It is, indeed," she murmured. "It is, indeed."

Doreen continued. "So, tell me about this other friend of yours who was also affected."

"Oh, Sandra. Sandra Brown." Lily nodded. "It was much harder for her. She didn't find another partner to her liking, and, when her husband came crawling back, she took him back, mostly because she was so lonely and had loved him so dearly. I don't think it was ever the same afterward, but she did find some level of happiness and peace in her life."

"Interesting that she took him back."

"You've got to think about the times way back when. It wasn't that men were allowed to do that thing without attracting negative attention, but, in Sandra's case, she found it better to still be married than to be divorced."

"And yet not for you."

"No. Goodness no. I would rather have stayed single for the rest of my life than to be with a two-timing lying son of a gun like that."

Doreen chuckled. "And you found that special someone who loved you for you."

"I did," she stated, "though I'm so sorry I didn't meet him earlier in my life. It would have made a huge difference to me."

"If you had met Gordon and your husband-to-be at the same time, do you think you wouldn't have married your husband?" Doreen asked.

"Oh no, definitely not," Lily declared. "That's a given. But I was young, single, and stupid, and it seemed as if the whole goal for young women back then was to get married. Otherwise you were seen as an old maid, unwanted and left sitting on the shelf." She gave a sad shake of her head. "Thankfully times have changed, and now, if you're divorced, you can go get married again and again if you please. But back then, you only got remarried if you were literally a widow," she explained. "Until then, you were a divorcee, and God help you," she muttered. "Regardless of the details, the shame rested with the woman, who was seen as unable to keep her husband at home."

"Do you think Sandra would be open to talking to me about it?"

"It's possible, and I do see her every once in a while. If nothing else we did stay friends because of that, even when I encouraged her not to take her husband back. Yet, at the time, she told me that she didn't think she could be alone."

"It's not for everybody," Doreen noted. "And we can't always know exactly what's going on in somebody else's world. Sandra made a choice, and hopefully she was happy with it in the end."

"She wasn't, but I think, for her, it was still better than

the alternative."

"So where would I find her?"

"She still lives in the same house she shared with her husband. I told her that she should move in here, but she still thinks she might not be fully welcomed. Her life changed so much afterward, when they were separated, and she was ostracized from so many things. Then, once she was back with her husband again, while there was talk for a while, eventually that died down, and she got her life back. So, for her, it was the lesser of two evils."

"Sad to think that's how the world works," Doreen muttered.

"Very sad, but it is definitely how the world worked back then. It was seen as much better to stay with a cheating husband than to be a divorcee," Lily shared, "so Sandra made her choice, and I made mine. There were pros and cons to each, but I think it really came down to our personalities and what we each were willing to endure."

"Yes, that makes perfect sense to me. On another topic, do you know anything about Rose having a sister?"

"Yes. She definitely had a sister, maybe still does. I don't know what became of her."

"Did your husband not tell you about her?"

"No, trust me that Rose was not a topic of discussion between us. Who did she end up marrying anyway?"

When Doreen told her about Milford, Lily stared at her. "Good God, you've got to be kidding."

"Not kidding."

"Rose would never have had anything to do with him in the prime of her life," Lily stated. "I still can't believe it."

"And yet they spent about fifty years together, the last twelve or so married."

Lily stared at her, still shocked. "Gosh, that makes no sense to me. For that many years? They'd had been together while she was seeing my husband too? Then again, I think a lot of men were seeing her at the same time."

"And why are you surprised that Rose chose Milford?"

"For one thing he was poor and wasn't the best-looking man around. He may have been a good man, but he wasn't her type, you know? He wasn't exactly the heartthrob type she usually went for. She was accustomed to having her pick of the men around her all the time, and Milford doesn't seem to fit the pattern at all."

"And yet she stayed with him."

"There had to be a reason," Lily stated, frowning at Doreen. "Believe me that the only reason she would have stayed with him was if he had something on her or was doing something for her."

Lily may have dealt with some of her anger issues, but she wasn't necessarily unbiased in her assessment. So Doreen thanked her for her help and headed off to contact her friend.

When she got Sandra Brown on the phone, Sandra suggested, "I can meet you in a coffee shop or something. I don't get out much, but I would prefer not to have this conversation in the home of my husband."

"Of course," Doreen agreed. She wondered just what that meant in this instance, but, hey, she was up for it.

Chapter 25

FINDING OUT WHERE the coffee shop was located took a bit longer, and, by the time Doreen pulled up, she watched an older woman walking slowly but steadily toward the front door of the café. Doreen smiled as she stepped toward her and asked, "Sandra Brown?"

"Yes." The woman smiled. "Come on in with me. I could use a cup of tea."

They quickly ordered tea for two and headed to a table in the far back corner. The other woman sat down a little heavily, as if it had been a long day.

"Are you doing okay?" Doreen asked.

"Surely you know that you're bringing up memories I'm not very comfortable with," she replied. "Did you talk to Lily Dale?"

"I certainly did, and she told me all about her heartache," Doreen noted.

Sandra sighed. "That was one of the hardest things I've ever been through in my life. You don't know what it's like, until all these people you thought were friends suddenly step away, or worse, pretend to be your friend, then lead the distribution of gossip about you. When the people you thought you could rely on are suddenly nowhere to be found, it changes you."

Doreen smiled at her. "I do understand."

Sandra eyed her for a moment and nodded. "Maybe you do. I did hear some rumors about you too."

"Of course," Doreen noted. "Apparently I've gained a fair amount of notoriety in the area."

"You sure have." She looked around and whispered, "I so wish you had the animals with you."

"If I hadn't been to the retirement home to see Lily Dale earlier, I probably would have brought them along. As it was, that home had so much paperwork to even apply to bring in my animals, I would still be trying to fill it all out," she quipped, with a smile. "Speaking of which, I need to get home to them soon."

"Of course, of course. So, what is it I can help you with?"

"You can tell me what you know about this man Bartlet Jones, who went missing fifty years ago, yet another man who Rose had an affair with, plus more about Rose and her sister."

"Ah, for one thing, Rose and her sister looked very much alike, almost identical twins in fact," she stated, "and I wouldn't be at all surprised if they hadn't gotten up to some shenanigans by trading places."

"But they weren't twins, right?"

"No, they weren't twins at all, but they had an uncanny likeness that was quite striking. It's just that Rose knew how to work it, I guess, whereas Poppy wasn't worried about working it. She was calm and happy just being herself."

"Which is always nice," Doreen noted.

"It is nice, but it's not necessarily a very workable scenario when your own sister is out to get you. Rose stole many a boyfriend from Poppy."

Doreen didn't say anything for a moment, then nodded. "That would have been very difficult for Poppy, I would think."

"Exactly, and it was, indeed. I did see her every once in a while, and we smiled, you know, both victims of the avalanche called Rose that swept through our lives and destroyed everything, then moved on. Unfortunately that was how you had to look at Rose."

"Which is very interesting," Doreen muttered, "because I wouldn't have thought that people would speak of Rose's sister as fondly as many do."

"The only reason they wouldn't speak about Poppy like that was because she didn't destroy their lives. Rose did," Sandra declared, frowning at Doreen. "For those of us who paid the price of having Rose in our world, believe me that there was a high price to pay, and that included Poppy too."

Doreen winced at that. "I am really very sorry to hear that and sorry that you went through that."

"It was a long time ago now," Sandra stated, "but thank you. The day I found out remains one of the worst of my life."

"What did you do?" she asked her.

"I screamed and railed at my husband and basically kicked him out of the house. Then I called Rose and yelled at her."

"And her response?"

"She laughed," she shared. "She just laughed."

"Ah." Doreen winced. "And that would have been the worst thing."

"Absolutely the worst," she agreed. "So many things

went wrong in our world back then, and we had so little recourse."

"Did you ever go on to have a family?" Doreen asked her.

"I already had a family when Rose blew it apart. That was another reason for taking my husband back again," she shared. "We had two daughters, and I had no idea how I was supposed to raise them on my own. I didn't have any money and no job skills, so it was all I could do to survive while he was out of the picture. When he came back, there was a certain amount of relief, knowing I could get some help," she explained.

"There was no child support, or even courts for that thing. You were left to rely on help from the people around you, neighbors and friends, but having been ostracized the way I was, I didn't get much in the way of assistance. Plus, by then, I made such a pitiful picture, I didn't want anybody to see me."

"That must have been terribly frustrating, since you had done nothing wrong," Doreen stated.

"In the eyes of many, my crime was clear. I simply wasn't woman enough to keep my man. So, they somehow felt justified to talk about it endlessly among themselves." Sandra shook her head.

Doreen frowned. "When it came to Rose, you mentioned that you thought she dressed up as Poppy every once in a while?"

"I know she did because Poppy told me so. She was devastated because Rose had gone out with somebody Poppy was dating and had completely destroyed things ever after because he was suddenly so enamored and so in love and wanted to get married, except it wasn't Poppy he wanted to marry. It was Rose. Yet he hadn't realized it was Rose he'd been out with instead of Poppy. Rose went out with him several times because it was just a big lark to her," Sandra muttered.

Doreen stared at her. "Nobody really wanted to say that Rose may not have been a very nice person."

Sandra laughed. "That's because people don't wish to speak ill of the dead, but, once you've been brutalized by someone like Rose, you stop having any concern or worry about that," she muttered.

"What Rose did to her own sister sounds so awful. Such an awful thing to have happen to Poppy or to Lily, or to you."

"It was. It absolutely was," she muttered, "but what could I do about it? It happened, and I was devastated. Just as Poppy was devastated. But we had no better options, so we all moved on."

"What about Poppy, did you stay friends with her?" Doreen asked.

"I did, and then she up and left, a long time ago."

"Interesting," she muttered. "I wonder why?"

"I think her sister pulled even more games on her, and finally she'd had enough of it. I did see Rose every once in a while after that, but I never spoke to her. I wouldn't talk to that woman. She was the scarlet woman, yet somehow she became a scarlet woman everybody was jealous of, which I never understood. Yet that's how it was. Men showered her with attention. They gave her gifts, gave her jewelry, took her out to the nicest places, and did all kinds of things, all to find favor and to win her hand, yet nobody ever really won over Rose."

Doreen wasn't even sure what to say after that. "And

you've never spoken to Poppy since?"

"I lost track of her quite a while ago. She moved back east, I believe," she muttered, with a wave of her hand. "But who could blame her? It's just one of those things."

"Right," Doreen said. "Do you know anybody who would have any information about this man Bartlet Jones who went missing fifty years ago?"

"Times were different fifty years ago, and we didn't have the same law enforcement as we do now. We had no way to keep in communication. We had phones, of course, but landline phones. Depending on what time you were talking, the lines were even shared with neighbors."

"Right," Doreen muttered. They talked for a few more minutes, and then Doreen added, "Sandra, I want to thank you very much for your help."

The other woman laughed. "I've hardly been of any help."

"If you get bored, you may want to go say hello to Lily Dale," Doreen suggested. "I got the distinct impression that she's in that home, just waiting to die, and she could really use a friend. All her family is dead, and she's the last in line."

"That's what those homes are all about," Sandra grumbled, "and frankly that's why I refuse to go there."

"And yet probably a lot of people you know are there or are visiting someone else there. Surely you don't count them among your enemies at this point, do you?" Doreen asked.

"The only true enemy I ever had was Rose," she stated. "Poppy was wonderful, but we were tied together by nastiness that neither one of us wanted to recall." Sandra shook her head. "So, it's not as if we wanted to remember."

"No, of course not," Doreen agreed, with a knowing smile. "Understood." With that, she got Sandra's phone number, in case Doreen had any other questions. Then as she stood to leave, Sandra stopped her.

"How did you get over your husband?" Sandra asked.

Doreen turned to her and smiled. "I found Mack, and that gave me a whole new perspective on life."

"Good for you," the other woman replied. "I guess I should have tried someone new, but I just couldn't see it. My good-for-nothing husband was the one person I'd always loved all my life."

Doreen nodded. "You don't need to feel guilty about that. The only person who gets to make choices about your life is you. And you chose to accept him back. I presume he was good afterward?"

"As good as gold," she said, with a nod. "I think he realized that life as a single man wasn't exactly what he thought it would be."

"Then it worked out for both of you," Doreen noted, and, with that, she turned and left.

Chapter 26

BACK HOME DOREEN quickly made a sandwich and ate it, then looked down at the animals and noted, "You've been inside all morning, I think it's time we headed out to let you guys have a bit of freedom now." And, with them eager to go, she quickly cleaned up the kitchen. As she went out the back door, she heard a voice calling her to the front door. She turned and, taking her animals with her, opened her front door, and her neighbor Richard stood there. "Problems?" she asked.

"No, no problems," he replied. "I was just wondering if you got anywhere on the missing person, you know, that poor woman's father?"

"No," she admitted, "I haven't gotten anywhere on that one. His name was Jack Mahoney. I just keep finding more missing people."

"Finding them?" he asked, his eyebrows raised. "Already?"

"No, no, not finding the people themselves but realizing there probably are more cases of other people missing than we know of. Likely because recordkeeping wasn't done as much back then."

"Yes, and you could move all over the place, and nobody knew all your business back then, not the way they do now, with cell phones and internet and databases. It was great back then."

She smiled at him. "And I'm guessing you don't have any information to offer."

"Nope, I sure don't, but you did say something about Rose earlier."

"Yeah, Rose is definitely somebody I'm interested in."

"Any reason why?" he asked, looking at her intently.

"No, not necessarily her. She's dead and gone now," Doreen noted, "so it's not as if I'm thinking she committed a crime."

"Right," Richard replied. "Did you check to see if any unidentified person was on her property, what with the bloody garden plot event?"

"Mack's looking into it," she replied, "but that's a good reminder. I need to check to see if he got that far."

"You know, it used to be that they would just bury anybody they didn't have a name for. And it seems there were a few of those dead bodies with no ID almost every year. You know, when somebody on the road was found or somebody was off in a corner and found dead. I'm not saying that's what happened in your cold cases. I'm just saying that it's possible, and that you should check that angle."

"Of course, thanks." Then she locked up and headed down the road.

He called back, "I'm not much help in this field of finding info or people, but I know my brother might be better at this. So, if you ever need help, after all you did for him, he would be more than happy to help you."

She thought about it, considering Roscoe's age, and

frowned. "I wonder if he knows anybody connected to Rose, not just twenty-five years or so ago but even as far back as fifty years ago?"

"Not sure that he would, but he knows a lot of the old-timers around town. So, who knows? He might. You could always give him a call."

"I'll see." She then lifted a hand to wave at him. "Thanks."

She wandered down the river, not heading toward Rosemoor in particular. She was just trying to figure out what was going on in her own head. Something was there, nudging at her, but she wasn't so sure what that was all about. And yet it was important. She just couldn't figure out how or in what way. Confused and a little perturbed, she walked down farther, and then Mack called her. She looked down at the phone and smiled. "Hey," she answered.

"Are you all right?" he asked.

"Yes. Why would you ask that?" she muttered. "Of course I'm okay."

"You sounded a little relieved to hear from me."

She chuckled. "Or maybe it's delight."

"In that case," he teased, with a bright laugh, "that's a good thing."

"It absolutely is a good thing," she replied.

"Oh, and here's something you've been waiting on. It took some man-hours, but our team traced Bartlet Jones to Boston, Massachusetts, where he has settled down with one woman and married her almost immediately after leaving Kelowna. So, at least in that missing person's case," he shared, "you should be good to go."

She laughed. "I'm glad your guys figured it out and told me. I'll update my Solomon file accordingly. So that takes care of Bartlet Jones, but I still have the body who bled out in Milford's zucchini patch and also Jack Mahoney," Doreen muttered. "Listen. Did you ever check into whether you had any unidentified remains, any Jane Does or John Does?"

"We do, and that is one of the things I'm calling about."

"Interesting. Do we know anything about them?"

"Not yet. I'm just getting the files pulled. We never did find identification for two of them over the years."

"One'll be a Jane Doe, and one'll be a John Doe," she announced.

Dead silence came on Mack's end. "Pardon?"

"Yeah, … though I should probably wait until you tell me when they disappeared before I jump to conclusions. I know you're always getting on to me about that anyway."

"Maybe you need to fill me in on just what you've been up to. How you seem to know what I'll say is a definite concern."

"Yeah, wouldn't that be nice," she muttered. "I'm literally walking the river right now, trying to sort out what's going on in my head."

"You sound as if you've had a very interesting morning."

"Yeah, you could call it that," she agreed, "but I don't have any answers yet."

"What? You mean the crazy Doreen's Deputies groupies don't have it all solved for you?"

"Oh gosh," she muttered. "Please don't call them that. They'll never live it down."

"No, they won't." He chuckled. "I told the captain, as a word of warning, in case they come up against them anywhere."

"And what did he think?"

"He thought it was hilarious," he quipped.

Doreen could easily imagine Mack with a big smirk on his face. "Yeah? Just wait until you see their outfits."

"Outfits?" he asked, his tone rising in comical laughter. "Are you serious?"

"Oh yeah, I'm very serious," she muttered. "And I hope you get to see them on your own, without my having to witness it again."

"Ooh, this is sounding better and better," he said, still chuckling. "So, will you tell me about these dead bodies you think you might know about?"

"Not yet," she muttered, "absolutely not yet, but I'm getting there." And a long pause ensued as she pondered what to tell him.

"Ha, you're just not ready to tell me. But, if it's connected to my shooting case, the death of Lynda Mahoney, you will eventually tell me, right?"

"I absolutely will tell you, once I figure it out," she stated. "However, right now, I have a lot of pieces and a few suppositions, but it's not necessarily clicking into place yet. Or it's clicking into place, but I don't have …" And then she stopped.

"You don't have one ounce of proof, do you?" he asked.

"Exactly. And I'm not sure anybody is left living to get it from."

"That is one of the problems with cold cases. People don't live forever, and sometimes they take their crimes and their secrets to the grave, and we can do nothing about it."

Chapter 27

DOREEN AND HER animals walked along the river, and it was cold, the wind biting at her cheeks. The animals didn't seem to be affected and were happy to trundle along beside her. She really missed the warm weather right now. Just a chance to sit by the river and to let some of these questions wander through her brain. She hadn't realized just how much she needed to let things churn away in her mind, not until this cold weather hindered part of her process. She had a slight idea of what was going on with the two unidentified bodies but needed more information to convince Mack.

Mack was happy enough to send her the little bit they had on the John Doe and Jane Doe they had in their missing person's files. They were cold cases, but, because they didn't have any real information on these two bodies, they would need DNA in order to solve anything to do with them. Even then, the DNA did them no good as far as IDs went if that DNA did not match some other DNA on record somewhere.

Doreen thought she might come up with something where they could go after these old cases, but now she wasn't sure.

For all she knew, even more people were missing in this valley, which, given the number of years these cold cases went back to, really wasn't out of the question. A lot of transient people came through Kelowna looking for work, people moving in, then leaving, and, in this Rose-related case, husbands leaving their wives, and then ending up who-knows-where, like Bartlet Jones. There were certainly a lot of families damaged, if not completely blown apart, by Rose's philandering actions, who seemingly didn't care about those families that she had hurt too.

Doreen stopped at one part of the river to just let the animals sniff away. When she heard a yell, she looked up to see Lynon's son, Nate, walking toward her. She looked at him and smiled. "How's your father doing?"

"He's doing okay," he replied, with a note of hesitation in his voice. "Has my … Has my nephew been making a nuisance of himself?"

"No, not at all. He's come by several times," she replied. "Gavin brought me the puppy he and Randy found."

Nate winced at that. "Right, and now Gavin won't leave me alone about it."

"It might be a good answer for him though," she pointed out. "I get that, for you, it's one more thing to look after, one more chore, but for Gavin? It's something he can love, and I think he's really missing that right now."

He stared at her. "I don't know that I'm up for it though," he admitted.

"I get that," she said, "and I'm not trying to tell you one way or the other. I'm just saying that, to help Gavin and maybe as an answer to his pain, having something else that he can love right now might be the thing that changes his behavior. He must be held responsible for the puppy too."

"Definitely something in his behavior has to change," Nate declared, as he stared across the river. "And I don't know if this would do it or not. I don't even know how we would tell. The problem is, I'm not cut out to be a father," he muttered. He pushed his hair off his forehead. "Honest to God, I think I've bitten off too much to chew as it is."

She looked at him in alarm. "You're not thinking about giving up on Gavin, are you?"

"I don't know what to do," Nate admitted. "Gavin's caused me no end of trouble, and I'm not sure I'm the answer. I'm not sure I can give him what he needs."

"No, you can't," she stated. "Nobody can give him everything he needs. Right now, he's grieving. He's lost his mother, and no easy answer will fix him. But replacing some of that which he lost with something he can love could help."

"But it could also make it worse," he pointed out, "and then I'll have a puppy to get rid of because I can't possibly keep a puppy either."

"Are you traveling a lot?"

"I was, but I changed my job and reduced a lot of the traveling because of Gavin."

"Of course," she replied. "And he doesn't appreciate that because he's still too caught up in his own pain to even realize that you are making sacrifices."

"Right," Nate muttered. "I would absolutely love to go back to my old job, but it seems as if that time is over."

"That time maybe," she pointed out gently, "but that doesn't mean it can't come back again at another time."

He smiled. "You're really an optimist, aren't you?"

"I don't know," she muttered. "I've been through a lot myself sometimes. However, when I hear about all these hardship stories of other people, I realize I got off easy."

He tilted his head to stare at her quizzically. "Most people wouldn't say you got off easy."

"Oh, I don't know," she said. "People are funny. If you didn't suffer enough, they're not happy. Yet, if you suffer too much, apparently they're not happy either."

He burst out laughing. "So true. Did Gavin mention to you how I won't take in the puppy?"

"Oh, yeah, he sure did," she confirmed. "I don't know what his life was like beforehand, but I know how he feels about his life now, and it feels very much like nobody cares about him, and nothing he wants or says or does will make a bit of difference."

"And yet if he would just cooperate a little bit …"

"Maybe you should have that talk with him," she suggested. "Maybe you should discuss with him what life would be like if you did give him the puppy and how much he would have to smarten up. Otherwise the puppy has to go."

"Yeah, but—"

"Listen," she said, interrupting his protests. "I am an animal lover to doomsday, and I would hate to have a puppy used as a tool for behavior, but Gavin does have to understand and to respect the fact that life and death happens. It has already happened, and it's been a bad deal for both of you," she noted, "and, if Gavin wants something like a puppy so badly, it'll require monumental changes on his part."

Silence came from Nate.

Doreen continued. "Maybe you could take the puppy in as a foster scenario for a month or two and see if Gavin's prepared to turn things around or not. He is old enough to understand that. It's a risk, and I certainly don't want you to take the puppy, then have to give it back, because I think the pup herself rather desperately needs to be loved too. I don't know what happened to her or how she ended up in such dire straits to begin with, but the fact is that Gavin literally saved her life by getting her out of the river and bringing her to me. If you take her on, I would absolutely want you to keep her, to give her some stability and love. However, if Gavin isn't willing to put in the time, effort, and work, then I understand your original decision," she stated. "On the other hand, if Gavin is motivated by this puppy, it could be a brilliant answer for both of you."

Nate groaned, as he stared back at the river. "You do put up a convincing argument."

"At this point we don't even know for sure if the puppy is okay or if she'll need something else other than what you can give her. That could potentially get you off the hook too."

He snorted. "Doesn't seem as if anything will get me off the hook right now," he muttered, almost morosely.

"What would your life be like if Gavin adapted, if he went to school and didn't cause you problems? What's the biggest thing in your world that he's destroying right now?"

"Probably the fact that I can't sleep at night because of the phone calls from the school, telling me that I'll have to put him into some special care facility, or a military school, or whatever soon."

"Then maybe that's what you need to tell him. Tell him that's the one big thing that you cannot live with and that's the one big thing Gavin has to change."

Nate regarded her with a contemplative expression. "That," he noted, "is smart."

"I don't know about *smart*," she replied, "but Gavin

can't change if he doesn't know what the problem is, and if he doesn't see any motivation to change. He has to realize that change needs to happen, or nothing else will improve. If he keeps up the same old, same old, then he can't expect a different outcome."

"Maybe." Nate nodded. "I'll think about it."

"You do that," she said, "and maybe you should go take a look at the puppy yourself."

"You think I'll fall in love with it?" he asked, with an eye roll.

"No, I don't think you'll fall in love with it, but you might see why Gavin did," she shared. "And that understanding alone might help the two of you get onto the same page."

Nate laughed. "I do hear what you're trying to do," he declared.

"Not sure it's working, but a puppy is only an issue if you make it an issue," she replied.

"A puppy will chew things, terrorize things, destroy things," Nate described. "It requires food, medicine, vet visits, walks every day. Taking on a puppy is not a simple commitment."

"Yes, and that's why you must speak with Gavin because it also needs to be *his* commitment."

Nate just groaned again. "Okay, fine, fine. I'll think about it, but no promises. However, the foster puppy thing? That's possible," he muttered. "*Maybe* anyway."

"Exactly, so you must talk to the vet clinic," she added. "I don't know exactly how that works because I've never had to take in any foster animals, but it would be something I would do in a heartbeat if necessary."

"Of course you would," Nate declared, "because you're

already set up for that."

"I am, though I hadn't really considered it." She looked down at her animals roaming about and particularly Mugs, who was sniffing away at the river, trying to get himself as soaked as possible.

"Oh, boy," Nate muttered. "Just the thought of a wet dog is bad news."

She laughed. "A wet dog dries, and broken things can be replaced," she clarified.

Nate grumbled, "What can't be replaced are broken hearts over lost parents. And, for a young boy who needs something special to get over this, a puppy won't be enough."

"No, it isn't," she agreed, "but it's a step in the right direction, one that would allow Gavin to reach out and to trust you a little bit more. Obviously this has been a huge change in Gavin's life, and unfortunately you're the face of it, so he doesn't want anything to do with you."

"Yeah, you're not kidding," he muttered, swearing under his breath. "If I get one more phone call from that school, I don't know what I'll do."

"And that's what you need to tell him because it's not just your life you're fighting for. It's his too. Yet, if Gavin doesn't want to make changes, then maybe he does need to go into special care, and that would break everybody's heart," she said gently. "But it's also not necessarily a good idea for him to be with you if you can't stand being around him."

"I love him dearly," Nate grumbled. "That's not the issue."

She smiled. "In that case, all the rest can be worked out."

Chapter 28

DOREEN WOKE UP in the middle of the night and jerked upright and swore. She slapped her hand over her mouth and stared around the room in shock. She was alone, except for Mugs, who was stretched out beside her. She saw no sign of Goliath, and Thaddeus was up on his roost, sound asleep. She sat here on her bed, with her covers pulled up tight, shivering in the chill and wondering what on earth was going through her mind that she woke herself up, swearing like a sailor.

Even as she sat here, considering the language she had used, it came back to her what her brain had been going on about. It had to do with those bodies, and she knew it. Now the question was, who was where and why, and what did any of this have to do with that poor woman, Lynda Mahoney, who was shot in a friend's driveway as she sought answers on her father's disappearance? Doreen had so many pieces, and yet none of it was coming together. However, she knew the final conclusion was right there, lingering at the edge of her brain. If only she could pull it out.

She sank back on her bed, struggling to figure out how this all worked together. She remained here for a good hour, before just giving up. She got up, had a hot shower, and then went downstairs and put on coffee. She soon got a large piece of brown butcher paper, stretched it out onto the kitchen table and started to map out what was bothering her.

This would take a little bit, even though not a whole lot was going on. Her problem was just that everything was disjointed and yet crisscrossed each other somehow. She knew that the answers at the end of the day would be very simple, but, as far as she was concerned, the key to all of it was Rose. If Doreen could map out Rose's life, then Doreen could get to the rest of this puzzle without any trouble. At least she hoped so.

She didn't want to tell Mack what she was up to though. Yet, as soon as he walked in the door—and she always expected him to walk in her door—he would have some idea. Still, he wasn't here now, and she had to get it sorted out before she asked Mack to start exhuming bodies. She was sure that would have to be done next.

Grabbing another cup of coffee, she picked up her pen and sat down. She had Jack Mahoney, still missing and maybe connected to Milford's bloody garden patch, or maybe not. She had no idea. She had a dead woman, Lynda Mahoney, who had been shot on a friend's driveway, after asking questions about her missing father, Jack Mahoney. Doreen added Jack's timeline and Lynda's two visits here to find her father to Doreen's map. She mapped out the location of Milford's farm up in the Joe Rich area, noting the bloody garden patch.

Too bad forensics had been a bust. She only had Milford's word on the blood's existance. Still… why would he lie?

Supposedly Milford had called in law enforcement all

those years ago, yet the cops didn't do anything but then again, that was before DNA so…. That was an interesting conundrum though. As she sat here working on it, she mapped out known events in Rose's life too. As far as Doreen was concerned, she had to focus on Rose, no matter how sketchy Doreen's info was. The third supposedly missing person was Bartlet Jones, gone some fifty years ago but recently found and connected to Rose in that he was one of the men she had had an affair with. So, that prompted Doreen to do what she really needed to do next, as she reached for her phone.

It rang just as she went to pick it up. She looked down at it and then grinned. "You must have read my mind," she said cheerfully.

"Why?" Mack asked.

"Because I was just going to call you."

"That's good, or maybe it's good," he clarified, a note of humor evident in his tone.

"I would like to think it's good," she replied.

"Did you solve something?" he asked.

"No, but I need the DNAs on those John Doe and Jane Doe bodies." There was silence on the other end for a moment.

"I don't know if we have samples set aside or if they would have to be exhumed," he replied. "They were buried in unmarked graves, which was a common thing back then."

"Of course," she noted, "but we do need the DNA in order to find out who they are. It's too bad they don't just keep them in a morgue drawer."

"Yeah, that's not exactly something most families would agree with either," he noted in a dry tone.

"I realize that," she admitted. "Some of these have been

there for a while."

"They were all down to bones, I believe, if I have the reports in my head correct."

"I'm not surprised," she said. "They were probably lost for a long time."

"So, who is it that you expect them to be?" When she went quiet, he asked, "You're not planning on telling me yet?"

"There's a good chance that I'm wrong."

"Sure, that's always the case," Mack replied, "and obviously we are missing some people, down to two now that Bartlet Jones has been found. Yet you do realize that none of the years given for when the other two who went missing match up, right? You've got Jack Mahoney missing twenty-something years ago, which was confirmed by witnesses who spoke with his daughter, Lynda."

"I know," she agreed, "but the two dates are iffy, not definitive."

"Right. I've already talked to the captain about getting DNA, even exhuming the bodies," he shared. "I had that discussion with him this morning."

"Oh? And what did he say?"

"He cautiously agreed. But only if you come up with more evidence to justify it."

There was silence at first, then she cried out, "Really?"

"Yes, but it's mostly because you have such a good track record."

"Oh, *great*." She winced. "That'll just put added pressure on me."

"Yeah," Mack said, "but these are very old cases, and I wasn't even looking at them necessarily because we have nothing on them to proceed with. We just have bodies, and they're skeletal remains at that."

"If you have any information on them, I would like to see if I can fit any of it into the lovely little hypothesis I'm working on."

"Yeah, but will you let me know what your hypothesis is?" he asked, with a note of humor.

"If and when I can figure it out in my head, yes, of course. But the problem I still have, as you know, is no proof of any wrongdoing."

"The one body had a lot of animal activity on it, so it was thought to be a hunter, or somebody who had just gone out for a hike and either had a heart attack, or was dropped by animals, but we have no way to know."

"Of course," she noted. "And it could also just have been somebody who had died and had been left there. Even with bones left behind, you could still have missing body parts."

He sighed. "That's another good point. On the one body, I'm not sure we have all of it."

"And, with a death like that," she added, "you might not easily find cause of death. Once the animals get going on a dead body, it's all the more difficult."

"And," Mack clarified, "if it was a natural death, or somebody killed by strangulation yet with no broken hyoid even left to examine, you and I both know that it would be hard to prove murder now."

"Exactly. Yet I'm pretty sure they were both killed," she shared. "I've been sitting here contemplating the butcher paper I've laid out on my kitchen table and all that I have mapped out."

"I'll come over this evening," he said, "but I'm organizing the exhuming process now. DNA will take a while. I know you don't want to hear that, but DNA does take a while."

"And yet these bodies have been here for a long time," she noted, "so I guess another day or two won't matter."

"I'm surprised to hear you say that," he joked. "You're usually the one jumping all over me to make it go faster."

"And I usually would be, but I suspect that their murderers may not be alive now to be charged for their crimes."

A moment of silence came before he spoke again. "You really think you know what's going on?"

"Unfortunately, yes. The thing is, I'll need another body exhumed as well." She heard him groan on the other end of the phone.

"And who is that?" he asked.

"I'll need Rose's body exhumed," she replied.

"I doubt that the captain will want to hear this," he muttered. "And Milford will be upset for sure."

"Yeah, I know."

"Hang on, let me call the captain at least."

She heard voices in the background. Almost immediately she felt her doubts assail her. As soon as Mack came back on, she repeated, "I could be wrong, though."

Mack laughed. "Look. We know that, and none of us will be at all upset if you are wrong. The fact is, we don't have anything in the way of promising leads right now."

"Right," she said, with a nod.

Then the captain's voice boomed through Mack's phone. "Why don't you just come down and talk to us? Let's see what you've got."

"Sure. ... Like, now?"

"Yes, now," he declared in that tone that wouldn't give anybody any option to do otherwise.

As soon as she disconnected, she looked down at the

animals and asked, "Are you guys ready for this?" Mugs woofed several times, and started turning around, chasing his tail. Goliath smacked Mugs twice on the head, then flopped back down, as if to say, *Whatever*. Thaddeus faced her from his living room roost and declared, "Thaddeus is here. Thaddeus is here."

"Thanks, buddy. Let's all get going." So she grabbed up all the related paperwork she had gathered, along with her multiple timelines map, and loaded up the animals into her car, already parked on the driveway. With a heavy dose of sarcasm, she said, "Okay, this will be fun." As she looked up and walked to her driver's side door, she saw Richard, sitting there on his front porch, staring at her. She shrugged and smiled.

"Did you solve it?" he asked.

"I don't think so, not yet," she muttered, "but I'm close."

In a rare vote of confidence, he just waved his hand and said, "You've got it. If you're that close, you're bound to get it in no time." And, with that, he walked back inside his home.

She stared in his direction for a moment, then frowned at her animals. "I didn't expect that."

As soon as she drove down to the police station and got out, Nan called Doreen on the phone.

"Where are you?" she asked, in that tone requiring an answer right away.

"I just parked at the police station. Why?"

"Ooh, do you have it figured out?" she called out in excitement.

"No, I don't have it figured out. I just have more questions."

"Oh."

The disappointment in Nan's tone was so deep that Doreen felt the need to temper her response. "However, I think I'm very close to figuring it out," she muttered, then rolled her eyes, knowing that was the last thing she should tell Nan.

"Then I'm coming down there."

"No, you're not," Doreen said in alarm. "I'm having a meeting with everyone at the captain's request, so this isn't the time for you and the gang to show up."

"It should be because, if you're almost there, you'll need us to go ferret out the rest of the details," she explained, "and we're ready." With that, she disconnected.

Doreen groaned and walked into the police station. Darren stood there, talking with Mack, and they looked up as she walked in. Mack smiled, and she looked over at Darren and muttered, "I'm so sorry."

He closed his eyes and whispered, "Please, no. Don't tell me that Rosemoor residents will soon descend on all of us."

"I won't be shocked if they turn up here," she replied apologetically. "I didn't mean for it to happen and told Nan no, but, well, you know how that goes." When Darren just stared at her, she nodded. "Honestly, they are a force unto themselves."

"You're not kidding," Darren muttered. "It's definitely lunchtime for me. I'm leaving."

"Oh no you don't," the captain roared. "If Richie is coming here, you're staying."

Darren's shoulders sagged as he looked at Doreen, hoping she might take mercy on him.

She laughed. "I can handle most of them, including your grandfather, but you know what happens when they go off on their own."

He nodded. "I do know, and that's why I want to go for lunch." Then he turned and glanced back at the captain. "Please."

"No. You stay here. You'll need to wrangle your grandfather, as they'll cause complete chaos."

She laughed. "That they definitely will."

"Did you tell them that you solved it?" the captain asked her.

"No, I told Nan that I came down here to ask more questions. Then I also said I was close to solving it, and, of course, she jumped on that, saying they needed to be here at the ready to go ferret out the rest of the information."

He just stared at her, shook his head, and muttered to himself.

"I know," Doreen added. "I'm sorry."

"Wherever you go, it seems chaos follows," The captain turned to look down at Mugs, who was straining at his leash. "At least give us some puppy love today."

She dropped the leash, and Mugs raced to him.

The captain dropped to his knees and hugged Mugs. "Honest to goodness, this is the best thing about having you around."

Doreen chuckled. "I'm glad somebody appreciates me."

"We do and we don't." Then the captain chuckled. "I have to admit it's a challenge having you around sometimes."

She nodded. "And I am sorry for that. I don't try to be difficult."

He shrugged. "You may not *try* to be difficult, but, I swear, you are."

"Yet I don't mean to be," she muttered.

"I get it. I really do, but unfortunately you come with

some big handicaps. Come on. Let's get the bulk of this over with, before the Rosemoor people arrive and find out."

With that, she headed into one of the boardrooms, where she walked over to the whiteboard and started putting up the timeline map she'd drawn on brown butcher paper. The captain came to stand behind her, and Mack was right beside her.

"You know that's as clear as mud," Mack pointed out in a low tone.

She looked back at him and explained, "It's not as if I was planning on presenting it to anybody. It was intended just for me."

Yet Darren looked at it and nodded. "It makes sense."

She snorted. "I'm glad to hear that because I'm hoping it won't be such a big deal. Now look," Doreen began, "we started off with three missing people, two named, one not." Then she took a red pen and drew a circle around them. "I could be way off here, but I'll just say it." Then she stopped to face them. "I'm thinking the vague twenty-odd-years-ago date when Jack Mahoney went missing and the generic twenty-five-years-ago date when Milford first saw his bloody garden bed are actually the same date. My theory says they *are* the exact same date. And Mack and I both heard Milford himself say that he doesn't remember the date when he married his wife. So any date he gives us in this investigation must be suspect. Plus, I understand the local old-timers and even forensics can't give us a definite timeframe on these two events. With Lynda dead, we can't ask her to refine her date for her father going missing. So that's why I need the DNA."

"Hang on a minute. Hang on. Let's start at the beginning," the captain stated.

She frowned at him and asked, "You mean, it's not self-evident?"

"No, it's not," he barked.

Just then her phone rang. She glanced down and moaned. "Oh, it's Milford, Rose's husband. And I need to ask him about exhuming her body."

"Unless he has a hairbrush," the captain suggested, "or something like that, where we could get the DNA from that instead."

She looked at the captain in delight and answered her phone. "Hey, Milford. Are you okay?"

"Not really," he muttered, his tone dark. "I'm parked outside in the police parking lot." She looked at the captain, her eyebrows shooting up, and whispered, "He's here."

He frowned back at her in surprise.

Doreen asked Milford, "Do you want to come in and talk to us?"

"Are you here?" he asked.

"Yes, I sure am."

"Okay, that'll be perfect," he muttered. "Besides, it's time."

"You're right," she agreed. "It is time." Then she ended the call.

At that, the captain looked at her. "Do you think he murdered his wife?"

"No, I don't think he murdered anybody. However, I don't think his wife was Rose."

Chapter 29

A s Doreen waited for Milford to walk into the station, the detectives just stared at her.

Then Mack asked, "The big question is, what difference does his wife make?"

"The question is whether Rose is buried in Milford's zucchini patch, or was someone else involved in that, or was it something completely different."

Just then the receptionist from the front brought Milford into the conference room to join them.

He took one look at all the cops and winced. He had his hat clutched nervously in his hands. He looked at Doreen and asked, "May I talk to you privately?"

"You can, but honestly, I'll have to tell these guys anyway, so maybe you should tell us now."

He winced again and looked around nervously.

She added, "Maybe I can make it easier by asking some questions."

His eyes widened, and he swallowed nervously, then nodded.

"Why don't you tell us who your wife really was?"

He looked at Doreen blankly for a moment, then all the

color fell from his face. "You know?" he cried out. "How is that possible? I just found out myself."

"Oh boy," she muttered, staring at him, as the pieces fell into place.

Then out of his hat, he pulled a small journal, along with a hairbrush. "After you were gone, I realized how little time I have left, so I was trying to clean up the place. Who knows if the town would even sell my place. I don't even know what they do with property that's just left with no family left behind for it to go to," he explained. "So, while cleaning up the place, I found this journal under her side of the bed. I don't even know what to think."

Doreen walked over and gave Milford a gentle hug. "You were married to Poppy, weren't you?"

He stared at Doreen, wearing a dazed expression, and nodded. "But I don't know how or why."

"Poppy was very jealous of her sister, and I think Poppy loved you very, very much."

He nodded. "I never could understand why Rose would have been so happy to go from that busy life she had to just being with me."

"And did Poppy explain it in her diary?"

"I don't even think it's a diary," he clarified, staring down at the journal. "It's more of a confession."

"Ah, right."

"Were you looking for that too?" he asked, staring at Doreen, obviously in shock.

"No, not necessarily. It depends on if Poppy killed anybody—deliberately, not accidently."

He looked at her with tears in his eyes, and he nodded. "Rose."

"That's what I figured." She turned and looked at Mack.

"Rose will be your Jane Doe."

Mack stared at her in shock, then back at the old man. "Did she say anything about where or how?"

Milford nodded. "It's all here in her journal," he whispered. "I'm still …"

"Of course you're still in shock," Doreen replied, "because you absolutely adored your Poppy."

He nodded, tears in his eyes. "How did I not know?"

"Because, for one thing, you never spent a ton of time with Rose. Secondly, you *wanted* to believe you had married Rose. And finally, Poppy never gave you any reason to doubt it. You didn't have a ton of time with Rose, and Poppy would have known that. So she didn't have to cover up very much. Then if she made a few rules about never talking about her history …"

Milford nodded. "That's exactly what she did. We couldn't talk about the past. She didn't want to talk about any of that, and I was just so happy she had chosen me that I didn't care." He eyed Doreen suspiciously. "Do you know how the real Rose died?"

"Yes and no. I'm pretty sure she died in childbirth."

Again he just stared at her, his eyes almost bugging out. "My God. How do you know when I'm just finding out?"

She winced. "Sometimes things just have a habit of coming to me that way."

He blinked at her several times. "So Poppy didn't kill Rose, or did she?"

"It depends," she replied. "Maybe Rose needed maternity care, and Poppy couldn't help her, couldn't save her."

He nodded. "I think that is closer to what happened," he muttered, staring at the journal. "I didn't know anything about it.'

"Did she tell you whose baby it was?"

He shook his head. "No, I'm not sure I even want to know."

"Right," she muttered. "And do we know for sure that the baby died too?"

Milford frowned at her.

Doreen noted, "You seem surprised. I'm thinking that the baby didn't die with the mother," she muttered.

"Oh, but then where is the child?" Milford asked.

"Good question," Doreen admitted, looking at him.

Milford glanced around blankly and just seemed to nod, as if not really seeing anybody else.

"Will you be okay?" she asked him.

"I buried her as my wife."

"Honestly, Poppy was your wife," Doreen pointed out. "She may not have been the woman you thought she was, but she was your wife." He blinked several times, and she asked, "Did you love the woman you lived with?"

"Absolutely," he declared, then frowned. "But she's not the woman I thought she was."

"No, and maybe keep in mind how desperately in love with you that Poppy was. Enough that she would have done whatever she did to protect her marriage."

That seemed to help settle him.

"Right, … the whole thing is just unbelievable." Milford shook his head and glanced at the journal in his hand. "It's really just unbelievable."

"I'm sorry," she whispered. "And you're right. It's a very hard thing to take in."

He sagged. "I didn't do anything to hurt her, you know?"

"I know that. Now, do you know what happened that

brought all the blood onto your zucchini patch?"

He held out the journal. "Apparently she did something. I was away, and I didn't even think about it," he began. "I wasn't even in town at the time. I was up north with a logging load to deliver, and she told me all about finding the blood. Honestly, I'd forgotten about it, except for the fact that she wouldn't let me ever plant anything there. … I couldn't read any more."

"Right."

He nodded, but he still looked a little lost.

"Do you mind if we come to your farm with some equipment?" she asked.

At that, the captain's eyebrows went up.

She turned to him and nodded. "A body is up there."

The captain frowned and asked, "Whose body?"

She looked back at Milford. "Did she ever tell you more about it?"

"No. … Tell me about what?"

"I suspect it's the father of Rose's child, somebody who came looking for Rose but found Poppy and realized that Poppy wasn't Rose at all."

"Good God," Milford groaned, as he just stared at Doreen. Then he held out the journal again. "I guess you don't need this then, do you?"

Mack snatched it from his hands. "Maybe she doesn't," he said, with a long-suffering sigh, "but we do."

At that, Darren snorted. "Yeah, you're not kidding."

Just then more chaos erupted as the double front doors to the station opened noisily, and the Rosemore gang soon found them in the nearby conference room.

"Oh, Lord, Nan." Doreen seemed horrified as she turned to them. "I love you, but there is a protocol in place here."

Nan waved her hand. "Hush, child. The captain and his men are happy to have us come help. Look at them. They're all smiling."

Looking at the grins on the faces of these professional policemen, Doreen knew those had far more to do with the troupe of elderly sleuths in full Sherlock Holmes regalia.

"In some ways your granddaughter has already solved it all," the captain declared.

Nan looked at Doreen in disappointment, only to have the joy of knowing her granddaughter had closed the case win over, and she exclaimed, "You could have told us, child."

"No, I couldn't," she whispered. "That's the agreement, remember? Mack rules this one."

Mack chuckled beside her and quipped, "That's nice. Thank you for letting me know."

She glanced back at him with a smile. "I am trying to uphold and to maintain our agreement."

"I can see that," he confirmed, with glee on his face as he caught what she was certain was a monocle on Richie's right eye. Shaking his head, Mack asked Doreen, "This settles quite a bit of stuff, but are you saying that Poppy murdered this man, this supposed father to Rose's child?"

"Yes," Doreen replied, "and I highly suspect that you will find this man to be Jack Mahoney, the missing father of Lynda Mahoney, the woman who was recently shot and has since died."

The captain stared at her in shock, as the other cops looked at her too.

"Then who shot Lynda?" cried out one of the detectives in the background.

She looked around at everybody and frowned. "Someone

who didn't want Lynda finding her father, who maybe hated her, maybe hated her father. And that would be … Clive." When Mack frowned at her, she nodded and explained, "Remember? He owns that corner store nearby where Lynda's shooting was and has to work double shifts there because he's financially strapped? He was the one seen walking around the area at the time of the shooting."

Nan shook her head in confusion.

Doreen and Mack both caught that motion. Mack groaned, finally catching up with Doreen's theory, then explained, "Clive killed Lynda, so he would be the last remaining heir of Jack Mahoney."

"Exactly," Doreen exclaimed, giving him a beaming smile.

He grunted, as he glared at her. "I really wish you wouldn't look at me as if I'm your favorite student when I say something."

She burst out laughing at that. "I believe that Clive is Lynda's half brother."

"Oh, good God," Nan muttered. "That makes so much sense."

"But," Doreen added, pointing to Mack, "you'll have to prove that one too."

Mack just stared at her, glancing around the room at the captain and the other officers, then noted, "Wow, you mean you didn't totally lock up this one for us?"

"I was focused on getting the DNA for Poppy. Milford has now resolved that issue for us, bringing us a hairbrush." She asked Milford, "I'm not sure how things evolved, but maybe Poppy's journal can tell us more?"

Milford shook his head. "I stopped reading it. Have your fiancé read it and tell you. I'm not sure I want to know more, not right now."

Doreen nodded. "I understand. So here's what I have in theory so far. First, twenty-some years ago, I think Jack may have heard the gossip about how Rose went missing to have a baby. So Jack was inspired to find Rose and to see if he had another child that she didn't tell him about. So Jack finds out she is living with Milford in the Joe Rich area, which didn't compute to Jack. So he went to confront her. Instead of finding Rose, he found Poppy. Poppy couldn't take the chance of her secret coming out, so she pops Jack and buries him in Milford's zucchini patch.

"Then more recently I believed Clive wanted answers about his birth parents, so he ordered a genealogy search. You'll have to ask Clive more about that. Does it notify both parties when there is a match? I don't know. But, let's say, Clive orders the DNA search a year ago, gets the results six months ago, and finds his birth father to be Jack Mahoney, but he is noted as missing for twenty-some-odd years. Maybe Lynda is notified of this discovery of her half brother, but wouldn't that work in reverse too? If so, Clive finds out he has a half sister and agrees to meet with Lynda ten or so days ago and shoots her, hoping to be the only heir to Jack's estate. That's just my working theory though."

They all continued to stare at her.

The captain asked, "Do you have any proof of this?"

"No, but, if you test Clive's DNA against Lynda Mahoney's, the woman he shot and killed, you'll find that they are half siblings. Then, if you test Clive's DNA against Rose's DNA, you'll find confirmation of his maternal DNA. Then do the same with Jack to confirm paternity."

"Good God." The captain turned to face the old man Milford, who nodded.

Milford replied, "Poppy did write in her journal that she never knew who was the father of Rose's baby boy, but the baby survived, and Poppy passed off the baby to somebody in town, but she doesn't give any names."

Doreen added, "Yet the whole town is a gossip center, and everybody knows exactly who raised Clive as his own child. With Poppy knowing so well how Rose's mind worked, Poppy could have told any of the men Rose had been sleeping with that the baby was theirs, asking them to raise the child, telling them that Rose had no motherly instincts to stick around, never explaining that Rose was dead. I spoke to two different women who had their marriages damaged by their husbands having a dalliance with Rose. I'm sure there were many more men involved with Rose."

"Ya think?" Mack quipped. "You burst into Rose's life and didn't really let go."

"Yeah, I sure did," she muttered. Then she turned to Milford. "Does any of that make sense to you?"

"It makes more sense than you know because Poppy did mention a couple different times that she'd been involved with handing off a baby to foster parents because she was a nurse."

"So both Poppy and Rose were legitimately nurses back then, weren't they?" Doreen asked.

"Yes. They both worked at the same place too, and often got mistaken for each other, even though they weren't twins. It really bugged Poppy, I think, because Rose got all the attention. Poppy intentionally wore her hair completely different and dressed differently and everything. Until I guess, at some point, Poppy decided to take over her sister's life."

Doreen agreed. "By doing that, she got to have you, without having to live Rose's exciting life, because, if Poppy had wanted to, she certainly could have. She had the opportunity," Doreen explained, "particularly looking so much like her sister, Rose."

The cops shuffled around her and her whiteboard timeline, as if still trying to sort out everything.

Doreen smiled at Milford and added, "But Poppy didn't ever want to be her sister, not unless she had some very motivating reason. And part of that motivating reason was the fact that Poppy likely had something to do with Rose's death, just by not rendering aid in a timely manner. Plus, Poppy wanted you out of it. By doing what she did, she just said her sister *Poppy* had moved far away to the east coast, removing suspicion from herself and stepped into the life she wanted with you and no longer had to live in her sister's shadow."

Milford stared at her and nodded. "You're right, … about all of it. I just don't know how. I don't know in what way your mind works that you could figure that out. However, if one of you read all of Poppy's journal, that's likely what happened. Yet I feel as if I need to go home and take a shower," he admitted. "This whole thing is making me sick to my stomach."

Chapter 30

WHEN DOREEN WOKE up the next morning, she was tired and groggy. However, as soon as her brain kicked into gear, she bolted out of bed, raced downstairs, and put on the coffee. She was just pouring her first cup, when Mack called.

"Talk to the captain," he began, then a muffled sound came as his phone was passed over.

"Good morning, Doreen. We'll do the DNA off the hairbrush Milford found to confirm Poppy was his wife," he explained, "and we're running DNA on the two samples that we have, as John Doe and Jane Doe. We may have something back in a couple days to confirm the John Doe as Jack Mahoney, Clive's birth father. We expect the Jane Doe should confirm that body to be Rose, Clive's birth mother. And your theory is probably correct that Clive found out through a genealogy search that he had a half sister, Lynda Mahoney."

"Yes," Doreen agreed. "Clive probably went looking for his real mother and probably uploaded his DNA, hoping for a hit, and, as a result, he could have found his half sister. Maybe even Lynda was notified of that match too."

"Yes," the captain replied. "Mack will go talk to Clive, before we proceed further on him."

"Ah, I want to talk to him myself."

"No way," the captain declared, his voice sharp. "If this guy is the one who shot Lynda, he's already got one murder under his belt. So another won't faze him."

"I know." She groaned. "I just didn't want to walk away at this point."

"*Sure.* Why walk away now?" he barked, but so much humor filled his tone that she groaned. "You've made all of us look like idiots again."

"You know I don't try to do that, right?" she asked the chief.

"No, apparently you don't even have to try," he declared, his laughter filling Doreen's kitchen. She smiled with relief when Mack took over the phone.

Doreen sighed. "I'm really glad that you are so content and so strong in who you are that you don't feel the need to be worried about your ego, when it comes to being a good cop."

"Oh, that's not an issue," he said, "but, if you and I ever break up, I can tell you right now that the captain will hold me responsible, and he won't be a happy man."

"Goodness, why?" she asked. "You would think he would be happy to be rid of me."

"No, because you're his secret weapon," he stated in a dry tone.

Doreen clarified, "You do realize this is merely a hypothesis at this point, a working hypothesis?"

"Of course. Then your grandmother and her merry gang arrived, zeroing in on whether you were right or not, asking whether we would bet for or against you."

"Lord, did she really set up a betting pool?" she asked, fascinated. "I was hoping she hadn't gotten that far."

"Oh no, she was right there in the mix, like a dirty shirt," he declared, a note of humor in his tone.

"Sorry." Doreen groaned. "She seems to think that, if you guys bet too, it's not illegal."

Mack burst out laughing at that. "I don't think anybody would even mind, except for the fact that they're forever losing. So, this time everybody bet that you would be right."

"*Uh-oh*, I don't think she'll take those odds."

"No, in fact, I'm pretty sure she was rushing to get away before she could accept any bets along that line. She was pretty sure that you were right too, and nobody was willing to take the chance of betting against you."

Doreen burst out laughing. "I guess there are worst things in life."

"You're right, and, speaking of that, you're still not allowed to go down to that corner store."

There was dead silence, before she asked, "How did you know?"

"Because, just as you know me, I know you. You're not going down there, do you hear me?"

"Yes, I hear you," she muttered. "You really know how to ruin a good time."

"Yeah, by keeping you alive. Remember that we think this guy has already killed somebody, so we're not taking any chances."

Just then came a knock on her door. "I've got somebody at the front door," she said, as she walked, still talking to him. She couldn't see anything out the window, but Mugs was barking heavily. "Mugs is not a happy camper over this one." She laughed, as she went to open the door.

"Don't open the door then," Mack roared.

"Too late," she said, as she looked outside, and her smile fell away. "Oh, hi. What can I do for you?" There in front of her was Clive himself, a gun in hand.

"Get off the phone."

"Oh, I don't know that I want to get off the phone," she argued, now in a crabby mood and hoping that Mack would quickly pick up on what was going on.

In her ear, he was like, "Who is it? Doreen, who is it?"

"You're the guy from that corner store, aren't you?" she asked, breathing into the phone, trying to get that message to Mack.

"Yeah, now get off the phone."

"Okay, I've got to go, bye." And she put her phone into her pocket, but she never ended the call. As she faced Clive expectantly, she knew Mack would be racing to her. "Now, what can I do for you?"

Mugs was sniffing around his feet, and Clive gave him a hard kick. Mugs yelped, and she turned on Clive.

"How could you hurt a dog like that?" she cried out. "What did he ever do to you?"

He just glared at her.

"Speaking of which, what do you want anyway? You're ruining my morning coffee."

He snorted. "That's not all I'll ruin either," he warned. "I didn't realize who you were until somebody mentioned that you got into your car full of animals and drove away. I went out and looked for you after you were nosing around, asking questions. I didn't have a clue until one of the kids who has worked there forever told me," he muttered. "He said you were that detective lady with the dog and the cat." Clive looked around behind her. "If this is what you're calling a dog, that's a pathetic excuse. Not even the size of a real dog. You've got to have one that stands upright. Not some squatty thing like this."

"Don't talk about Mugs like that."

He stared at her. "*Mugs.* Yeah, that's a good name. It figures. He's got an ugly *mug* all right." With that, he burst out laughing, then the laughter abruptly cut off, and he glared at her. "What were you doing asking questions down there anyway?"

"I was looking for information about your half sister," Doreen stated. "Wondering just how much Lynda had told you. After all, you decided to claim the family fortune and had no intention of sharing it, did you?" His glare turned even darker and more solemn than anything she could have expected.

"Good Lord, you really are dangerous."

"I don't know about dangerous," she said, with a wave of her hand. "Yet people do tend to underestimate me."

"I won't underestimate you," he stated, and suddenly the gun was pointing right at her head.

"Oh goodness," she muttered, staring at the gun. Mugs growled, then barked several times.

"Shut him up," Clive yelled, "or the first bullet is his."

She looked at Clive, aghast. "You would shoot a poor dog?"

"He exists, and he's annoying me."

"Right, so apparently your half sister existing was enough to get you going too."

"She wouldn't stop. She wouldn't stop looking into Father's death. The old fool had a real family, who all lived together and grew up. Not that he ever claimed me as his family. I didn't even know Lynda existed. I had just recently found my birth father, so imagine my surprise when I found out that my father had this whole other family that I didn't even know anything about."

"How did you find your mother?" she asked.

"Genealogy, and then I found out who my father was. That was great. So I managed to get all that paperwork together, though I already knew of him. My adopted father told me that he had been led to believe that he was my birth father but asked me not to share that with my adopted mother. She would not take kindly to hearing the truth, and I wasn't to ever tell her. Yet he knew all along that I wasn't his biological son, and he figured out who my father was. He told me that money was there with Jack Mahoney, what with his big-time cattle ranch and the quarter horses and how I should go after it. So, that was my plan. I was the only family member left. It will take a while still to get Jack declared dead, but, with that taken care of, I'll be set up for life. Then all of a sudden, this half sister turned up—the half sister who had been living with my birth father and who had had an actual relationship with him," he stated, staring at her. "Like how fair is that?"

"You mean, you were upset about the lack of a relationship with your real father, or was it the fact that Lynda showed up before you finally got your hands on the pot and you didn't have to share it?"

"I don't have to share the pot now," he declared, with a wave of his hand, "but she would have had a case against me if she'd wanted to push it."

"Considering the fact that, as far as she was concerned, Jack was her father, and you were the interloper, she might very well have done so."

"She might have tried," he conceded, the threat evident

in his tone. "She wouldn't have succeeded."

"But that's what she told you that she would do, isn't it?" He didn't respond. "Did you talk to her that morning of the shooting?" He continued to stare at Doreen. "I assume that, if you were on that street, you had been talking to her already."

"So what? What if I was talking to her? We had a good row, not that anybody would have heard us out in the empty park that morning," he said. "I always kept things on the down low, but, yeah, she was pissed off." He laughed. "And I was livid. So angry. I followed her, and she went to a house in my old neighborhood. I knew she would leave there soon, so I just waited outside, then popped her when she stepped out. It was easy, and then I just kept on walking to work. *Nothing wrong here.* I just kept walking."

Doreen sighed. "I'm really glad to hear you say that. I'm not sure the cops would have had very much evidence to try you for this otherwise."

"They don't have any evidence."

"The gun you're holding would be the same one that you shot Lynda with, so that will go against you."

"That would imply that you walk out of here with it. What will you do, jump me?" he asked, with a laugh.

It was all Doreen could do to keep her expression under control as she watched several cops pull up quietly behind them, sirens off. Parking at the street, a few houses away, the men came silently on foot and raced upward.

"The thing is, we never really know what other people can do. And, just when you think you're safe, *boom*, you're not."

He glared at her. "I don't know what you think you're up to, but you're just one interfering old busybody."

She glanced at him and then nodded. "You're not the first person to tell me that."

He snorted. "Yeah, ya think? What a pain in the …"

"If you hadn't shot your half sister—" Doreen interrupted.

"Whatever," he snapped. "If she wanted to have any family life with me, she was way too late, just like the rest of them."

"Meaning that you missed growing up with your birth mother and your birth father?"

"No. God, no." He frowned at her. "You think I didn't hear all the stories about Rose? I heard you were asking questions too."

"Sure, it's what I do." She winced. "Sometimes it has a tendency to upset people."

"You—"

"And again, it's not personal, it's just—"

"Shut up. Don't speak. Just move into the living room. Just go."

"I could move into the living room," she noted, still standing in the entranceway, "but it'll get really full very quickly."

At that, Mugs moved forward, staying out of reach of getting kicked, but he was right up against Doreen's legs, peering up at the gunman.

"Stupid dog," Clive muttered.

Just then Thaddeus poked his head out from the fall of her hair and cried out, "Thaddeus is here. Thaddeus is here."

Clive stepped backward, startled. "What the …?"

"They're my pets," she stated, looking at him. "We already know what your attitude about animals is."

He glared at her. "There you go, making assumptions

again. I had a dog growing up. I loved that thing."

"Yeah, until what?" she asked. "Until you killed it?"

"No, not me," he muttered. "It died of old age."

"Good, though I'm sorry it died. That's always very hard."

"It happens. I mean, it's an animal. What else do you expect it to do?"

She stared at him. "Right, so you weren't terribly bothered."

"Of course I was bothered, but I won't sit here and cry about it."

"No, of course not," she muttered, staring at him. "That would be way too human." He looked at her, confused. She just shrugged. "Never mind. It's obvious that we would never be friends."

He laughed. "I have no intention of being your friend. Besides, you won't be around long enough to worry about it."

"Oh really?" she asked. "You'll use that gun on me? Is that the idea? Shooting your own half sister wasn't enough?"

"I should have shot her a long time ago, when she came up the first time."

"Wow." Doreen shook her head. "And why didn't you?"

"Back then I was just a kid and didn't know about her relation to me, that's why. Only after I uploaded to the genealogy site did she find out about me and reached out. Then there was all this whining about how her poor father was missing, and, since it was in my area, did I know anything about it and all that garbage." He stared at Doreen. "What could I say? He's dead. I didn't know where or how, and I didn't have anything to tell her, and all she wanted to do was raise money to find him."

"So instead you shot her."

"When she started poking around, I had to do something. So I agreed to meet her. We had a big fight and after that. I realized she wouldn't go away."

"She could have sued you for her part of her father's estate, whether she found her father or not. Yet she didn't do that. She wanted to get to know you. Doesn't that count for anything?" Doreen asked.

"Now she can't sue me," he snarled. "And stop talking. Now get inside."

At that, Thaddeus pulled out again from under her hair and screamed, "Thaddeus loves Doreen. Thaddeus loves Doreen." And then the bird shrieked, and it sounded like the sirens on cop cars.

"Holy Moses," Clive roared, as he jolted backward several steps. Mugs, already having him on the run, jumped forward, hitting him in the kneecaps and pushing him farther away from the front door. Even as Clive stepped backward yet again, Goliath appeared out of nowhere and jumped straight up to the middle of his chest, his claws dug into his shirt, and used his full body weight to slide down. Clive screamed and roared, trying to get the cat off him.

Doreen was more concerned about his gun hand.

But Mack reached around the whole melee, grabbed Clive's gun arm, and removed the gun from his hand, then clapped a set of handcuffs on him, so casual and relaxed.

Doreen grinned. "Look at that," she said, with a happy smile. "It looks as if we solved them after all."

Mack groaned. "I don't know how you do it, but you get into trouble and somehow—"

She looked up at him, her smile turning brilliant. "And somehow this absolutely wonderful man comes to my rescue."

Mack glared at her. "That won't get you out of trouble this time."

Clive looked from one to the other, completely confused. "What is this? Are you two an item or something?"

She smiled at him. "Or something, yeah." Then she twirled the ring around on her finger.

"You're marrying a cop?" Clive asked, as if that were the worst thing ever.

"I sure hope so," she replied, laughing. "Unless he decides to quit and join me full-time in solving cold cases."

"Never," Mack declared, glaring at her still. "You're trouble enough when you're on your own."

She looked at him and nodded. "Can you imagine how much fun the two of us would have together, solving cold cases?"

"Nope, not happening. Besides, you'll need somebody on the inside to keep you out of jail."

She turned back to Clive. "I hope you've got somebody on the inside to help you because you've just confessed to murdering your half sister, and that won't go down very well."

"I didn't confess to anything," he snapped. "You've got no proof of that."

She pulled her phone from her pocket and looked over at Mack, who nodded.

"I've got it recording at the office."

She smiled. "See? The phone is still on, and we've been recording your confession the whole time."

Clive frowned at her, glanced at Mack, and asked, "What? No way."

Mack shrugged. "You can spend the rest of your life in jail figuring it all out, but I bet you won't. There is just something different about Doreen."

Epilogue

A Couple Days Later ...

DOREEN POURED A cup of coffee and stepped out onto her deck. It was not quite mid-January and still too freaking cold. She didn't know what she was thinking, but she continued to hold on to that misplaced hope that it would warm up at least a little bit, so she could sit out here comfortably. Still she couldn't stop smiling as she'd heard from Nate who'd given Gavin the best New Year's gift ever—he could keep the puppy. The two had a serious talk and had come to a compromise where Gavin would be responsible for looking after the puppy, as well as keeping his nose out of trouble and his marks up as his part of the bargain. Nate would cover the cost of keeping the puppy as his part of the bargain. It seemed like both were happy with the deal. She was thrilled.

Mack stepped up behind her. "Why are you out here in the cold?"

"I don't know," she muttered. "It's just funny that I still want to sit out by the river right now. The only reason I like winter is because I know that very quickly it'll be spring, and we can enjoy being outside again."

"And by then you'll have a huge appreciation for the nice weather too."

She smiled and nodded. "Good point." She leaned back against him.

"My brother's been trying to get a hold of you."

"Of course he has," she replied noncommittally.

"And is there a reason why you haven't responded?"

She shrugged. "No. No reason other than the usual, which is that I'm busy," she replied. "It's been a crazy ten days, you know? And I haven't told him about this case."

"Ah," Mack said, with a note of amusement in his tone. "Even he will be impressed. I think you solved, what, three cold cases all at once? Plus my current murder case. Believe me that the captain is just crowing."

She sighed. "At least then maybe he won't argue so much about the cost of DNA testing in the future."

"I wouldn't count on that. He likes to argue. Besides, you've solved so many of the cold cases already, so how many more DNA tests could you ask for? Although … another one bothers all of us. Maybe one day we can get there."

"What is it?" she asked.

"A case of bones in a box. A baby's bones," he began. "We have the box, and we have the skeleton, but not much else. They're still on a shelf at the coroner's office."

"Oh my," she muttered, twisting around to look up at him. "Seriously?"

He nodded. "Yes, they were found in a patch of yams, a very long time ago. I don't even have the details, but the captain brought it up, wondering if maybe it was time for that poor case to be resolved. Just rehashing that one case hit all of us pretty hard."

"And yet you don't remember much."

"No, I don't. I was just a youngster at the time of the original find. My mom might have more answers about it than I do. But, if you're interested, the captain told me to give you the file and to let you run wild."

She looked at him in delight. "Seriously? You're not joking?"

"No, I'm not joking. I would say the captain is a happy camper and must be to invite you to rummage around, settling these cold cases."

"I do cost him money though."

"You do, indeed," he agreed, with a laugh, "but that's okay."

"A baby? That's sad," she muttered.

"Yes, and"—he winced—"it sounds terrible, but there are definitely bite marks on the bones."

"Of course," she said. "Anytime bones are left out in the wild, that could happen. And yams? Those grow really well here. So could have been in anyone's garden."

"Do they?" he asked.

She nodded. "Yes, they do, especially in these parts. I'll take a look at the case, though the thought of a baby dying is just heartbreaking."

"I know," he muttered.

Then she giggled and quickly stifled it.

"What?" he asked suspiciously.

"Nothing, nothing at all," she said. "I'm going to the burial this weekend. Are you coming?"

"You mean for Rose to have a proper funeral? Yes, and I guess we'll have one for Jack too."

"Yes, now that he's been dug up from Milford's zucchini bed," she muttered. "Who would have thought that Poppy could do that?"

"They had farm equipment at the time, remember? A tractor. She just used the bucket and worked away at it, I presume, all in Milford's absence. It's what I would do." He nodded. "I guess it's what all of us would do, and, being out in the middle of nowhere like that, there was a certain level of privacy."

"But what about Jack's vehicle?" she asked Mack. "He had to get there somehow, right?"

He frowned at her. "I have no idea."

Doreen suggested, "I bet Poppy drove it off in the middle of nowhere and just left it parked there or maybe drove it into the lake and sunk it there."

"Maybe. I can check to see if we've got any abandoned vehicles found in that area."

"Oh, you keep track of those things too?" she asked, her eyebrows raised.

"No, not always, it depends on the circumstances," he replied. "Much more can be done now with the advances in technology, but, back then, not so much. Yet, if we find a vehicle, and it's in the way, we'll tow it in. Often they are held for the legal owner. … Poppy was smart and devious. I guess we'll never really know the whole truth about Rose's sister."

"Maybe not, but I'm guessing that, if nothing else, Poppy walked away when her pregnant sister needed help."

"Maybe," Mack agreed. "It sure sounded as if there was absolutely no love lost between them."

"No, not at that stage," Doreen pointed out sadly. "It seems there's only so much love when it comes to jealousy between siblings, and, once somebody crosses the line, well, it's all over."

"Yet I'm not sure what it would take to cross that line."

"I don't know," she said, "but I can guarantee you that Rose did it."

"And what would that have been?"

Doreen sighed. "I would assume Rose seduced Milford, the man Poppy loved."

"So, Poppy gets rid of her sister and took over Rose's identity, in order to have the man Poppy loved?" he asked, with a headshake.

"Yeah, and that just deepens the mystery about Rose. Nobody really knew what happened to her because they didn't need to know. Poppy took over Rose's identity, and she could say that her sister *Poppy* had moved to Alberta or Vancouver or wherever, and nobody would be any the wiser."

"Smart," he repeated, with a nod, "but also devious."

"Poppy didn't always choose wisely, but I guess it worked because she got Milford, and she got to die in peace in the arms of the man she loved. She sure left him a heck of a mess to clean up afterward."

"And yet I wonder if he was ever intended to find out the truth. She probably assumed he would stay there on his own farm and maybe never would even find that journal."

"I would like to think that she meant for him to know something at some point in time. Otherwise why bring up the zucchini patch? Why press him to find out about the blood there? Why even write out her confession?"

"Maybe so, but I suspect that she couldn't stand the thought of him hating her, even then, even after her death. Or finding out the truth beforehand because, what if, when she needed him the most, he found out the truth and left her?"

"That may have been Poppy's greatest fear," Doreen

whispered.

He wrapped his arms around Doreen and asked, "What was that laugh about earlier?"

She smirked and looked up at him. "Well, I just closed out the *Zonked in the Zucchinis* case."

He rolled his eyes. "You don't know he was *zonked*."

"I'll bet you that the autopsy will prove he was hit with a shovel or a pitchfork to the head. You know that means he must have been extremely drunk or exhausted or blindsided to have been taken out by her. … So zonked at the time."

He groaned. "Okay, that's quite possible, but that still doesn't explain your laughter." She looked up at him and giggled again. He smiled. "What?"

"We now have yams."

"Yeah, what about yams?"

"And we have animal bites. That means animal sounds …"

"Yes, so?"

"*Yipped in the Yams*," she cried out triumphantly.

"Oh, Lord, I'm so sorry I asked."

Instead of continuing that ridiculous conversation, he pulled her into his arms and kissed her.

This concludes Book 1 of Lovely Lethal Gardens Rewind: Zonked in the Zucchinis.

Read about Yipped in the Yams: Lovely Lethal Gardens Rewind, Book 2

Lovely Lethal Gardens Rewind:
Yipped in the Yams
(Book 2)

When the Captain suggests that Doreen might want to break her boredom spell by looking into an old case, she jumps at the chance. Anything new is always great, and anything that the Captain gives her means she has his permission—which gives her a lot of leeway in getting the information she needs.

However, when she realizes the case is about the long-forgotten and unidentified bones of a baby, ... she knows this case will hurt in so many ways. Still, the thought of this case remaining unsolved for so many years makes her all that more determined to solve it.

However, the more digging she does, the more people try to clamp down on talking to her, as she learns that family members of that little girl are still alive. No one is willing to talk, except one—who dies the morning after ...

When her case dovetails with another case and an old big-business local family, the gloves are off, and Doreen wades into the mix as always ...

Find Yipped in the Yams here!
To find out more visit Dale Mayer's website.
https://geni.us/DMSYipped

Author's Note

Thank you for reading Zonked in the Zucchinis: Lovely Lethal Gardens Rewind, Book 1! If you enjoyed the book, please take a moment and leave a short review.

Dear reader,

I love to hear from readers, and you can contact me at my website: www.dalemayer.com or at my Facebook author page. To be informed of new releases and special offers, sign up for my newsletter or follow me on BookBub. And if you are interested in joining Dale Mayer's Reader Group, here is the Facebook sign up page.
http://geni.us/DaleMayerFBGroup

Cheers,
Dale Mayer

About the Author

Dale Mayer is a *USA Today* best-selling author, best known for her SEALs military romances, her Psychic Visions series, and her Lovely Lethal Garden cozy series. Her contemporary romances are raw and full of passion and emotion (Broken But … Mending, Hathaway House series). Her thrillers will keep you guessing (Kate Morgan, By Death series), and her romantic comedies will keep you giggling (*It's a Dog's Life*, a stand-alone novella; and the Broken Protocols series, starring Charming Marvin, the cat).

Dale honors the stories that come to her—and some of them are crazy, break all the rules and cross multiple genres!

To go with her fiction, she also writes nonfiction in many different fields, with books available on résumé writing, companion gardening, and the US mortgage system. All her books are available in print and ebook format.

Connect with Dale Mayer Online

Dale's Website – www.dalemayer.com

Twitter – @DaleMayer

Facebook Page – geni.us/DaleMayerFBFanPage

Facebook Group – geni.us/DaleMayerFBGroup

BookBub – geni.us/DaleMayerBookbub

Instagram – geni.us/DaleMayerInstagram

Goodreads – geni.us/DaleMayerGoodreads

Newsletter – geni.us/DaleNews